Carl Weber's Kingpins:

Queens 2: The Kingdom

Carl Weber Presents

Carl Weber's Kingpins:

Queens 2: The Kingdom

Carl Weber Presents

Erick S. Gray

www.urbanbooks.net

Urban Books, LLC
300 Farmingdale Road, N.Y.-Route 109
Farmingdale, NY 11735

ISBN 13: 978-1-64556-417-1
ISBN 10: 1-64556-417-7

First Trade Paperback Printing March 2023
Printed in the United States of America

10 9 8 7 6 5 4 3 2 1

Distributed by Kensington Publishing Corp.
Submit orders to:
Customer Service
400 Hahn Road
Westminster, MD 21157-4627
Phone: 1-800-733-3000
Fax: 1-800-659-2436

Carl Weber's Kingpins:

Queens 2: The Kingdom

Carl Weber Presents

Erick S. Gray

Chapter One

"On the chow!" the guard shouted.

It was noontime. Rafe muscled the sliding door the rest of the way open and stepped out into a single file of inmates. Then with his face directed down at the polished concrete floor, he moved forward with short, sliding steps to a flight of stairs down to the first floor. The forty-two residents of the cell block stood to the left of a thick yellow line painted on the floor. The inmates paused and began their ten-minute walk to the mess hall. They trooped forward clad in green state-issued shirts and pants, some immaculate and sharply dressed, while others were rumpled and messy. Almost all of the block mates were either black or Latino, and they all were young and ruggedly built.

Rafe crept with the others toward the mess hall. He continued to cast his face toward the ground, minding his business. Rafe was doing twenty-five years to life inside Elmira Correctional Facility, a state prison known as "The Hill" located in Chemung County, New York, in Elmira. The prison housed some notorious inmates throughout the years, from contract killer Frank Abbandando of Murder, Inc. to Nathaniel White, a convicted serial killer who'd confessed to beating and stabbing six women.

Rafe was a shell of himself, crippled by gunshot wounds he suffered from his feud with Sincere four years ago. Now he walked with a slight limp. Though his reputation preceded him, Rafe had lost everything:

a criminal empire, his little brother, Drip-Drip, and his right-hand man, Malik. He was alone, but he was still feared and respected—and he still resented Sincere. The man had taken everything from him. Now four years later, Rafe still wanted to take everything from him. The two were at odds with each other on Rikers Island. When Rafe became healthy enough, he placed a hit on Sincere in Rikers. It failed. Sincere found out about the hit, and he tried to come back at Rafe. Sincere personally attacked Rafe in the jail hallways while in passing, but Rafe dodged death that day.

"I swear to God, nigga, I'm gonna destroy your fuckin' life," Rafe had shouted. "You killed my little brother. I know about your little sister, nigga, and I'm gon' have the bitch slaughtered!"

The threat infuriated Sincere. It took nearly half a dozen guards to stop him from charging at Rafe. Sincere wanted to tear Rafe apart limb by limb for threatening Denise. As a result, they both were placed in isolation for weeks.

The men were fierce adversaries, and they wanted to kill each other and had tried several times. Nevertheless, transfers to different correctional facilities in 2001 ended that. Sincere went to Clinton, and Rafe was transferred to Elmira.

Rafe had little interest in the fifteen-minute mess-hall meal like others high in the prison pecking order. He'd been living well in Elmira, eating macaroni and tuna fish from the commissary in his cell. This afternoon, Rafe was headed to the mess hall to nod hellos across the wide stainless-steel tables and check for new faces. For two years, Rafe had kept a low profile in prison. He did more reading, got into art, and enjoyed the view from his cell. Rafe discovered that from his jail cell, he could see through a layer of grime-coated Plexiglas to the city of

Elmira and the forest beyond, and Rafe became obsessed with the view. It was a temporary escape for him, providing a bit of tranquility.

He would sit and view for hours the milky sky hanging above ranges of oak, red, and silver maple, beech, and pine trees, many shades of green in the bright autumn sun. Rafe was a city thug who had fallen in love with the beauty of Upstate New York. This would be his home for the rest of his natural life. Most of his rivals were either dead or doing lengthy sentences themselves. So when he heard the news about Mob Allah, it was not surprising to Rafe. It was the world they lived in, an endless game with high stakes. You are a king one day, and then the next you're either toppled over by a rising pawn or knocked entirely off the chessboard. Mob Allah tried to reform himself, and he was killed for it, no doubt by one of his underlings or his second-in-command.

While sitting in the mess hall, Rafe saw the unthinkable: Sincere. The sight of him made Rafe frown. "What the fuck!"

It had been over two years since the men crossed paths with each other. Now right away, an old flame of revenge and hatred had been sparked inside of Rafe. Seeing Sincere in Elmira made him somewhat ambivalent. He had found some peace there, accepting identity and self-awareness, but now his old beef came barreling back at him.

Sincere was diesel thick, tall, and physically intimidating. However, it was clear to everyone that he took care of himself and lifted weights while incarcerated. He had a thick and well-groomed beard, and he sported a bald head. He was a man who had been through hell and back ample times. But gradually, over three years, he had built his name up throughout the system and earned the respect of everyone around him. Furthermore, Sincere was now a shot caller.

Sincere had been moved from a different prison because he was listed as a "known enemy" of another inmate at that prison. Throughout his incarceration, Sincere had become a violent and dangerous man. He had been moved from one institution to another because of incidents with guards or fights with other prisoners. There was an incident where he slashed an inmate several times then dodged the guards through the vast mess hall of the facility.

The federal and state prison systems were vast but at the same time microscopic. So word would spread quickly to other penitentiaries whenever something big happened. Convicts out in California would know if a riot jumped off in New York before the last drop of blood was cleaned up. Moreover, Sincere's reputation was spreading. He was a man who went after two notorious drug organizations on the streets of New York, killed several men, and survived. He was intelligent, calculating, and ruthless, and becoming a shot caller was equivalent to being the CEO of a powerful conglomerate.

Looking up from the stainless-steel table, Sincere finally noticed Rafe glaring at him. It was a shocking moment. *Oh, shit,* Sincere thought, and then he smirked. Sincere wanted to take Rafe's head off right away, but now wasn't the time.

While Sincere kept his cool, eating his meal, another inmate, named Row, took a seat next to him and greeted Sincere with dap and respect.

"My nigga, I didn't think I would see you again," said Row.

"Different house, same rules, right?" said Sincere.

Row nodded.

Row was dark, stocky, and short, no taller than five six. He was diesel thick like Sincere, and his neck was as wide as a grown man's thighs. The two men met in Clinton, where Sincere's rise to domination was catapulted. In the pen, everything was broken down into races. Inmates lived, ate, and associated with men of the same color as themselves. A race riot had erupted in the yard, things got ugly fast, and Sincere took out two rival men belonging to the white supremacists. Then a few months later, he killed a high-ranking Latino.

Before the men left the mess hall, Row read Sincere's mind. "You're going after Rafe, right?" he whispered.

Sincere didn't respond to him, but the look he had in his eyes said it all. These two had history, so it was surprising that they were placed in the same state prison. Sincere figured it had to have been a clerical error. Still, he would take advantage of the situation before the prison officials realized the mistake.

It was a beautiful bright autumn day. The sky was so blue you could drown in it, and the temperature was inviting. But the beautiful weather was in contrast to the towering brick walls, double rows of fencing topped with razor wire, metal detectors at each gate, and an ominous gun tower looming overhead. The activity happening in the prison yard was common. Inmates came together to visit with friends, exercise, and participate in leisure activities. Others were bartering and scheming or engaging in social activities. The yard was where alliances were forged and, unfortunately, where many disputes were settled.

Sincere and Row stepped out into the yard where areas of the yard were rigidly staked out by racial or geographical groups. Tension was thick. Sincere had been there two weeks, and already word was spreading throughout the facility about an incident brewing. Although things seemed copasetic with inmates playing basketball, exercising, or simply chatting, any hellos or greetings were replaced with menacing stares. Sincere didn't want to waste any time in taking out Rafe. It was an "either him or me" mentality.

Sincere quickly learned the lay of the land. With Row by his side, he had established a crew of loyal supporters ready to do his bidding, including murder. Sincere wanted to kill Rafe himself. As far as he was concerned, Rafe was unfinished business, and although the threat he'd spewed against his sister happened years ago, it was still fresh in Sincere's mind. As long as Rafe was alive, he believed Denise's life was in jeopardy.

Sincere spotted Rafe among other hardened inmates by the workout section. Rafe was busied bench-pressing, lying on a bench and pressing weight upward with a barbell. Staying fit inside was beneficial to your survival and health. There were men at Rafe's side watching him work out. Sincere glared at everyone from across the yard. Row had worked it out with a guard and was able to sneak a weapon through the metal detectors and into the yard. A shank was mandatory. You became the prey if you didn't want to be part of the hunt.

Communication between Sincere and Row was through eye contact, nods, and body language. Row knew it was time to set things off. Row faintly gave a nearby inmate a clever nod, and from there, things went from calm to chaotic in a heartbeat. That inmate quickly and unexpectedly attacked a Hispanic inmate of a rival gang. Seeing this, his allies hurriedly went to defend him, and this set off a chain of violence throughout the yard. The prison alarm sounded, and guards hollered commands and threats, but they were unheeded.

Amid the chaos, Sincere moved dynamically toward Rafe with the shank protruding from his fist. The men by Rafe's side seemed in cahoots with the planned attack.

Sincere stealthily charged at Rafe and quickly ran the sharp blade across his neck, opening his flesh like a zipper. He was drunk with revenge. Rafe gasped and grasped at his bloody open wound, struggling to breathe. He collapsed to his knees, blood pouring from him like a geyser. Rafe couldn't speak, choking from his blood. He could only stare up at Sincere clutching the weapon that had taken his life. Their four- or five-year feud had finally come to a violent end. Rafe toppled to his side, dead.

Sincere grinned. His destiny was sealed. It was hard to believe that he was on the edge of becoming a police officer four years ago. Now he was a seasoned criminal, a shot caller, a muthafucka becoming highly feared in the state prisons.

Correctional officers used pepper spray and blasted grenades to break up the skirmish between thirty inmates. When the dust settled, two men were dead. Sincere and Row lay facedown against the ground, surrendering to the authorities.

Chapter Two

The Q100 bus crossed over the Rikers Island Channel of the East River and Bowery Bay. To the left, passengers on the bus had a distanced view of LaGuardia Airport while departing from the prison. Recently released inmates were blended with the visitors coming from seeing their loved ones.

Nasir stepped off the MTA bus and stared up at the sky. He took in a breath of fresh air. After serving eighteen months inside the notorious jail for drug possession, he was finally a free man. The air was crisp, and the October sky appeared ominous and ferocious, with clouds racing across the sky, throbbing with the charged energy they desired to release in a stormy day. Whatever the weather, the day felt like paradise to Nasir.

Wearing an oversized white football jersey and a dark blue Yankees baseball cap pulled down low on his head so that his round face seemed to begin at his eyes, Nasir began his journey off the jail grounds. Instead of taking the Queens bus into Long Island City, Nasir decided to get into a cab.

The tapping sound started against the windshield to the cab, and it soon turned into a pitter-patter. The clouds had finally burst, and a downpour began. People began to hurry for protection outside, and umbrellas were opened. Nasir sighed heavily from the back seat of the cab. A thunderstorm was his welcome home gift. The heavy rain sounded like many angry bees. *What a day,* he thought. Nasir didn't carry much with him: some cash, his personal belongings, and an address.

The cab idled outside a two-family home at the end of a dead-end street in Jamaica, Queens. It was near a train trestle that carried the Long Island Rail Road. Nasir stared at the sturdy two-story residence designed without the slightest imagination. He released another deep sigh, paid the cab driver, and hurried from the vehicle toward the home.

Nasir hurried to the side of the house, descended the concrete steps toward the basement, and knocked on the side door. While he waited for it to open, Nasir felt like a man without a country. He'd lost everything being locked away in Rikers Island. Two years ago, he was a rising star. He had money, women, and respect. His best friend Sincere had done him a favor when he got rid of Rafe and Mob Allah. With those two gone, it left the streets wide open for opportunity. The only competition in Jamaica, Queens, was Zulu, and fortunately for Nasir, Zulu was a reasonable man, and the two came to an agreement. There had been enough bloodshed in the neighborhood. Nasir would buy his work from Zulu at an affordable price, create his crew, and let bygones be bygones.

The money was good. Nasir was a natural-born hustler. But an anonymous snitch brought down some heat on Nasir, and cops raided his home and found a gun and drugs. It was his second drug arrest within three years, and a lengthy minimum drug sentence loomed over his head. However, his money was well spent on an adept lawyer who was able to have the drug charges dismissed.

Nevertheless, Nasir would do time for the unregistered gun and pay a minimum fine of $2,500. Though it was a sweet deal, it was the beginning of Nasir's downfall. While he was incarcerated, his baby mama moved out of state with his daughter, his crew disbanded, and Zulu cut ties with him. Eighteen months later, he came home to nothing.

The side door opened, and Nasir was greeted by his cousin, Lou.

"Cuzzo, good to see you out," Lou greeted Nasir with dap and a brotherly hug.

"Out to what?" Nasir replied dryly.

"Just be grateful you have a second chance," said Lou.

Lou stood six feet and was 180 pounds. He was indeed slim. However, he had a reputation for being icy calm in sticky situations, and he was known to be a ruthless, vicious man.

Nasir entered the basement apartment. It was outdated with peeling paint, crumbling plaster, unhinged doors, green shag carpet, and sparse furnishings. The seventy-five-inch flat-screen TV mounted on the wall was the only luxury in the place.

"I got you, cuzzo. My home is your home," Lou said wholeheartedly.

Nasir looked around. It wasn't the ideal place to stay. But he trusted Lou, and Nasir needed someplace he could trust to regroup, think, and make moves again.

"You got the second bedroom," Lou added.

Nasir walked into the second bedroom. It was small with clean white walls, a twin bed, a desk, and closets with sliding doors opposite the bed. Nasir sighed. *It is what it is,* he thought.

"I know it isn't much. But you know, make the best of things for now. I know you'll be back soon running shit in these streets."

Nasir nodded. He didn't have a choice.

"Follow me. Let me show you something," Lou said.

Nasir followed his cousin into the main bedroom. The decor was as bad as the rest of the house, unkempt and sparse. Lou moved toward his bed and lifted the mattress to reveal an impressive arsenal. He had everything from handguns to assault rifles and shotguns. Nasir was taken aback.

"Whoa!"

"Yeah, impressive, right?" Lou smiled.

"Who you ready to war with, nigga?" Nasir joked.

"You always knew I got a thing for guns, cuzzo. Like money and pussy, you can't have enough of it," Lou proclaimed. "But I got your back out here."

Nasir nodded.

"Pick one, whatever, it's yours," Lou suggested.

Nasir stared at the heavy arsenal for a moment, then soon his eyes became fixed on a Smith & Wesson SW99. He picked up the gun and inspected it.

"You got great taste, cuzzo," Lou uttered.

Indeed, it was a remarkable weapon. Lou picked up a Remington 870 with a folding stock, cocked it, and uttered, "Whenever you ready to get this money again, let me know, cuzzo."

Nasir stared at his cousin quietly. He knew Lou could be a handful—a crazy muthafucka, a firecracker with a short fuse, a gunslinger if this were the Wild West—and he could be helpful when the time was right.

"Where did you get these guns from?" Nasir asked him.

Lou's twisted smile was like a sudden beam of sunlight illuminating the darkest corners of the room. He replied, "I got connected with some white boys upstate. We did a late-night smash-and-grab at this gun store. Nearly cleaned them out. I sold off a few shits but decided to keep the best toys for myself. You never know, right, cuzzo?"

Nasir chuckled. Lou was a maniac.

"What you drinkin' on, cuzzo? You home now. We gotta celebrate, pussy and liquor. Which one first?" Lou laughed.

The two men sat on the couch in the living room sipping vodka while watching rap videos play on the mounted flat-screen TV. The bottle was half empty. Lou was rolling a blunt while Nasir lounged on the couch, brooding. Then out of the blue, he uttered, "I was ready to take it all, my nigga. Wear that crown."

Lou looked at him.

Nasir continued, "And one snitch took it away from me."

"You know who it was, cuzzo? 'Cause we can hunt for that nigga right now and take care of that," Lou uttered enthusiastically.

"Unfortunately, I didn't take my case to trial. Took a plea deal. Therefore, the snitch's identity wasn't revealed, but I have an idea who it might be."

"I haven't caught a body in over a year. Feels like I'm slippin'." Lou laughed.

Nasir took another swig of vodka. He stared at the TV, still brooding, then proclaimed, "My baby mama took my daughter and moved out of state while I was locked down. Bitch came to see me, pregnant, while I was in Rikers, and the bitch didn't bring my daughter to see me. She told me she met someone special, they were getting married, and she was moving out of New York, wouldn't tell me where. She talkin' some shit about wanting a better life and didn't want my wrongdoings crossing paths with her new family. I think about my daughter, Jazzman, every day. I miss my daughter. She's ten now."

"Sorry to hear 'bout that, cuzzo. We can find that bitch, too, get your daughter back," said Lou seriously. "Fuck that bitch."

A quiet moment came upon them, each man in his own thoughts for a split second. Nasir felt like he was a man who had fallen from grace. Sincere, his best friend, was doing hard time in an upstate prison. He had no family around besides his crazy cousin, and he'd hit rock bottom. Nasir took another swig of vodka and sighed.

50 Cent's rap video for "Many Men (Wish Death)" started to play on the TV. Lou became excited seeing the video. He cranked up the volume, then jumped up and shouted, "Nigga, this my fuckin' shit right here! This that new nigga comin' up, 50 Cent. He nice. Jamaica, Queens, stay on the fuckin' map."

Nasir stared at the music video while Lou moved around the living room animatedly, blunt in one hand, his cup of vodka in the other.

Blood in my eye dawg and I can't see
I'm tryin' to be what I'm destined to be
And niggas tryin' to take my life away
Put a hole in a nigga for fuckin' with me

Lou rhymed with the song, and Nasir watched him with a deadpan gaze.

"This your life he rhyming about, cuzzo. It's your time," Lou added. "You back home, nigga. Eighteen months ain't shit! You Teflon, muthafucka, and we gon' start putting holes in niggas for fuckin' with you! What's that shit you and Sincere used to say?"

Nasir grinned. "Real niggas ain't scared of shit. Real niggas take care of shit."

"Yo, I used to love hearing that shit from y'all niggas," Lou exclaimed. "You and Sincere were the two livest and most real niggas on the block, real talk. We goin' to the strip club tonight to fuckin' celebrate. I need some pussy, too. You down, cuzzo?"

Nasir shook his head and chuckled. "Yeah, I'm down."

Lou was definitely a live wire, but he was family.

Chapter Three

The nondescript two-story residence in Valley Stream, Long Island, appeared to be the hallmark of family and friendly. With its manicured lawn, attached two-car garage, small flower garden, and oak front door on the picture-perfect street, the residence looked warm, inviting, calm, cozy, and comfortable—appearing to be a world away from the drugs and violence of the urban city. It was a beautiful fall day with sprawling blue skies and warm winds. But inside the place, it was a different story.

A dark blue 2002 Mercedes-Benz E-Class cruised through the community, slowly turned into the driveway to the residence, and entered the garage. The driver killed the engine, and a man named Cook Gamble climbed out of the driver's side. He was sharply dressed in a charcoal three-piece suit, a master of his style. Cook believed that we live in a judgmental world. People are quick to judge and make assumptions—folks like to categorize individuals based on what they see. So dressing nicely drew positive attention.

Cook Gamble was a handsome black man in his early thirties. He was nearly clean-shaven with just a thin goatee, and he had cropped hair. He kept to himself but would take the time to say hello to his neighbors in passing. Everyone believed Cook was a businessman, a stockbroker working on Wall Street who owned a few clothing stores in Queens and Brooklyn, including on Jamaica Avenue. He was intelligent and motivated. He liked to talk about fashion and money so much that he had the initials F&M tattooed on the right side of his chest.

However, there was a side to Cook that was dark and sinister. Cook was a drug dealer. He was part of the inner circle of Zulu's sprawling drug empire. The criminal organization moved hundreds of kilos of cocaine and heroin a month, with Cook at the helm. The lovely house, the neat suit, and the clothing store were all a front for money laundering. The three-bedroom home in Valley Stream was one of many stash houses in the city, a distribution magnet for millions of dollars.

Cook opened the trunk of the Benz and removed a brown duffle bag from it. Then he went into the kitchen that was adjacent to the two-car garage. The place was stylish. The rooms had a lived-in comfort with the furnishings, warm colors, and accessories that displayed the life of the person who lived there, a history, a warm color appreciation. It was someplace anyone would like to sit and enjoy a welcoming cup of tea or a glass of wine and good company.

Cook placed the duffle bag onto the kitchen island and unzipped it. Inside was a ton of cash. He then stepped into the living room, where his partner, Winter, was busy on his laptop while watching CNN on the mounted flat-screen TV, a 9 mm on the coffee table next to the laptop. Winter was a charismatic, tattooed thug who stood six two with an attractive physique. His body was pretty ripped as he worked out daily. Winter sat on the plush couch, clad in a wife beater and basketball shorts watching the stock market live.

Winter looked at Cook and asked, "How much this time?"

"A quarter of a million," Cook responded.

Winter nodded. "I can have that into the banking system by tomorrow and transferred into one of the shell companies by noon."

"Do what you do best," said Cook.

Winter took a pull from the blunt and continued to work on his laptop. What looked like rocket science to many—numbers, percentages, inflation, compound interest, balance sheet—was easy to him like ABC. He was intelligent, good with numbers, and great with laundering money for Zodiac. Winter learned in his teens how to build a business portfolio, diversify wealth, and monitor investments, and he knew how to short a stock. Winter and Cook were two of if not Zodiac's best goons for laundering and distribution.

Cook Gamble, along with Zodiac, owned several clothing stores, dry cleaning businesses, strip clubs, and a few other cash businesses, something pleasant and joyful with easily manipulated books and no credit card receipts. Winter used them to launder money by physically mixing the drug money in with the takings paid into the bank, artificially inflating the businesses' revenues, and exaggerating the businesses' outgoings.

Winter was able to make millions of dollars disappear like butter on a hot skillet.

"What about that other thing? Did they eat?" asked Cook.

"Maybe some lunch," Winter replied with his eyes on his laptop, typing.

Cook removed his suit jacket and tidily placed it over the back of a chair. Then he turned and went to the basement door. He unlocked it, turned on the lights, and descended into the cellar. Below was where the merchandise was stored, nearly fifty kilos of cocaine and a little over a million in cash. Though the house looked quaint and typical outside, it was a fortress. Security cameras were subtly placed everywhere. There were motion detector lights for the backyard that could light up a soccer field and a hidden arsenal, and each door was reinforced.

The basement was sizable with bright white walls and light-colored flooring, and it was windowless. If it weren't for the kilos placed on the shelves ready for wholesale, it would have been the typical live-in basement with a dehumidifier to prevent mold and mildew and improve air quality.

But something else was stored in the basement besides the kilos and cash that were valuable to Cook and Winter. Cook moved toward the end of the room, where an architectural detail gave the area a sense of mystery, a secret door leading to a hidden room. Using a remote IR signal, it activated the wall behind a bookshelf. A discreet corridor was tucked behind the sliding wall leading to several hidden rooms. The concrete passage was pocket-size and brief. Cook opened the door to one of the isolated secret rooms, which looked a world away. He pulled the cord of the dangling light bulb to reveal a young girl chained to the wall by her ankle, held like a prisoner of war. She was naked, a bit dirty, and afraid. Right away, the presence of Cook made the girl cringe and cower against the wall. He stared at her expressionless.

"Are you hungry?" he asked her.

"Please, I just want to go home," she pleaded.

Cook moved closer to her. He stood over her godlike and smirked. "This is your home. Get used to it."

Near the girl was a small, stained mattress and a plastic toilet she was forced to use, and it was emptied infrequently. The room was nearly the size of a janitorial closet. She had been locked in the dark room for a month, forced into sexual conduct among other horrors, and continuously anticipating the next abuse session.

Cook stared at the girl with apathy and uttered, "Don't worry, I'll soon find you a new home. You're young, curvy, and white. They all love your blue eyes and blond hair. You'll sell well. Pictures of you got my site blowing up."

He pivoted, leaving the room. He turned to her with an afterthought. "I'll leave the light on this time, a bit of courtesy for now."

Cook closed the door and locked it. Then he went to an adjacent room, unlocked it, and opened the door. He turned on the lights to reveal a naked black girl. She was 19, pretty, shapely, and chained to the wall by her ankle. However, she was a lot more aggressive than the other girl. The moment the light illuminated the small room, she took a wild swing at Cook but missed.

He chuckled. "You're still a feisty little bitch, aren't you?"

"Fuck you!" she heatedly cursed. "Get me the fuck outta here!"

"It's been a week now, yet you still haven't comprehended your situation," Cook replied nonchalantly. "It's okay. We have time to get you acclimated to how things work here."

Cook started to unbutton his crisp, clean white shirt. The young girl's stern glare transitioned into fear when she realized what was about to happen to her again.

"Please. I can't," she beseeched him.

"Oh, you can, and you will," he contested.

Cook undressed, becoming naked. He neatly hung his clothes against the wall not to get them wrinkled or soiled, and then he reached for a Taser and baton he kept outside of their rooms. The girl cowered into the corner, shrinking away from him with absolute terror.

"I just want to go home," she cried out.

"Oh, I'm going to fuck you and punish you at the same time, and it's going to be so much fun for me," Cook stated with his callous eyes torturing her soul.

He lunged at her, forcefully grabbed her throat, squeezed, and slammed her against the wall. He then threw her against the mattress and proceeded to rape her while Tasing her body in different places. He got off from her pain.

When he was done with her, the girl lay sobbing in the fetal position against the soiled mattress in her blood and urine. Cook glared at her and uttered, "Next time you try to attack me, I'll make it worse."

He got dressed, turned off the lights, and locked the door, sealing his kidnappee into a room of darkness but in a world of hurt and pain. There were four small spaces in the hidden section of the basement, and three out of the four rooms were occupied with young, scared, and abused girls. Each one dreamed of someday escaping and being reunited with family. Instead, they suffered from physical and emotional abuse. They were treated like animals with daily threats of being killed and allowed to shower once a week. They missed the lives they once enjoyed.

Cook emerged from the cellar, looking satisfied. He locked the door, looked at Winter, and said, "Feed them bitches in about an hour."

Winter nodded. "Where you about to go?" Winter asked him.

"I got to take care of some other business."

"You going to Zulu's birthday celebration tonight?" asked Winter.

"Yeah. He would want us there," Cook replied.

Cook exited the same way he came in. He climbed back into his Mercedes-Benz and left the premises. His neighbors believed he was a nice, successful man with a bright white smile. But behind that catchy smile was a ruthless young black millionaire rooted in the drug and sex trades.

Chapter Four

Outside a club called Spotlight was a convoy of expensive cars. The crowd to get inside was massive. There was a sea of expensively dressed men and beautiful-looking women standing before two huge, menacing doormen clad in black. Their faces were clear. *You act up, you get fucked up*. No one dared to act up. The violent reputation of one of the nightclub owners made everyone inside and out respectful and patient. The last thing they wanted was to anger the man and get on his bad side—especially on his birthday.

Inside the nightclub were a lively party and a birthday celebration designed for a royal king. The popular nightclub incorporated cutting-edge design and a sophisticated feel. A state-of-the-art sound system and a stunning lighting/visual display captivated the revelers. Several scantily clad beauties danced in cages, while impeccable bottle service provided an arena for everyone to revel in the party atmosphere.

It was a birthday celebration designed for a king—Zulu. He watched the energetic activity from his VIP/office perched above the club. The joint was jumping, a crowded, young gangster's paradise. But the place had everything for everyone to enjoy. There was a crowd of elegant black teenagers gambling, top-shelf liquor, beautiful women, and a premiere DJ.

Zulu watched everything from above dressed in an Armani suit with his ego on high. This was his night.

Everyone came out to celebrate his birthday, including a few pro athletes and celebrities. He owned the city, running a multimillion-dollar drug organization with distribution centers in various states of the US. The organization employed hundreds of people. He had money, power, and respect, and Zulu stood above it all like a god, feeling untouchable.

Zulu watched the revelers below, drunk with power.

Since he and Zodiac killed Mob Allah four years ago, a man who was once a mentor to him, and with Rafe's timely incarceration, there was nothing to stop his rise to the top. Business was good, with his organization bringing in $5 million a month, and Zulu had an estimated net worth of $60 million. There were beautiful women, luxury cars, lovely homes, expensive trips to the Caribbean, fight nights in Vegas, and yachts and beaches in Miami.

Life was good. No, life was great!

Zulu took a swig from the champagne bottle and nodded his head in approval. DJ Gotcha was spinning a few of his favorite throwbacks, Rakim, LL Cool J, Nas, Run DMC. Finally, he was ready to join the others on the dance floor and show off a few moves of his own.

Zodiac approached him. He threw his arm around Zulu, hugged him close, and said ecstatically, "Happy birthday, my brother. You like what you see out there?"

"This is love, no doubt," Zulu replied.

"Everyone came out to show their respect. But listen, I just received some news I think you want to hear," said Zodiac mindfully.

Zulu looked at him, anticipating bad news on his birthday. He uttered, "What the fuck now, nigga?"

Zodiac suddenly smiled and chuckled, then stated, "Rafe is dead."

Zulu was taken aback by the news. "What?"

"Yeah, my nigga. He was killed in Elmira State Prison not too long ago. And guess by who?"

Zulu had an idea.

"Sincere. I heard the muthafucka ran a blade across his throat in the yard like hot butter, ended that nigga right there. He's becoming a name, Zulu, a shot caller, and I'm hearing he's one nasty and ruthless muthafucka," Zodiac proclaimed.

"He got twenty-something years. He's no threat to us right now," Zulu replied. "Shit, if he were home, I would put that nigga on my payroll."

Zodiac laughed.

"But anyway, it's my night, right?" uttered Zulu.

"True. Indeed, everyone's waiting to show you some love."

"The night's still young, right?" Zulu smiled.

"The night's always gonna be young for us," Zodiac replied.

Assembled in the office for a toast on his birthday was Julie, one of the female goons left from the old crew, Nappy, Catch, Leroy, Kareem, and Big Joe. They were all dressed stylishly, looking like they were torn right out of the pages of *GQ* and *Vogue*. They were not only there to celebrate Zulu's birthday but to celebrate their massive success in the underworld. Each one had their bottle of champagne, and each one belonged in the organization's inner circle. They'd all proved their worth by putting in the needed work to help Zulu excel in the game, and they were determined to keep him on top.

Zodiac looked at his friend proudly and proclaimed, "Today we celebrate the birthday of a legend, a king, a friend, someone I'm proud to call my brother. We go back years on these streets and definitely put in some work. Shit isn't always easy, but we did what always needed doing, and now look at us. We're here. We got it all, my brother. This is the fruit of hard work, the belief in the entrepreneurial spirit. The new American dream. Top of the world. So a birthday toast to you, Zulu. Happy birthday."

Everyone raised their champagne bottle to the ceiling and proclaimed, "Happy birthday."

Everyone took a swig from their bottles. Now they were ready to mingle, drink, party, and find that right person for one night only to continue their after-party. But there was more. Zodiac motioned to one of the staff members of the club. The woman disappeared and arrived again moments later, pushing a cart with a giant birthday cake. It was a two-layer chocolate cake, candles of different colors were lit around the cake, and it had a replica of the city of New York on top. "I know chocolate is your favorite," said Zodiac.

Everybody gathered around the cake.

"Once again, a toast to my brother, in life to my brother until death. Happy birthday. To the family, on and on. I will treat my brother as I treat myself," Zodiac proclaimed.

Zulu, Zodiac, Julie, and the others waded through the oceans of revelers and happy-birthday wishers. Excited to see Zulu, partygoers reached to touch him like they would be filled with his special street magic. They went out of their way to tell him, "Happy birthday." Zulu visibly enjoyed the adoration.

They made their way to a VIP table beside the dance floor, where several Amazon-like strippers waited for his arrival.

"Yo. Yo!" DJ Gotcha shouted into the microphone. "I wanna give a special birthday shout-out to my nigga Zulu. Happy birthday, Zulu. The world is yours. We love you!"

Zulu saluted him and smiled. He then took his seat at the VIP table next to one of the beautiful Amazon-like strippers. This was his high. Zulu's drugs of choice were money, power, and respect. The world was his.

Moving through the crowd of partygoers was Detective Michael Acosta. While everyone was there to celebrate Zulu's birthday, Detective Acosta was there to spy and investigate the man who believed he was larger than life. Over the years, a cat-and-mouse relationship had developed between Zulu and the detective. The drug dealer was on his radar, and he was determined to arrest Zulu on criminal charges and bring down his drug empire.

The serial killer the Wolf made Detective Acosta well-known four years ago. He'd become the man of the hour, ending the killing spree of a stealthy and skilled killer who targeted and butchered young black prostitutes. The case was headline news for weeks, and Detective Acosta became the spokesperson for the NYPD. Now he had Zulu in his crosshairs. His violent organization was responsible for over a dozen homicides and flooding drugs into the neighborhoods this year. In addition, Acosta and his partner were investigating two cold-case murders linked back to Zulu's organizations. But unfortunately, there was no hard evidence or witnesses who were willing to testify against the organization. As a result, he was becoming a difficult criminal to take down.

Detective Acosta's six-foot frame was clad in a dark suit showing his badge. He stood out among the revelers in the nightclub. From the dance floor, he glared at Zulu reveling in all his glory and looking like he was the king of New York. The detective held a small gift and made his way through the crowd toward the drug kingpin.

Kareem hunched toward Zulu and whispered something in his ear. Then Zulu looked toward the crowd and spotted the detective inside his nightclub. He smirked.

"You want me to get rid of him?" Kareem asked.

"No. Have him come up," said Zulu coolly.

Kareem nodded. He and a second goon went to greet the detective, who was an anomaly among the celebrating partygoers. Kareem approached Detective Acosta casually and invited him to the table where Zulu and everyone sat. The detective was eager to greet Zulu and share a few words with him on his birthday.

"Detective Acosta, I'm glad you could make it to my celebration, though I wasn't expecting you," Zulu said. "And I see that you brought me a gift. How nice of you."

The detective locked eyes with him while everyone glared at him like he was the Antichrist.

"It's rude to show up to a birthday celebration and not bring something," Detective Acosta replied.

"Indeed," uttered Zulu with a smile.

He handed Zulu the small wrapped gift. Everyone, including Zodiac, was on alert, eyeing him intently. Though he was a cop, they didn't trust his reason.

"You're not trying to blow me up or anything, Detective?" Zulu joked, shaking the gift near his ear. "I don't hear any ticking."

"No. I want you alive when I come for you," the detective replied. "But you'll like this gift. I picked it out myself."

Zulu started to tear open the gift, revealing a black box. He carefully peeked inside and laughed.

"You're a funny man, Detective Acosta," said Zulu, removing a pair of handcuffs from the box.

"I'm not going to be so funny when I place those on you and arrest you for murder and every other crime you've committed. You're a menace and a monster, Zulu, and I will bring you and every clown dumb enough to follow you down," Detective Acosta said wholeheartedly.

His offensive statement didn't go over too well with everyone. They continued to glare at him, wishing they could kill him where he stood. He was ruining the night. But Zulu kept his cool. He replied casually, "I'm a businessman, Detective. I don't know what you're talking about. If I were this monster you say I am, why did so many people come out to celebrate my birthday?"

"The devil has his demons, too," Acosta quipped.

"And you're the NYPD's golden boy," Zulu remarked. "The man who brought down Mob Allah's brother. A fuckin' serial killer in the family, you believe that?"

"I'm going to pin his murder on you, too," said the detective. "You're nothing but a two-bit, stupid, selfish thug. But your time will come, and I will be there to enjoy it."

While the two went back and forth, Acosta's cell phone chimed. It was his partner calling him. He looked at Zulu with finality and uttered, "Catch you later."

As he walked away from the table, Zodiac uttered to Zulu, "He might become a problem for us."

"He's just fishing, that's all. Fuck him," Zulu replied.

Detective Acosta urgently moved his way through the crowd with his phone to his ear, with the loud rap music blaring. It was hard for him to hear what Emmerson was saying. Then as he made his way toward the exit, he accidentally bumped into a man.

"Pardon me," Detective Acosta said.

Cook Gamble glanced at him and replied, "It's cool. You're pardoned."

They held each other's stare and then went opposite ways. Once outside, Acosta finally heard Detective Chris Emmerson say, "Where are you? We got a call."

"I'm on my way."

Chapter Five

Detective Acosta arrived at the crime scene and was immediately familiar with the place. He climbed out of his gold Toyota Camry and sighed. It was going to be one of those nights. The police presence outside was thick with marked squad cars, yellow police tape, emergency vehicles, and uniformed officers making a perimeter around the home. Several bystanders stood across the street with curiosity in Hollis, Queens, a mostly Black residential neighborhood.

Acosta made his way toward the front door, where two uniformed officers stood guard. The two cops grinned and nodded. One uttered, "There he is, the NYPD's golden boy. I can't say I didn't see this one coming. The people won't be grieving for this muthafucka."

Detective Acosta ignored the statement and proceeded inside. He was immediately met in the foyer by his partner, Chris Emmerson.

"You're late," Emmerson said lightheartedly.

"The dead isn't going anywhere. Besides, I had to drop off a birthday gift," Acosta replied.

Emmerson chuckled, somewhat shocked. "You really gave him the gift?"

"It was his birthday. I had to. It was something needed for his future. I heard he likes bracelets," Acosta joked.

"You know he may consider it police harassment," said Emmerson.

"Fuck him. The asshole is starting to believe he's untouchable. It's been four years. I want to change that," Acosta replied.

The two men moved from the foyer into the living room.

"So is it him?" Acosta asked.

"He's in the kitchen. It's ugly," Emmerson replied. "Good news though, I believe this is a simple and straightforward situation without complications. The bitch was caught with the murder weapon."

Detective Acosta walked into the kitchen, and he was hit right away by the brutality of the murder. It was shocking, but he was used to seeing the horror of humanity. The body was sprawled across the kitchen floor in a pool of blood that covered more than half the kitchen. He only had on a pair of jeans and was shirtless. But there was a pistol near his feet.

"Damn, Coffee, what girl did you piss off now?" Detective Acosta uttered.

"Yeah, I guess pimping isn't easy," Detective Emmerson quipped.

There was smeared blood on the counters, cabinets, and walls inside the kitchen, and a couple of knives and a meat cleaver were in the sink. The medical examiner stood after inspecting the victim's lethal stab wounds, amazed. He looked at both detectives and said, "I count over one hundred and twenty stab wounds so far, and his skull has been fractured."

"What the fuck?" Emmerson uttered in disbelief. "Talk about overkill."

"Where's the girl?" Acosta asked.

"She's in the bedroom," Emmerson answered. "What do you think, a crime of passion?"

"Knowing Coffee, he had it coming."

The detectives moved through the house. It was a combination of luxury and extravagance with licentiousness and brutality. Coffee was a wealthy pimp with a stable of beautiful women head over heels in love with him—or brainwashed. Four years ago, he'd lost two girls to the serial killer the Wolf. But despite the loss, business had always been good to him. Pussy sold better than bottled water in the desert.

Detectives Acosta and Emmerson walked into the main bedroom, where a young, pretty girl named Maria was being detained for now. She wore a blood-covered nightgown and sat at the foot of the bed, cursing and ranting.

"Fuck that muthafucka! I hate him. I told him not to fuck with me, and he wouldn't listen to me, and he was fuckin' them other hoes, too. I told him I loved him, and he fuckin' dissed me!" she shouted and cursed heatedly. She was hysterical.

Detective Emmerson looked at the officer guarding her and said, "Give us a moment."

The cop nodded and exited the bedroom, closing the door behind him. Acosta coolly approached Maria with her tearstained face. Acosta noticed the cuts on the palms of both of her hands. It was common for offenders to sustain that during a stabbing due to losing their grip on the handle.

Maria's aggressive and angry attitude quickly transitioned to grief and despair when Acosta stood over her. She cried out, "Oh, my God. Is he dead?"

"When you stab a man over a hundred times, death tends to happen," Detective Emmerson scoffed.

Maria continued to cry. "I loved him. Why did he do this to me?"

"What happened?" Detective Acosta asked her kindly.

"I don't know. I just fuckin' snapped. I didn't . . . I didn't mean to," she whimpered.

It was clear to both men that there was a violent struggle.

"It . . . it was self-defense," she added.

"Yeah, we saw the gun. But the problem, sweetheart, is when you stab a man over a hundred times, it's no longer self-defense. That's overkill, and you fractured his skull," Emmerson let her know.

"He slipped," she commented.

Emmerson chuckled.

"What's going to happen to me?" Maria asked them.

"We're going to do our jobs and investigate this thing. In the meantime, you'll be taken to the hospital for your wounds and an evaluation. But you're going to be placed under arrest for first-degree murder," Detective Acosta proclaimed.

Emmerson tapped on the bedroom door, indicating for the cop to come back into the bedroom. He did.

"Stand up," Acosta ordered Maria.

She reluctantly stood, crying. The officer approached her with handcuffs. While he placed the handcuffs around her wrists, Detective Acosta read her her rights.

"You have the right to remain silent. Anything you say can and will be held against you in a court of law. You have the right to an attorney. If you cannot afford an attorney, one will be provided. Do you understand the rights I've just read to you?"

Maria was beside herself with grief and regret. She didn't respond to him, and then she was escorted out of the bedroom by the officer. Acosta and Emmerson shared a glance. It was a tragedy. Before leaving the bedroom, Emmerson glanced at the area, finally taking in the decor. There was a $3,000 king-size bed with a high thread count, a sixty-five-inch plasma TV mounted on the wall, and a walk-in closet, and the man had an extensive shoe collection.

"This muthafucka lived like a king from selling pussy," Emmerson commented. "Every good thing eventually comes to an end, huh?"

The men walked out of the bedroom as the coroners placed Coffee's remains into a body bag. Maria continued to cry as officers now escorted her from the home. As they walked her out the front door, everyone heard the commotion. The detectives hurried from the house to see what was happening.

Coffee's stable of women was trying to charge at Maria from behind the police tape with a barrage of cops trying to hold them back.

"You stupid fuckin' bitch! You killed him!" one of the girls screamed.

There were nine ladies in short skirts, tight jeans, long weaves, and stylish stilettos cursing and screaming at Maria while she was being led to the marked cop car in handcuffs. It looked like it would take an army to hold them back. They were upset and angry, and they wanted to tear Maria apart.

"You gon' get yours, bitch, for what you did to Coffee!" another woman shouted heatedly.

Detectives Acosta and Emmerson couldn't believe their eyes. The control Coffee had over his stable was unbelievable. Each girl was grieving and heartbroken by their pimp's demise. Finally, the cops were able to take control of the situation and whisk Maria away from the scene.

Detective Emmerson laughed and uttered, "Gotta fuckin' love this job and this city."

Chapter Six

Lights. Camera. Action. Platinum Plus was a popular Queens strip club in LeFrak City. The place was teeming with men, young and old, on a Friday night, looking to unwind, get drunk, and ogle at beautiful topless women. The lighting was dim, the floor and stages were sizable, and the furnishings were plush with leather couches and a nice, long bar. 50 Cent's "In da Club" blared throughout the place, and the atmosphere was lit.

Nasir and Lou paid the $20 cover charge and walked into a whirlwind of ass and titties. The girls were stomping around in their heels, and the customers looked like they were about to drown in their beers.

"What you drinking, cuzzo? I got you tonight," said Lou.

"Get me whatever. I don't care," Nasir replied.

Lou smiled and nodded. He went toward the bar while Nasir stood among the crowd taking in the lively atmosphere. Two years ago, he would have been making it rain with thousands of dollars. Now he was a broke nigga with barely $100 in his pockets. It wasn't very comfortable. But Lou insisted on having a good time tonight and not thinking about his troubles.

Lou rejoined Nasir with two beers. Nasir took a mouthful. Then he eyed the ballers seated in the VIP booths popping champagne, with beautiful strippers swooning over them and flossing money like it grew on trees. Nasir frowned at their activity, becoming reflective. But Lou placed his arm around his cousin, encouraging him to have a good time.

"Forget about that, cuzzo. You'll be back on top soon. Watch and see," Lou said wholeheartedly.

Nasir had a lot on his mind. But Lou was a ball of charged energy ready to be released. He was excited to be in the strip club with his first cousin, surrounded by beautiful, scantily clad women. Lou guided Nasir toward the main stage with his arm still around Nasir. Lou immediately set his eyes on a topless, big-booty stripper in a G-string twirling around the pole. Men sat by the stage and openly tossed money her way.

"We're gonna have some fun tonight, cuzzo," Lou uttered gladly, squeezing Nasir close.

Lou removed a few hundred dollars from his pocket and handed Nasir a few bills. He wanted him to have a good time because he believed his cousin deserved it. Though Nasir wasn't incarcerated in a state or federal prison, doing eighteen months in the city jail wasn't anything to sneeze at. Rikers Island was a very violent place.

Lou and Nasir sat by the stage, with "Never Scared" by Bone Crusher blaring. A thick yellow-bone stripper with butterfly locs twisted her figure around the pole while spreading her legs skillfully in midair. The sultry act captivated everyone. The stage was littered with money, which she casually tucked into her knee-high leather boots or a garter. She coolly made her exit from the scene when she was done while another curvy young girl took her place.

Lou beamed and uttered, "I'm 'bout to see if I can get a lap dance with that bitch. Be right back."

"Have fun," Nasir replied.

He departed from Nasir. Once again, Nasir stared at the ballers in the VIP booths dripping in jewelry, swimming in champagne, and surrounded by women. He couldn't help but feel a bit envious of them. He reached into his pocket and removed the only cash he had to his name, less than $100. His fall from the top was embarrassing. But on the other hand, he was appreciative that no one recognized him inside the place. LeFrak City felt like a world away from home.

While Nasir drowned in nostalgia, the DJ began to spin some R&B. A young, curvy ebony stripper with silky skin hit the stage in clear stilettos. She was scantily clad in a one-piece candy pink fishnet romper that featured a halter neck and multicolored crisscross. The reaction from everyone was, "Oh, my God!"

It was bold, daring, and irresistible.

Her name was Skyla, and she fired up the dance floor with her flesh and metal blending under the hot neon lights. The DJ began to turn it up in the booth perched above the main stage. She was moving in slow motion as she rocked her hips, making ripples snake into tsunami. Her well-oiled body was choreographed against the stage as she became topless. All eyes were on her, everyone becoming turned up. Once again, the scene became littered with money, and Nasir couldn't turn himself away, but there was something familiar about her he couldn't place his finger on.

From one R&B hit to another, Skyla put on the performance of a lifetime by hypnotizing her audience with her sultry and damn near-pornographic performance. When she neared Nasir, and the two finally got a good look at each other, a slight pause in her act was followed by instant recognition.

Nasir mouthed, "What the fuck? Denise?"

It was Sincere's little sister. But she was all grown up, beautiful, shapely, and not a little girl anymore. Denise, aka Skyla, returned to her performance while Nasir was left stuck in shock. It had been years since he'd seen her. She was 16 then. Now she was 20 years old and out on her own. Nasir knew she had no one left. Marcus and her mother were dead, and Sincere was locked up.

Knowing Skyla was Denise, seeing her naked hit him differently. Sincere was like a brother to him, and knowing that his little sister was stripping, probably to survive and make ends meet, Nasir was hit with some guilt. Nasir felt he should have done more to look out for Denise. Maybe he should have reached out to her when he was making money. But they'd lost contact after Sincere's incarceration.

Ending her performance after three songs, Skyla quickly collected her money and garment and hurried off the stage. But Nasir was in pursuit of her. They needed to talk. He weaved his way through the crowd, trying to catch her before she disappeared into the dressing room. Skyla was popular, and men wanted a piece of her time. Before disappearing into the dressing room, a man in a brown FUBU T-shirt leaned toward her and politely grabbed her arm.

"Excuse me, but you are so beautiful. Can I get a dance with you?" he asked.

Skyla smiled. "It's twenty-five for a lap dance."

He couldn't reach into his pocket and respond fast enough. The look on the man's face was pure excitement. But as she was about to lead him to an area for a lap dance, Nasir intervened.

"Denise, we need to talk," he uttered, revealing her government name.

Skyla frowned at him and griped, "Nasir, are you fuckin' serious? You calling me out by my real name in here."

"I'm sorry. I just want to talk."

"Nasir, my time is money," Skyla responded.

Nasir quickly placed $50 into her hand. He then glared at the man in the FUBU T-shirt and exclaimed, "Get the fuck outta here, nigga."

The man became intimidated, and he had no choice but to pivot with his tail between his legs and walk away. Skyla chuckled and said, "That was rude."

"Fuck him. If I could scare him off that easy, you don't need him," he countered. "Broke-ass nigga."

Skyla/Denise sized him up, smirked, and said, "Shit, you don't look like you're doing good your damn self. I heard you were locked up in Rikers. When did you get out?"

"Today."

"Damn, and you ain't waste no time being up in the strip club trying to find you some pussy, huh?" she quipped.

"My cousin wanted to bring me out," he replied.

"Anyway, you paid for two lap dances. So c'mon. I got you," said Skyla.

"Is there somewhere where we could talk in private?" Nasir asked her.

"In the VIP rooms. But that's gonna cost you."

"How much?"

"A hundred dollars," she said.

Fuck it. Nasir placed another $50 into her hand. Skyla smiled. "It's your time and money. Follow me."

Nasir followed Skyla up a short flight of stairs leading to a narrow corridor with curtained rooms on each side. She pulled back the curtain to one room, revealing a black leather couch and privacy. Nasir stepped into the space, and Skyla closed the curtain. He reclined on the leather couch while Skyla towered over him in her six-inch stilettos. They held each other's gaze for a moment. R. Kelly's remix of "Bump n' Grind" played. Then Skyla began to dance for him. Nasir still couldn't believe how much she'd changed.

He chuckled.

She stopped dancing and asked, "What's so funny?"

"I can't believe how much you've grown," he replied.

"Believe it. I'm not that little girl anymore," Skyla returned while straddling him. "And I'm gonna show you how much I've grown."

She started to perform a series of sexual moves sitting on his lap, sensually grinding and gyrating on him. Nasir couldn't help but become aroused. Skyla's ample backside rippled on the downbeat against him, and he couldn't help but start exploring with his hand snaking up her thigh.

"Fuck," Nasir groaned.

Skyla grinned. She continued to tease him and touch him. He reached up to cup one of her breasts, but she playfully swatted it away. "No touching," she purred. "Only I can touch you."

Nasir grinned. Her sexual performance was becoming so exciting that it damn near felt like a lead-up to sex.

Then out of the blue, he asked her, "When was the last time you heard from your brother?"

Skyla's mood quickly altered. She abruptly removed herself from his lap, frowning. "What the fuck, nigga? Why would you ask me that?"

Nasir was taken aback by her reaction. *Did I do something wrong?*

"I was having a nice time with you, and you had to bring him up. I wasn't thinking about my brother. Fuck him!" she cursed.

"Damn. I'm sorry I even asked."

Skyla sighed. "You know what? This was a fuckin' mistake."

Nasir stood. "Denise, what the fuck? I ain't mean to offend you."

"Well, you did."

"Sincere's my nigga. He's my day-one homie from back in the days—"

"And here you are, fondling his little sister in the VIP room, trying to fuck me," she countered.

Wow! Nasir was shocked by the response.

Skyla collected herself, ready to leave the private room. "Anyway, your time is up. I guess it was good seeing you again, Nasir," she uttered gruffly.

"So that's it? It's like that, Denise?"

"Look, nigga, I've moved on from my brother, my past, and all that bullshit that went down with him. He got himself locked up for being stupid and selfish! And I tried to forgive him for leaving me, but it hurt. I don't have any family anymore. So now I'm makin' my money and living my life," she heartily proclaimed.

She glared at Nasir for a twinkling, and her final words to him were, "Thank you for the tip."

Skyla pivoted and marched out of the private room, leaving Nasir behind, dumbfounded. But he wasn't going away that easily. There was an attraction between them. Oddly, he was excited about Denise, and she was right. He wanted to fuck her.

Chapter Seven

The scene inside the strip club started to wind down a bit. It was getting late. Several dancers were still twerking for their dental bills, car notes, and cable bills. Nasir and Lou sat at the bar, with Nasir nursing his beer. Lou was drunk, but Nasir was focused on one thing: Denise. From the barstool, he observed her entertaining the men in the VIP booths, bending over, and having them over the moon.

She would often glance at Nasir sitting at the bar with his cousin, giving him a distinct look that he couldn't read. Then she continued dancing, bending over, twerking for their entertainment. But she had the specific interest of a man named Gino—a local hustler making serious bank moving weight out of state. He clutched a handful of cash and wasn't shy in sharing his earnings with her.

"I need me some pussy tonight," Lou uttered out of the blue.

Lou's comment snapped Nasir's attention away from Denise. "What happened to that redbone bitch from earlier?"

"Bitch too expensive. She was trying to hit a nigga up for two hundred dollars to fuck. Fuck outta here wit' that shit," Lou griped. "Two things I want cheap: bottled water and pussy. Both should always come free anyway."

Nasir laughed.

Lou continued, "We need to bring something back to the crib tonight. I ain't tryin' to go home empty-handed. My dick ain't gonna forgive me."

Nasir turned his attention back to Denise.

She was now straddling Gino, grinding her pussy into his lap. The man couldn't get enough of her. He was all smiling while running his hand from the small of her back down to her ass, squeezing one of her ass cheeks. Denise smiled and coolly moved his hand from her ass.

"You know, you're beautiful," Gino complimented her.

Denise smiled.

"Your name is Skyla. But what's your real name, shorty?" asked Gino.

"I can't give you that," she responded.

"Why not? I really want to get to know you," he said.

"You're getting to know me now."

Gino laughed. "I can take care of you," he added.

"I'm sure you can. But I'm not that bitch who needs someone to take care of her," Denise responded.

"You sure? Everyone needs someone looking out after them. It can be a cold world out there, shorty."

"I'm a fuckin' polar bear. I'm used to the damn cold," she retorted.

Gino laughed again. "I like you."

"I bet you do."

Gino continued to toss money her way, and it kept the show going for him. Denise, dancing as Skyla, became so sultry and seductive that Gino seemed to be under some spell. She knew how to implement the seduction strategy to negotiate anything she wanted. Denise used sex or her sexuality as a weapon. She was gorgeous with her beloved curves and rich ebony skin.

"Damn, you so soft, shorty," Gino cooed. "I wanna see you naked."

"I can't do that here, sweetheart. Sorry."

"Where can we do that then? I'm willing to pay whatever to see all of you. Whatever," he insisted. "How much? Just give me a number."

Her clients' desire or desperation to want more of her wasn't unfamiliar to Denise. Typically, men wanted sex more than women did. So Denise became overtly sexual in appearance but played hard to get. She controlled everything. One of her seduction strategies included the art of conversation and sexual role-playing. She learned early to use sex as a tool to manipulate men. Gino may have been the boss on the streets, ruling blocks or neighborhoods, but Denise became his boss in the Platinum Plus strip club.

She ground against his lap and felt his erection protruding underneath her. He was hard.

"I know you feel that," Gino uttered.

She did.

"What are we gonna do about that?" he asked.

Denise giggled. She didn't respond to his harassment. Instead, she switched positions on his lap, pivoting into the reverse cowgirl position. Then she leaned back into him and felt his hands move between her thighs. While teasingly gyrating against Gino, her attention shifted to Nasir by the bar. They held each other's stare. Since she was 8 years old and he was 14, Denise had known him. Nasir always came by the house to see her brother. The two men were so close that Nasir became family, and as a surrogate, he was a third older brother to her. He had always been cute and friendly to Denise. She had a crush on him. But in Nasir's eyes, she would always be Sincere's little sister to him.

But there was this unexpected unspoken chemistry between them. Denise couldn't take her eyes off Nasir, and it was the same with him. Seeing Nasir again was exciting for Denise, but she remained standoffish because he was a part of something she wanted to forget. He looked good, though.

Denise suddenly felt her right titty squeezed by Gino and his hand on her crotch. She immediately removed herself from his lap. He was becoming too touchy-feely for her, and though it was frustrating, Denise kept her calm and her smile.

"I'm gon' keep it one hundred. How much to fuck you?" Gino persisted.

"You can't afford me, sweetie," she countered coolly.

"That's bullshit. Everyone has a price," he opposed, removing a wad of cash.

Gino counted $500 and placed the cash against his crotch, believing it would bait Denise into doing whatever he wanted from her. "And that's pennies to me, shorty. I got much more where that came from. I can change your life right now," he proclaimed.

Denise scoffed.

"What, you don't like making money, shorty? That's five hundred for you right now. You know what I want. So what's up? You know you want that fuckin' money. That shit got your pussy wet, right?" he laughed.

Now he was becoming disrespectful. She stared at him, knowing his kind. Like how she used her sexuality to manipulate means to coerce men into doing what she wanted by promising to give them something they wanted, Gino used money and intimidation to force people into giving him something he wanted.

"Take it bitch, and let's go somewhere so you can suck my dick," Gino exclaimed, becoming impatient.

Wow. His goons laughed. Gino believed his money controlled her. Denise frowned. She stepped closer to him, leaned forward, and picked up the money from his lap. Gino thought she'd finally surrendered to the cash and sexual advances.

"See, every bitch has a price," Gino said with a cocksure smile.

Denise scoffed at the cash, and instead, she threw it back into his face and shouted, "Fuck you! You little-dick muthafucka!"

Gino fumed. He leaped from the couch and snatched Denise by her arm. He was embarrassed and angered by the insult. "You dumb bitch! You know who you fuckin' with?" he angrily shouted.

"Get the fuck off me," she shouted.

Seeing the confrontation, Nasir was already charging toward the incident at full throttle. Lou was right behind him. Nasir threw a thunderous punch toward Gino, striking him in the jaw, and shouted, "Get the fuck off her!"

Immediately, Gino's crew went into action, attacking Nasir. But Lou was right there to have his cousin's back. First, he angrily picked up a chair and slammed it into one of the men. Then fists flew. The cousins were outnumbered five to two, but they were fierce. Lou loved the action. He didn't care how many men he was fighting. It was all about protecting his cousin and knocking niggas out. Lou punched a man so hard he felt his eye socket break, and then the man staggered back and dropped into a sitting position.

Jewelry, champagne bottles, chairs, punches, and kicks flew everywhere. But surprisingly, Lou, Nasir, and Denise got the best of the five men. Denise was no wallflower. She grew up in a turbulent home with older brothers in the streets, and fighting was in her blood. First, she attacked Gino with a series of punches, three lefts and a right in the face. Then Nasir cocked him with a champagne bottle. He stumbled back, blood rushing from his nose. Meanwhile, Lou banged another man's nose with his forehead, pushed him away, and hit him with a right cross, and the man fell over the table.

Though the fight seemed like it was forever, it was quick, and several bouncers rushed to the VIP to break it up with force. They pulled an angry and ranting Denise off Gino, and it took two men to control Lou. He was like a bull in a china shop.

"Fuck them niggas!" Lou screamed.

"Y'all muthafuckas is dead!" Gino threatened with his nose coated with blood.

Everyone was fuming. Threats and insults were traded back and forth, but the adrenaline the trio felt was enriching. Nothing brought a group of folks together than a good brawl.

Lou and Nasir were quickly escorted out of the strip club. But they weren't ready to leave yet.

"We gotta wait for Denise," Nasir said to his cousin.

"After tonight, you better fuck that bitch," Lou joked.

Both men were badly bruised from the fight. Lou's hands were sore. Nasir's face was bruised, and his lips were cut and bleeding. But they remained in good spirits. First, however, Lou went to get his gun from the car. After that, he was ready for any backlash from Gino's crew.

A moment later, Denise stormed out of the club, fully dressed, cursing and ranting. When she saw Nasir and Lou, instead of being appreciative, she angrily pushed Nasir. She shouted, "You got me suspended, nigga."

Nasir was taken aback by her reaction. "Damn, no thank you for having your back?"

"I had things under control, Nasir. I'm no damsel in distress," she retorted. "I grew up with two older brothers, remember? Fuck! That's my money."

Nasir chuckled.

"What the fuck is so funny?" Denise exclaimed.

"You have changed. Damn. You tougher than G.I. Jane," Nasir joked.

"Fuck you, Nasir," she laughed. "But are you okay?"

"I'm good. You know me. I can take a few punches. I ain't got a glass jaw."

Denise smiled. "I see."

"So are y'all two gonna fuck here or take it back to the crib? 'Cause I gotta take a piss," Lou chimed in.

"Really, nigga?" Nasir reacted, shaking his head.

"Yeah, really, nigga. Let's go before I have to kill a nigga tonight," said Lou.

Denise left with them, climbing into the back seat of a dark green Pathfinder.

Back at Lou's place, Denise treated Nasir's wounds by placing some ice cubes into a bowl, running some water, and placing his hand in it to soak while treating his bruised eye with ointment.

"Don't get used to this," said Denise.

Nasir laughed. "I won't."

"But I'm going to say this once—thank you," she said.

"You family, a'ight? And any nigga put their hands on you, they fuckin' with me. That muthafucka lucky he's still breathing after tonight," Nasir proclaimed to her wholeheartedly.

Denise smiled. It was flattering. They stared at each other for a moment, and it was apparent there was some chemistry developing between them. They were connecting on every possible level. Denise felt Nasir understood her, supported her, and accepted her for who she was. She was relaxed, but sparks started to ignite.

Denise continued to treat Nasir's wounds, but an awkward silence fell between them as they held each other's stare. Both of them were reading each other's minds. Then unexpectedly, Denise straddled his lap, wrapping her arms around him.

"Do you really want to take it there?" asked Nasir.

"Just fuck me already," she replied.

She began to kiss him passionately.

"I want you," Nasir panted through the hard kissing and touching. That did it for Denise. She peeled off her shirt and pressed her chest against Nasir's, running her hand over his crotch. He kissed her breasts, unbuttoned her jeans, and pulled them off, and then off came his shirt. Denise unbuckled his belt, and they both became naked in the kitchen. Denise climbed on top of Nasir as he sat in the chair, and she slowly descended onto his erection as it opened her like a good book.

"Aaaah," she moaned and smiled, feeling the penetration.

Nasir's breath became ragged, his voice barely above a whisper. "Oh, shit. Damn, your pussy feels so fuckin' good," Nasir groaned while thrusting inside of her.

The heat was intense. Nasir was intoxicated with her scent. She was giving herself to him, and they were about to become one. They hugged each other while they fucked in the kitchen. She loved being penetrated by a muscular thug, a black roughneck who had her back. She pulled Nasir close and dug her nails into his neck and back with her weight against him and that hard dick deep inside her, pumping her and filling her with ecstasy. Denise didn't have any second thoughts or doubts. What she now had was desire and passion for Nasir.

They were lovers now.

Chapter Eight

It was a lovely night, and the sky was aglow with bright city lights. The pale crescent moon excelled like a slivery claw in the night sky. The sounds of New York City could be heard for miles and were endless. But Harlem seemed like a world away from the city. Harlem had been the Black Mecca of the world for African Americans for years. The many streets and avenues were named for their famous leaders and residents.

Harlem was a goldmine for Zulu in legal and illegal businesses. Still, gentrification was a threat—and big money and bulldozers threatened Black history. Ironically, what Zulu criticized Mob Allah about, he became exactly—a developer. With his business in the streets expanding, he started to acquire property throughout the city with the help of an attorney who was skilled enough to put together bids and talk about strategies. Zulu started a company called East-Side Development, and business was great. Zulu also acquired a place in Mount Vernon, where he stashed his money and a few secret documents.

A 2002 burgundy Cadillac Escalade arrived at a luxury brownstone on West 119th Street, a quiet block with opulence. The moment the Escalade stopped, a young goon approached the back window. It rolled down, and Zulu loomed into view of the young thug.

"They in there right now," said the youngster.

"How long?" asked Zulu.

"About forty minutes now. They never left," the youngster replied.

Zulu sighed with unhappiness. Then he glanced at Zodiac seated next to him and uttered, "Where the fuck is the loyalty and love, huh? Everything I do . . ."

"In this business, it's hard to find," Zodiac replied.

"Do I need to worry about you too?" Zulu asked him.

"We brothers, Zulu. I'm always going to have your back," Zodiac responded.

Zulu swung his attention back to the brownstone. Three levels of a rich brown chocolate hue indicated luxury, middle-class, or wealth. Zulu, Zodiac, and two goons climbed out of the Escalade and approached the brownstone.

"You wait here and keep an eye out," Zodiac told the youngster.

He nodded while the four men entered the brownstone. They followed Zulu up the flight of stairs to the third floor. The way Zulu frowned and moved indicated there would be trouble soon.

The moans coming from the bedroom were soft, inviting, and natural. Things were hot and heavy in the bedroom as a couple was having intense sex in the missionary position, soiling the sheets passionately on the king-size bed. If there was a heaven for Cynthia, it was having the total weight of a muscular black man on top of her. He cooed into her ear with her nails digging in his ass, pulling him deeper and deeper inside her.

The two were so deep and heavy into each other that they didn't notice the bedroom door opening. Zulu, Zodiac, and his two goons coolly stepped into the bedroom to witness the heated intimacy between his lady, Cynthia, and Marcus, one of his underlings. Cynthia was the mother of Zulu's two kids. The sight of his woman being fucked by another man was disheartening, but he kept his cool.

"I don't think she ever fucked me like that before," Zulu said to Zodiac.

He quickly interrupted the sexual rendezvous. Marcus jumped out of the pussy so fast he almost caught whiplash. They both were shocked and wide-eyed at Zulu's sudden presence.

"Zulu! Oh, my God!" Cynthia hollered.

"Zulu, look, man, it just happened," Marcus tried to explain.

"Shut the fuck up!" Zulu shouted.

The room fell intensely silent. Marcus sat there with his wide, scared eyes and panic-stricken. *This isn't happening*. But it was.

"I warned you, nigga, to stay the fuck away from my bitch," Zulu growled at him. "Now you got her stealing from me."

"Zulu, I'm . . . I'm sorry. Look, I promise this won't happen again," Marcus stammered nervously.

"I know it won't. I'm going to make sure of that," said Zulu unequivocally.

Zulu moved closer to Cynthia as she held a clear expression of terror on her face. Her nude body still glistened with the exertion of what she had done with Marcus. Zulu couldn't keep his eyes from roaming up and down her beautiful flesh and admiring her perky, youthful breasts and toned body and legs.

"What did he promise you?" he asked Cynthia.

"What?" Cynthia stammered.

"I said what the fuck did he promise you to risk being with him? His heart? That's what the fuck he promised you?" Zulu exclaimed.

"Zulu, please, don't hurt him," Cynthia begged.

"Why, because you love this nigga?" Zulu chuckled. "Since this fool promised you his heart, then that's what you're going to get—his fuckin' heart."

Zulu nodded at his two goons on standby. They reacted without a second thought. They lunged for Marcus and heatedly snatched him from the bed. He tried to struggle, but it was futile. Cynthia cried out as they assaulted him. She watched two burly men repeatedly strike Marcus with the butts of their pistols then cover his mouth with duct tape to drown out his screams. Subsequently, they dragged him into the bathroom and closed the door behind them.

"You want his heart, then I'll give you his heart," Zulu repeated.

"You're a monster!" Cynthia screamed. "I hate you!"

Angered, Zulu backhanded her so hard she flew off the bed and hit the floor. He stood over her as tears welled up in her eyes. She could hear them torturing Marcus inside the bathroom. Though his mouth was covered with duct tape, his muffled screams echoed through the door.

"This is my fuckin' city. I run things and don't anything go down without me finding out about it. So what, you thought you and that fuckin' fool could steal half a million dollars from me and hide?" Zulu uttered through clenched teeth.

"I'm sorry!" she cried out.

Zulu glared at her and replied, "Yeah, you're sorry, and what about our kids, huh?"

"We'll give the money back," she exclaimed.

It was too late for redemption. Marcus's subdued screams continued until there was absolute silence. The sudden stillness indicated his demise. A great tremor overtook Cynthia. She couldn't hold the anguish any longer as her grief poured out in a flood of uncontrollable tears that raced down her cheeks.

Finally, the bathroom door opened. The two goons emerged with their hands bloody, one clutching a large blade and the second clenching Marcus's bloody heart.

They approached Zulu with it and handed him the heart. It was a cruel act, one that left them desensitized.

Shit! Zodiac thought.

They handed Zulu the man's bleeding heart, and he didn't cringe. He, too, was numb to the brutality and cruelty. Killing became second nature to them.

Cynthia was beside herself with grief. Zulu scowled at her clutching her lover's heart after he tossed it to her.

"There. I keep my promises, don't I?" Zulu mocked.

Cynthia was horrified. She covered her face with shaking hands.

Zulu looked at his two goons and instructed, "Clean this shit up, and make him disappear."

They nodded.

"What about Cynthia?" Zodiac asked him.

Zulu looked back at Cynthia, who was still fastened to the floor, her body racked with an onslaught of sobs and tears. He thought about it for a moment, then said, "Fuck her. She can go too. Jimmy Hoffa that bitch."

It was considered done.

"Bitch didn't even come to my birthday party," Zulu uttered.

Zulu and Zodiac stepped out of the bedroom, leaving behind a slaughterhouse. The pool of blood in the bathroom was so thick you could swim in it.

Both men exited from the brownstone with the youngster still guarding out front. Zulu reached into his pocket and removed a wad of cash. He peeled off a few hundred dollars and handed it to the youngster.

"You earned it," said Zulu.

The youngster smiled.

Zulu and Zodiac climbed into the front seat of the Escalade, with Zodiac at the wheel this time. Zulu looked distant for a moment, thinking about his decision to kill the mother of his two children. Zodiac picked up on his friend's disdainful look.

"You did what you needed to do. Unfortunately, she stole from us, and she was reckless," said Zodiac.

Zulu huffed, then he uttered, "Just get me the fuck out of here. I got some other business to take care of."

Zodiac nodded. He started the SUV and drove off.

Chapter Nine

Cook Gamble killed the ignition to his Mercedes-Benz E-Class. He climbed out of it looking fashionably sharp in a royal blue double-breasted custom suit and a fedora. He pressed the switch that activated the alarm to his vehicle and exited from the parking garage. The sky was gray and gloomy, the sun nowhere to be found, and a cool breeze scattered a few fallen leaves throughout the street and across sidewalks.

He walked toward Jamaica Avenue, a shopping hub in Queens where shoppers sought the ultimate bargains, perfect gifts, and up-to-date fashions. The closer he got to the avenue, the louder it got. Boom boxes promising the best deals blared from speakers between Sutphin Boulevard and 170th Street, traffic was dense, and the epicenter of it all was 165th Street.

Cook strolled down the commercial strip of 165th Street, catching fleeting stares from women and a few men. He stood out. He was the only man in the crowd dressed in an expensive suit, pricey shoes, and a fedora. He was handsome, too.

When he arrived at the entrance of his clothing store, Urban Boutique, a group of teenagers came strolling out of it carrying shopping bags and laughing. Cook smiled their way and entered his place of business.

Inside the brightly lit clothing store was a variety of primarily women's clothing, the best the store offered for reasonable prices. It was a young girl's dream. Cook had a staff of all young women working the store, and Kyra was working the register. Danielle and Michelle were working the floor, and Lonnie was in charge of stock in the back room. For the girls, working at the boutique was fun and unique because they got exposure to the latest trends on the market, and it helped improve their marketing skills.

They were his retail associates, and Cook trained his staff in processing payments and handling the returns of merchandise, bagging, or packaging clothing. The position also required the girls to have an eye for fashion in case customers asked them to help them put together or accessorize an outfit. Another benefit was that the job paid them well, and there weren't long hours to work or unrealistic job expectations.

"Use your body language," Cook would say to the girls. "Maintain a positive work-life balance. Ask for help when you need it. Let customers touch the product. Know the store's layout. Take accountability. Respond to your customers and prepare for the schedule." Those were Cook's main rules for all of his stores.

When the girls saw Cook enter the store, they all lit up and smiled.

"Hey, Mr. Cook," they greeted him.

"How are my girls doing today?" he replied.

Cook kept a generous attitude toward them, but he kept things professional, knowing that they were attracted to him. There was no reason for them to believe that behind the pleasant demeanor and his golden-boy smile, he was a monster and a ruthless sex trafficker who preyed on young women.

Cook stepped behind the cash register with Kyra. "How's business today?" he asked.

She responded, "Busy."

"Busy is always good. If it continues like this, then you might get a raise. Keep up the great work, Kyra," he said.

She smiled. The comment made her day.

Cook studied the floor, eyeing the customers and his staff, and it all moved smoothly like a ticking clock.

"If you need me, I'll be in the back," he told Kyra.

She nodded. "Okay."

Cook entered the office in the back and made sure to lock the door behind him. It was small and quaint but secure. He straightened the stuff on his desk, ensuring everything was square and adequately spaced. There wasn't much—a phone, laptop, and a legal-sized lined yellow pad—and there were security cameras monitoring everything happening in his store.

Cook went to the safe in his office. He crouched to hit the needed code and opened it, and inside was $50,000 in cash, a few documents, several floppy disks, and some pictures. He removed $25,000 cash and placed it into a small sack. Then he removed one of the floppy disks, took a seat at his desk, and opened his laptop. He immediately logged into the dark web using a secured service. Cook sat in privacy with the door locked and started to auction his stable of girls online on the dark web.

He typed: Three beautiful gems ready for their shine. The bidding starts at $3,000 each.

He uploaded their pictures and leaned back in his chair to watch the show. The price jumped for the blond-haired, blue-eyed girl named Amy. Cook smiled. It was like watching the stock market soar, and the numbers were increasing for all three girls.

An anonymous bidder typed: Are they virgins? I will pay $6,000 more if so.

Cook responded: No, they've already been broken in.

The bids continued to rise, and Cook looked at nearly six grand apiece for each girl. He grinned at the numbers.

"Keep showing me the money," said Cook excitedly.

It was business. Zulu knew nothing about his and Winter's involvement in sex trafficking young girls. Though Zulu's organization flirted with prostitution rings, he knew the boss would be totally against sex trafficking. Though it was profitable like drugs, it brought too much heat to everyone involved.

But Cook was an opportunist—a capitalist. He had a strong appetite for the finer things in life. He loved driving luxurious cars, wearing nice clothes, and living in the best homes. Cook felt moving drugs and girls was the best of both worlds. He was obsessed with getting more and more money. What drove him was his ambition for greed and power.

The bidding for all three girls ended. In the end, Amy sold for $7,000. Keisha sold for $6,500, and Karen sold for $6,000. He had made the arrangements for their delivery. White girls with blond hair and blue eyes always profited him more. Cook logged out of the dark web and leaned back in his chair, feeling accomplished. He removed his cell phone and made a call to Winter.

"What's up?" Winter answered.

"It's done. Get them cleaned up and ready. We move them tonight," he said.

"Okay."

Their call ended. Now it was back to focusing on his store. Cook stared at the security monitors and observed his workers throughout the store. Then something caught his attention. He stood up and exited the back office.

"What the fuck did I say, bitch! You stupid or what?" a pimp shouted at his woman inside the boutique.

He roughly grabbed the back of her neck and nearly slammed her into the clothing rack in front of them. Kyra tried to intervene, but he stood six two and was built like an athlete. His taste in clothing and jewelry was gaudy.

He sported a diamond-encrusted skull the size of a small boulder with dollar signs for eyes.

"You need to get off her and leave," Kyra exclaimed.

The pimp shot an angry look at Kyra and retorted, "Bitch, shut the fuck up before I make you my business too."

Kyra scowled. The pimp grabbed his woman again, a young girl named Anna. She was pretty with round cheeks, high cheekbones, and a slightly thin nose that gave her a European look. Her pretty face was surrounded by straight but still beautiful, shiny raven black tresses. Her hair flowed freely and framed her face and head perfectly. But she looked scared and defenseless against her man, and he wasn't shy about assaulting her in front of everyone.

The pimp turned his heated attention back to Anna and exclaimed, "You see this shit, bitch? You're embarrassing me."

Before things escalated inside the store, Cook coolly approached the dispute and uttered, "Is there a problem inside my store?"

He shot his eyes at Anna while the pimp glared at him. "Who you, nigga? Fuck off. This ain't your fuckin' business. It's between me and my bitch."

"I was about to call the cops," Kyra said.

"No need for the cops, Kyra. I can handle this," Cook returned. Then he held the pimp's stare. "What's happening inside of my store is my business. Let her go."

"What?" the pimp griped.

Cook buttoned his suit jacket and stepped closer to him. The pimp stood over Cook by three inches and outweighed him by a few pounds, but that didn't intimidate him. Instead, Cook continued his hard stare and repeated, "I said let her go, and I'm not going to repeat myself again."

An uncomfortable silence grew between them, and the way Cook looked at him, it was easy to deduce that he was not a man to be messed with.

The pimp relented, and he released his hold around Anna.

"Now get the fuck out of my store," Cook said gruffly.

"Fuck that bitch anyway," the pimp scolded. "I'll be back." He turned and walked away, leaving the store.

Cook looked at Anna and asked, "Are you okay?"

She nodded.

"Get her some water," he said to Kyra.

Kyra walked away to retrieve bottled water from the back while Cook comforted Anna. He took in the girl's angelic face and hazel eyes and was stunned. She was beautiful.

"What's your name?" he asked her.

"Anna."

"And how old are you, Anna?"

"Nineteen."

Cook smiled. "Well, Anna, you're in good hands right now. Do you have a place to stay?"

"I stayed with him," she mentioned.

"We'll get you back on your feet," said Cook. "Are you hungry?"

She nodded. Cook signaled Danielle.

"Listen, run to the deli, buy her and everyone something to eat, on me," said Cook. He reached into his pocket and removed a wad of cash. He peeled off a fifty-dollar bill and handed it to Danielle.

"No problem." Danielle smiled.

Her boss was the best. Anna had a hefty price tag, and Cook needed her healthy and well-fed. She was white, European, beautiful, and young. How she got mixed up with a street pimp was baffling. But Cook had plans for her.

***

It was a chilly night when a Lincoln Navigator arrived at an empty parking lot in Long Island at Hempstead State Park in the middle of the night. Their Navigator was the only vehicle idling in the parking lot, and their unlawful activity was ironically cloaked by park trees, playgrounds, cookout areas, and public restrooms. What was meant to be a family-friendly place was the chosen location for criminal activity. With no one around for miles, Cook lit a cigarette and waited. He and Winter remained calm, relaxed, and collected. At the same time, two of their captive girls were in the back seat blindfolded with their wrists bound, awaiting their fate.

"These fools are late," Winter griped.

"They'll be here," said Cook.

"I hate waiting around being exposed like this, Cook. You know that. We got these bitches in the back looking crazy. What if unexpected company shows up?"

"Just relax. They'll be here. We've done this transaction plenty of times. Don't become unhinged over a few minutes," Cook assured him. "Besides, who the fuck gonna roll up in a state park in the middle of the fuckin' night?"

"State troopers," Winter countered matter-of-factly.

Cook chuckled. "What? Are you ready to leave and not make this money? They already wired the money into our accounts. It's done."

Winter huffed.

Cook took another pull from the cigarette and stared out the window. He then looked at Winter with something else to say. "I have another girl for us, a cash cow. Maybe we can get ten grand from Handler for this one."

This caught Winter's attention. "You do?"

"She strolled into my store this afternoon as luck would have it. Beautiful white girl with these hypnotic hazel eyes. Young, too."

"And you say she happened to walk into your store?" Winter questioned.

"Yeah, with her pimp. He started abusing her. I had to intervene. Kicked him out, and she stayed."

"That's kind of odd, huh?"

"What is?" Cook asked.

"White girl in distress so happens to come into your store needing your help," Winter questioned.

"What are you trying to say? It's some kind of setup?"

"We need to tread carefully, Cook. That's all," said Winter.

"We've been doing this for two years, and we know the signs of a bitch in distress. But I'll vet the bitch, track the pimp down, and have a word with him," Cook said.

"We can't be too careful, right?"

Cook knew Winter was right.

A pair of bright headlights turning into the parking lot caught the two men's attention.

"It's about damn time. They're here," said Winter.

A dark blue panel van arrived. Two tall white males in tracksuits climbed out of the van and approached Cook and Winter.

"You got the girls?" the van driver asked them.

"Why the fuck you think we here, nigga?" Winter retorted. "And y'all late."

The passenger mockingly replied, "Traffic."

"You're funny," Winter uttered.

"Let's just get this over with," Cook chimed.

Cook opened the rear door to the Lincoln Navigator and roughly removed Amy and Karen from the back seat. They were in sundresses, whimpering, scared, and a bit resistant. Cook pushed them toward the two men. They nodded in approval, seized the two ladies into their grasp, and then forced them into the back of the panel van. The door closed behind them, sealing their fate.

"It's always good doing business with you two," said the passenger. "More girls soon?"

"Yeah. Give us a few days," Cook replied.

The passenger smiled. Then the two men pivoted, climbed back into the van, and drove off.

"Let's get the fuck out of here," said Winter.

They climbed back into the Navigator and left the premises.

Chapter Ten

Denise's body lit up with pleasure as she cooed beneath Nasir. She was angled on top of him as he was deep inside of her. Nasir gripped her ample, tight ass as her nails dug into his chest.

"Fuck me, baby!" Denise cried out. "Ooooh. Shit!"

She leaned forward, and their mouths hungrily devoured each other's lips as their tongues battled for dominance. Her legs tightened around him, and her nipples were hard as stones with the heat building inside of her. Denise could feel her juices leaking out of her while she rode him wild and fast. Her pussy pulsed nonstop around his hard dick, and it felt like Nasir's dick was being sucked on by a gulping throat.

"I'm gonna come!" Denise exclaimed.

Nasir continued thrusting upward into her, bringing her closer to an orgasm. Their breathing matched one another, becoming labored and low. Denise's legs continued to tighten as she locked eyes with Nasir, the inevitable happening. She showed her strength as her body shook beneath his as she orgasmed along with him. They both were lost in the enchanted haze of mind-blowing orgasms that never seemed to end.

When their orgasms finally rode their course, Nasir felt ashamed. Neither let go of the other, their bodies wrapped tightly together. Their mouths were just inches apart, ready to kiss the other.

"That was fun," Denise said.

He looked sadly into her eyes.

"Damn, was I that bad?" Denise joked.

"No. You were great. Shit, that was some of the best sex I ever had," he confessed.

"Then why do you look like I just took a shit in your oatmeal?"

He sighed. "It's Sincere. It's guilt. That's my best friend, and I'm fuckin' his little sister while he's locked up. If he found out . . ."

Denise huffed and arose, removing herself from his arms. "He's not going to find out. Besides, this is my life, not his. Don't ruin a good thing, Nasir," she replied.

"I'm trying not to."

"I really like you," she admitted. Then she chuckled. "In fact, I've always had a crush on you."

"You did, huh?" Nasir chuckled too.

"Yes. But you never used to notice me. I was always going to be Sincere and Marcus's little sister in your eyes."

"And now you're all grown up," he said.

"I am," Denise confirmed. "Are you having fun with the new me?"

"You have changed."

"Is that a good thing or a bad thing?" she replied, touching his chest soothingly.

"It's a good thing," he replied.

"How good?"

"It's good. Really good," he said.

"Are you sure? Because I don't want you doing anything you're going to regret later on. I'm sure about this, about us, and I'm never scared," Denise said with conviction and a teasing smile.

She continued to massage his chest. Then her pleasing touch gradually moved from Nasir's bare chest to underneath the sheets. Finally, her hand reached around his growing erection. She began to stroke his dick with the softest caresses Nasir ever felt a woman give him.

"I see one part of you is definitely sure about us," she teased.

Nasir moaned from the soothing hand job. "Oh, fuck."

"You like that?"

He did.

Denise then disappeared underneath the sheets to do what she did best. Her fingers continued to stroke Nasir to the height of his lust.

"What the hell are you doing?" he asked, peeking underneath the sheets down at the mass of black hair planted in his lap.

"If you have to ask, maybe I need to stop right now," she returned.

"Nah," he replied unequivocally.

She grinned. *Of course not.* Her lips started kissing and sucking on his shaft. Each stroke of her tongue brought rude thoughts to his mind. Then she took him entirely into her mouth, using her saliva as a lubricant. Denise moaned while giving him head. Nasir began to groan as well and moved with her. Her deep suction and salivating mouth continued to bring Nasir closer to another orgasm. She cupped his balls, and her manicured nails tickled the backside of his scrotum. Nasir was thrust into absolute bliss. Denise's mouth became like a vise as she sucked him harder and faster, and Nasir began to squirm in her grasp.

"Oh, fuck. Ooooh, shit! I'm about to come!" he cried out.

Nasir was so deep in enjoyment and gratification that it became almost unbearable. She simultaneously gave him head and a hand job. He could not keep his flood from rushing forward as her suction started to pull his semen out of him. Nasir howled as he felt his sudden release, and soon she sucked the last of his sperm from his dick. Denise freed her fingers around the base of his dick as her mouth rose to the tip. She had swallowed every last drop of him unflinchingly. Then she released his dick from her mouth but not her hand and looked up at him.

Nasir looked deflated. He'd become completely paralyzed from the pleasure she'd bestowed. His breathing once again became labored. There were no words for what he'd just experienced.

Fuck!

"Are you hungry?" she asked him.

"Yeah."

"I'll make us some breakfast," she said.

Denise removed herself from the bed, and Nasir eyed her ample, nude backside. *Damn.* She was a curvy but petite ebony woman with an hourglass figure. The sight of her nearly made his dick hard again.

While Denise threw on a long T-shirt and exited the bedroom, Nasir lay there and stared up at the ceiling. "Fuck me," he said to himself.

His mind began to spin with worries and thoughts. He had no idea what he was going to do next. Sex with Denise was lovely and a temporary escape from his reality, but now it was back to what he feared: his uncertainty on the streets. Nasir wasn't used to being a broke nigga, and something had to give.

He began to smell Denise's cooking coming from the kitchen right away. The aroma was as alluring as having sex with her. But whatever she was cooking, it shifted Nasir from his thinking, and he wanted to sink his teeth into it immediately.

He removed himself from the bed, donned a pair of shorts, and left the bedroom to join Denise in the kitchen. The day was young and bright, and the length of the day could be filled with either opportunities or challenges.

Denise was as skilled in the kitchen as she was in the bedroom. She played the radio while she cooked, and she moved about the kitchen gleefully.

"Whatever you're making, it smells good," Nasir announced.

She smiled his way, gave him a quick kiss, and replied, "You'll like it."

"It smells like I'm going to love it," he responded. "I didn't know you could cook."

"With my mother on drugs, a brother in the military, and another brother in the streets, I learned to take care of myself. It took some time, but I love cooking. It's one of the few things that gives me purpose and excitement," she said.

"I respect that. So what you cooking?"

"A classic Denver omelet."

"Never had it before," said Nasir.

"Never?"

"Shit, I never tried an omelet before. That's some white people's shit. Black people eat scrambled eggs, not omelets," he joked.

"You need to expand your taste buds and stop being so simple, especially when it comes to food," Denise countered.

"With you, I'll try."

She smiled.

Denise finally finished making breakfast and set the table for them to eat in the compact, outdated kitchen.

"You see my cousin around?" Nasir asked.

"I think he left. I think we got too loud for him this morning," she quipped.

"He'll be a'ight," said Nasir.

Finally, Nasir took a bite from the omelet, and immediately, his face lit up like the sun. "Damn, this is really fuckin' good."

"I knew you would like it."

"What the hell is in this?" he wanted to know.

"Pillowy scrambled eggs stuffed with smoked ham, melted cheddar cheese, sweet bell peppers, and onions," she revealed.

"It almost tastes like pizza but in an omelet form," Nasir expressed.

The dish was primarily savory, but he got some sweet crunches from the bell peppers. Nasir devoured the omelet and immediately wanted seconds.

"I got you," said Denise. "I knew you would want more."

If this was a dream, Nasir didn't want to wake up. Great sex, phenomenal head, and a delicious breakfast: it was a dream come true. Denise was a remarkable woman. But he had to ask that question.

"Mind if I ask you something?" Nasir uttered.

"What's up?"

"How you get into stripping?" he coolly asked. "I mean, since I've known you, Denise, you've been a smart girl, and Sincere had high hopes for you."

"You sure know how to keep fuckin' up a good morning, don't you, Nasir, constantly bringing up my brother?" she retorted.

"I'm just curious, that's all. No offense to you," he said.

"I had your dick in my mouth about an hour ago. I think we're far past being offensive," she countered. "And I don't wanna talk about it." Denise pushed her chair back from the table and stood up. "Thank you for the fun and the great fuck, but I think it's time for me to leave," she added.

"Are you serious?" he voiced.

"Call me when you can stop thinking about my damn brother and just wanna fuck me," she stated.

And just like that, everything went left. Nasir sat there dumbfounded. He wondered why she became so sensitive about her brother and her past. There was something she didn't want to tell him.

Denise hurriedly got dressed and marched back into the kitchen.

"That was quick," Nasir said.

She responded, "I really do like you, Nasir. But please, don't have me stuck in the past with my brother. It is what it is, okay? And if you wanna fuck me again, you have my information. Use it."

She pivoted and left.

Wow, was Nasir's reaction. *She has definitely changed.*

Chapter Eleven

It was happy hour at the local Queens bar on Sutphin Boulevard. It was a slow Wednesday night, and beer and drinks were $4 during happy hour for domestics. The jukebox was kept at a reasonable volume to allow for conversation. The crowd varied from the locals and frequent flyers, but it leaned heavily toward MTA and airport workers. The mixed drinks were solid and worth coming for—along with the bartender, Mary. She was cute, friendly, and skilled at making any alcoholic drink known to man.

A few blue-collar workers played a game of pool in the back while Nasir and Lou sat at the bar conversing while the Knicks were playing on a few TVs and losing in the fourth quarter. Then finally, Lou downed a shot and uttered, "The world's changing, cuzzo. You need to change with it, but don't let it make a bitch outta you. It's 2003. Rappers wanna be gangsters, and gangsters wanna be rappers, and everybody is fuckin' snitching. So what the fuck is goin' on?"

Lou was rambling, and Nasir let him talk. Nasir's mind was elsewhere, and he was thinking about Denise. It'd been nearly a week since he saw her. Something was going on with him. He wanted to see Denise again, but she ignored his calls for some strange reason.

Out of the blue, Lou asked him, "Yo, what happened to shorty you fucked in my crib? I liked her. She was banging."

"Shit happens," Nasir replied.

"How you fucked that up, cuzzo? She was into you."

"I didn't. She was off-limits anyway," Nasir replied.

Lou chuckled. "What the fuck you talkin' about? She was beautiful with a badass body, and you let that slip from your fingers. I know that pussy had to be good. I heard you moaning and groaning like a bitch in the bedroom. I knew that was you."

"Damn, nigga, just tell all of my business, will you?" Nasir replied, then glanced at the bartender, Mary. She was too busy with other customers to actually hear his business.

"I'm just sayin'. I liked her."

"I liked her too. But you know whose sister that was?"

"Nah."

"That was Sincere's little sister," Nasir mentioned.

Lou chuckled. "Get the fuck outta here. For real?"

"Yeah. She grew up."

"Yeah, she damn sure did. Damn. Crazy, I didn't recognize the bitch at first. Anyway. You still fucked her, though. I'm not mad at you, cuzzo. I would've fucked her too," Lou teased. "Heard that nigga Sincere's breaking heads and fuckin' shit up upstate. How many bodies you think that nigga got on him right now?"

Nasir shrugged. He didn't care.

"That used to be your boy, though," Lou added.

"We still cool," said Nasir.

"Yeah, but you know that nigga gonna feel some kind of way when he finds out you fucked his little sister."

"And how he's gonna find out? Only you and I know it," Nasir responded, looking intensely at Lou.

Lou chuckled. "Nigga, don't look at me like that. I ain't no snitch. But shorty, on the other hand, she might kiss and tell, let it slip to her brother."

"She doesn't talk to him anymore," Nasir revealed.

"Why not?" Lou questioned.

Nasir grew frustrated and spat, "Lou, what the fuck? Are you a journalist for *20/20* now? Why are you asking me so many questions?"

Lou chuckled. "Because I'm bored and horny, nigga, and your shit is entertainment."

Lou finished off his beer and signaled the bartender for another round. Mary nodded and smiled. She made her way to the pair with her meaty thighs peeking from underneath a short denim skirt. Lou smiled and licked his lips.

"What can I get you two men?" asked Mary.

"Another beer, love," said Lou, grinning her way.

"No problem," Mary replied.

She glanced at Nasir and then turned to retrieve two beers from the cooler. Lou fixed his eyes on her ample backside and said to Nasir, "By the end of the night, I'm trying to pull that skirt up, bend her over, and fuck her like crazy. I know that pussy's good."

Nasir chuckled and responded, "You think you can pull that?"

"I know I can. Watch and see, cuzzo."

Mary returned with their two beers. Lou handed her a twenty-dollar bill and uttered, "Keep the change."

Mary smiled. "Thank you."

When she turned to walk away, Lou called out, "Mary, have a drink with us."

"I would love to, but I don't drink," she told him.

Lou was taken aback by her statement. "What? You don't drink? How can you become a bartender and don't drink? That's like some oxymoron, isn't it?"

Mary laughed. "I have my reasons."

"I would love to hear about a pretty bartender who doesn't drink. Now that's intriguing," said Lou.

Mary smiled and replied, "You're amusing and funny."

"Oh, baby, you don't know the half of it. I can light you up like the Fourth of July." Lou smiled glibly.

He had Mary's interest.

"Yo, watch my beer. I gotta take a piss," said Nasir, removing himself from the barstool.

"I got you, cuzzo," Lou uttered, then he went back to flirting with Mary.

Nasir walked into the bathroom, which contained two urinals and one stall. It wasn't in the best condition, with graffiti on the walls, dim lighting, dirty fixtures, and soiled toilet seats. He had to piss like a racehorse. He occupied one of the urinals and relieved himself immediately. Nasir could hear the jukebox playing "My Life" by Mary J. Blige, and hearing the classic song stirred up some old memories. His baby mama loved that song. She used to play it all the time. Nasir frowned. The thought of his baby mama now married, pregnant, and living out of state with their daughter bothered Nasir. He had so many things going for him, money, cars, women, and respect, and though he wasn't together with his baby mama, it brought him some comfort to know that his daughter was close by.

Nasir thought, *how the fuck did I end up like this?*

He knew the answer: a snitch. He was lucky to take a plea deal for eighteen months, but eighteen months away from the game might as well have been a lifetime. The streets were regularly changing. Players were coming and going, blocks and neighborhoods switching leaderships. But there was one thing constant on the streets: Zulu's and Zodiac's authority. Since Mob Allah's demise, Zulu had taken over and ruled everything with an iron fist. He'd protected his newly acquired territory through top enforcers. As a result, Zulu had increased the cost of everything, from kilos to street taxes. Detectives and major crimes targeted Zulu's organization. They tried to infiltrate his organization using wiretaps and snitches. Still, they failed to link him to any murders or illicit activities. It seemed like Zulu was untouchable—the Teflon don.

Nasir didn't want to admit it, but he had a strong distaste for Zulu. He was jealous. He wanted to wear that crown, become the king of New York. He figured he earned it. Since he was 13 years old, Nasir had been hustling on the streets. He'd put in the work needed for his respect and rise—including murder. Now he felt like a has-been.

He wiggled the last drop of piss into the urinal, then zipped his jeans and washed his hands. When he exited the bathroom, he was shocked to see Denise entering the bar with some man. She'd ignored his calls for a week. Now it was a coincidence to see her tonight. He noticed her before she noticed him.

Lou was still flirting with Mary. She was all smiles.

Denise looked radiant in a pair of skintight jeans that hugged her fierce curves and firm ass. Her trendy top was tight enough that if she moved, one of her nipples would peek out, and her dark ebony skin shined as if recently oiled or sweating after a long, hard workout. Nasir gawked at her from across the room. Finally, Denise turned and noticed Nasir's eyes fixed on her. They held each other's gaze, and then she sneered and walked toward the bar with her date. The man she was with screamed hustler with flashy jewelry, long cornrows, exclusive Air Jordans, and a throwback Giants jersey.

What kind of game is she playing? Nasir thought.

Jealousy stirred inside of him. Nasir felt she was dissing him. There was no way he would leave the bar and not interact with her.

While the man entertained Denise at the bar, ordering drinks, Nasir coolly moved their way and positioned himself onto the unoccupied barstool next to Denise. He immediately grabbed her attention. They locked eyes, and Nasir uttered, "What games are you playing, huh?"

Denise giggled. "Why do you think I'm playing games?"

"I tried to call you for a week now. You've been ignoring my calls," he said. "I thought we had something. So now you're in here with this clown-ass nigga."

The disrespectful remark immediately caught the man's attention. "What the fuck you say, nigga?" the man exclaimed, glaring at Nasir.

Nasir didn't know why he said it. It just came out of him like a sneeze he couldn't control, probably because of jealousy. But the cat was out of the bag now, and Nasir wasn't someone to back down from a fight.

"This isn't your business, fool," Nasir uttered.

By now, Lou noticed what was happening, and he picked up an empty beer bottle by the small end and positioned it in a threatening method. He was ready to break it upside the man's head and protect his cousin. The tension between Nasir and Denise's mystery date started to escalate.

"You know who the fuck I am, muthafucka?" the man growled.

"I don't give a fuck who you are," Nasir retorted.

Denise had to come between them before they exchanged blows. She pushed Nasir away from her date and exclaimed, "Let's talk outside."

Reluctantly, Nasir stepped out of the establishment into the cool night air. Denise was right behind him, upset. The moment the door closed behind her, she shouted at Nasir, "What the fuck is your problem?"

"You're my problem," he retorted.

"Really? Why? Because I didn't give you a call back?"

"What's up with you, Denise? Why are you dissing me?" Nasir asked her.

"Damn, nigga, you pussy whipped that quickly," she quipped.

"This shit isn't funny, Denise," he growled.

"What the fuck do you want from me? We fucked, had a good time, but you don't fuckin' own me, Nasir," she griped.

"I'm not trying to own you. Why would you think that? And who is that clown you're with anyway?"

Denise grinned. "You're really jealous, aren't you?"

"I don't like people playing me," said Nasir.

"Damn, are you gonna be a problem?" she snappishly replied.

"I'm not trying to be a problem."

"You didn't answer my question," she said.

"And I thought you said you liked me," he countered.

"I do, but I don't want your friendship with my brother to be a problem with us. You keep bringing up his name at the wrong time. You think I'm trying to think about him when I'm intimate with you. It turns me off," Denise stated.

"I won't then. I promise you that," he assured her.

Denise huffed, wanting to believe him.

Nasir stepped closer to her. He couldn't take his eyes off her. He took her hand into his. He continued, "It'll be just you and me, a'ight? I got you no matter what. No lie, I like you too. There's something about you that I can't stop thinking about, and running into you that night, I believe it was fate. Let's go somewhere and talk."

"So I'm supposed to forget about Lee and run off with you?" she laughed.

"That's that fool's name, Lee?"

"Yeah."

"But yeah, fuck that fool. I'll go tell him myself, right now," Nasir uttered excitedly. "You ain't fuck him, right?"

Denise laughed. "Wow, you do get jealous."

"Not over everybody," Nasir replied.

"But no, I didn't fuck him," Denise answered.

Nasir smiled. Denise smiled with her eyes and mouth. Nasir was someone special to her, but she was conflicted about his loyalty to her or her brother. She figured time would tell.

"You coming with me?" Nasir asked her.

Denise's smile widened. Of course she was leaving with him. Lee wasn't that interesting of a man in the first place. "You lead. I'll follow," she kidded.

"I'm gonna go tell my cousin and let Lee know you changed your mind," Nasir said.

He walked back into the bar where Lou was flirting with some random girl, and Lee was still by the bar buying drinks and waiting for Denise to return. Nasir went to Lou and said, "I'm out."

Lou smiled. "Oh, shit, you patched shit up with shorty?"

"Yeah." Nasir smiled.

"My nigga. Have fun. I'm working on my own thing for tonight," said Lou.

They gave each other dap. Then Nasir decided to tell Lee the bad news with his ego and a smile. So he approached Lee and uttered, "Yo, partner, I got some bad news for you. Denise is leaving with me tonight. So go jerk off somewhere."

Lee immediately frowned and responded, "What, nigga? What the fuck you say to me?"

"You heard me, nigga!" Nasir exclaimed.

"Fuck you, and go tell that dumb bitch to bring her trifling ass back into this bar before I fuck both of y'all up," Lee hollered.

The assault came out of nowhere, and Lou blindsided Lee with the empty beer bottle. He smashed it over his head, having it shatter completely. Lee hollered, "Oomph!" while he stumbled forward, not knowing what'd hit him.

As Lee slumped forward against the bar, a bit dizzy, Lee and Nasir were all over him like white on rice. Nasir slammed his fist into his jaw, and Lou tried to crack his head open with another beer bottle. Lee then folded in half and fell to the ground. Nasir and Lou continued attacking him with heated kicks and stomps. Everyone in the bar stood there in shock and silence, including Mary, with her mouth gaping.

Someone shouted, "They're going to kill him. Call the police!"

Finally, Lou and Nasir stopped their violent attack against Lee. He lay there, his breath wheezing and eyes closed. Warm blood ran down his face and filled his mouth, the pain blinding.

"Bitch-ass nigga!" Nasir roared.

Denise, hearing the commotion, had stepped foot into the bar again to catch the end of the assault. She, too, was taken aback. Lou and Nasir were savages, but something about Nasir's willingness to go the extra mile for her turned her on. She couldn't believe what he'd just done, but it happened because of her.

"Fuck that nigga!" Lou cursed.

The cousins spun and stormed out of the bar with Denise.

Outside, Denise stared at Nasir with some admiration. Then she uttered, "Wow, you're really crazy, you know that?"

"He disrespected you," said Nasir.

"You better give this nigga some pussy tonight," Lou joked.

"Let's get the fuck outta here before the cops show up," Nasir uttered.

The trio jumped into Lou's Jeep and left the scene, while Lee, still alive, slowly got up, dazed and confused, and limped and stumbled toward the door.

Chapter Twelve

Detective Michael Acosta stared long and hard at himself in the bathroom mirror. He was shirtless, locking eyes with his reflection as the faucet ran cold water into the sink. Acosta was a physically fit man in his early forties sporting a five o'clock shadow and hard eyes that had seen it all. He had seventeen years on the force, and being an NYPD detective came with its perks, but it also came with curses and nightmares. He'd been a detective for twelve years and saw his fair share of troublesome crimes out there—some so disturbing, it would give the boogeyman terrible dreams. But one of the curses of being a detective, and one highly skilled at his job, regularly took him away from his family and into the line of fire with other people.

Michael Acosta had been divorced for five years. His ex-wife, Janette, took both of their young children and moved to New Jersey. She eventually remarried and lived happily ever after with her new husband, who had a lucrative career in investment banking. Acosta was left behind with the remnants of an ugly divorce, child support, and becoming estranged from his children. The only thing he had left was the job.

Ten years of marriage went down the drain because of the high demands of being a detective first. He worked long hours, evenings, weekends, and holidays, and constantly saw the darkest underside of humanity. He had to deal with it every day. There was no turning back. There was no taking it away.

Lying on the sink counter was his police-issued Glock 17, and next to the gun was a pamphlet that read, "Recognizing Symptoms of Trauma." The bathroom was neat and quiet. Detective Acosta lived alone in a three-bedroom house in Elmhurst, Queens. His therapist reminded him that he needed to shore up his inner resources so he could rebound easier from the things he'd witnessed every day.

"You should build a healthy, intimate relationship outside of work," his female therapist reminded him. "Leave work at work and go enjoy being with family. It is hard but necessary to do this. Separation between the job and home life is significant."

What family? Acosta didn't have any family.

"Are you dating anyone?" she'd asked him.

He wasn't. The job was his relationship.

His therapist had said, "Substance use and mental illness often go together for detectives who are struggling."

The good news was that he didn't drink or use drugs to cope with the job. But the signs of becoming burnt out from the job were surfacing. The Wolf case four years ago placed Acosta into the spotlight. It was glitz and glamourous headlines for the mass media, sensationalism at its finest to provoke public interest and excitement. But Detective Acosta remembered the mutilated bodies. He was there from the beginning to the end. The faces of butchered young girls whom society had discarded haunted him. The newspapers, television, radio, and media could effortlessly move on to the following exciting headline. Still, a piece of his cases would always linger behind.

"Don't fuckin' burn out," Acosta said to himself. His eyes stayed fixed on his reflection. "They need you. They fuckin' need you."

The job was affecting his physical and emotional states, causing mental exhaustion. His left hand started to cramp. Sometimes, he would feel self-conscious about his ability to manage work and wondered what value he brought to the workplace. Maybe it was compromising his health.

Keep it together. Keep it together.

Detective Acosta's one spark was wanting to arrest Zulu. He'd become obsessed with putting the drug kingpin behind bars. The man was a menace to society with murders, racketeering, drugs, extortion, money laundering, and prostitution. But unfortunately, law enforcement couldn't get any charges to stick. Zulu was clever, manipulative, dangerous, and feared. The man had political and conglomerate reach and maybe a few dirty cops on his payroll. The streets knew Zulu and Zodiac murdered Mob Allah to seize control of a multi-million-dollar drug empire. But they couldn't prove it.

Acosta snapped himself from the daydream he was having. He turned off the water and sighed heavily. He took one final look at himself, then picked up his gun and walked out of the bathroom. The hallways, bedrooms, and living areas had been absent of family for years. But there were remnants of his family left behind, from pictures of his wife and kids hanging on walls, toys that remained stagnant from the time his kids left, and Christmas presents that were months old meant for his kids.

The moment Acosta entered the bedroom, his cell phone rang. It was his partner, Chris Emmerson, calling. The call indicated there was another murder. Michael Acosta answered the call with some indifference.

"Talk to me, Chris," he uttered nonchalantly.

"You need to see this," said Chris Emmerson.

"Where at this time?" asked Acosta.

"Jamaica Bay, Brooklyn," said Emmerson.

"That's a bit out of our jurisdiction," said Acosta.

"It is, but they found a body that I believe connects to Zulu."

"I'm on my way there now."

Michael Acosta ended the call, and then he took a seat at the foot of his bed to collect himself. Evil was twenty-four seven.

Detective Acosta's Toyota Camry arrived at the pier, Jamaica Bay, where the place was inundated with police activity during the early morning. The day dawned crisp and clear with the sun pouring through the car's windshield. A new day was supposed to bring new hopes and aspirations. Instead, it brought death and misery.

Acosta climbed out of his Camry in his dark blue suit and coolly approached the pier where the seagulls and other birds were going about their morning rituals. There was a gentle cool breeze. NYPD officers and members of the FDNY had scrambled to retrieve a body found bobbing in the water just off Canarsie Pier. Onlookers at Rockaway Parkway and the Canarsie Veterans Circle had watched in dismay as police helicopters hovered overhead and emergency services had worked in tandem to retrieve the body floating face down in the bay.

Detective Emmerson met his partner at the beginning of the pier.

"It's a woman they've found," Emmerson said. "They believe she's been dead for about four days."

"And you believe she's connected to Zulu," Acosta uttered.

"Follow me," said Emmerson.

The detectives walked toward the bloated and decomposing body. It wasn't pleasant. After a few days, what water could do to the body was disturbing. Detective Acosta got a good look at the body and remained unflinching. The skin started to peel off, and the body began to emit an unpleasant smell. The body also started to swell and discolor. It was almost becoming unrecognizable.

But Emmerson asked Acosta, "Do you recognize her?"

It took Acosta a moment to do so. First, he crouched closer with his eyes fixed on her face and a few tattoos on her chest. Then Detective Acosta was taken aback.

"Cynthia Blackwell, Zulu's baby mama," he uttered in disbelief.

"You think it was a rival hit?" Emmerson mentioned.

Acosta wasn't sure. Zulu had many enemies. He remembered a few years ago when Rafe came after his family.

"They tried to weigh her down. It didn't work. She floated to the surface. If she had stayed in the water a few days longer, she would have been completely decomposed and unrecognizable," Emmerson stated.

"If it was a rival hit, then why would they try to make her disappear? Wouldn't they want to send a message and kill her in public?" Acosta suggested.

"So you think this was Zulu's doing?"

Detective Acosta's instincts told him that this was personal. She'd fucked up somehow, costing her her life. He'd run into Cynthia a few times while investigating Zulu several years ago. She was a beautiful woman with two lovely kids. It was hard to comprehend why she was with a brute like Zulu—maybe it was the money, power, nice things. It was easy trappings for a woman like Cynthia, who came from nothing. Unfortunately, benefiting from a life of crime came with a grave cost, and if Zulu had Cynthia killed, it was coldhearted, and Acosta wanted to arrest him right away and charge him with murder. Unfortunately, Zulu would have a sealed, tight alibi, and he most likely outsourced the murder. A man in his position rarely got his hands dirty, and besides, he and his partner weren't the primaries on the case. The body had washed up in Brooklyn.

"What did you do to get yourself killed like this?" Acosta asked Cynthia but talked to himself.

While Detective Acosta stared at Cynthia's bloated and disfigured body, Emmerson was chatting with two Brooklyn detectives. It was their case, their call. However, Acosta fumed inside. Cynthia wasn't a gangbanger, a drug dealer, or a thug. She was a black woman who happened to become involved with the wrong man. Cynthia had to be no older than 27. She was young, a mother, a daughter. Now she was a casualty of the drug game. This wasn't his case, but Detective Acosta started to take things personally. He stood up, pivoted suddenly, and marched back to his Camry. Detective Emmerson noticed his partner's sudden departure. He immediately chased after him.

"Mike, where are you off to so suddenly?" Chris Emmerson shouted.

"I need to take care of something," Acosta replied.

"Don't do what I think you're about to do. It isn't worth it," Emmerson blurted.

"I just want to talk to him," Acosta exclaimed.

"It's going to be considered police harassment," Emmerson countered.

But Detective Acosta didn't care what it was considered. He was tired of Zulu's disregard for human life. *How could he kill the mother of his two kids?*

"C'mon, Mike, you're smarter than this. Don't do anything stupid," said Emmerson, trying to prevent his partner from leaving.

"As I said, I'm just going to talk to him," Acosta uttered with finality.

He started the Camry and sped away, leaving his partner behind, looking concerned.

Chapter Thirteen

Jackson's Boxing Gym in Hollis, Queens, produced some of the greatest fighters in the nation. The place shaped some of the best boxers in the city, with three contenders training for the state and regional Golden Gloves and the Olympics. It was the place to be if you wanted to become the best of the best. The sizable gym came completed with a boxing ring in the center of the stage, punching bags, exercise benches, weights, machines, classes, showers, and changing rooms, and it was one of two businesses that Zulu owned he kept clean: no money laundering through the place. Zulu's love for boxing started when he was 13 years old. When he was 16, he became a serious contender for the state Golden Gloves. But his involvement in the streets ended his boxing career.

The boxing gym was busy with young and adult protégé training with one-on-one personal trainers or alone. A few other protégés were shadowboxing or hitting the punching bag. The gym was energetic with activity, and Zulu took it all in with a relaxed smile. However, one particular young trainee caught his attention. His name was Jaron Ortiz. He was a young, amateur bull ready to take the boxing world by storm, compete in the Junior Olympics, and become *The Ring* magazine's Prospect of the Year.

Zulu stood in the ring mentoring his protégé Jaron. Jaron was shirtless, slim, and muscular. He had on a pair of black and gold boxing gloves and was ready to spar with a fierce opponent named Nacho Cruiz, who stood five eleven and weighed 210 pounds. Everyone circled the ring, anticipating seeing Jaron spar with Nacho, who was once the world's light heavyweight champion. Though there was a wager for a quarter of a million dollars on the match, Zulu had a genuine passion for and experience in boxing. He loved both boxing and watching the matches and had even attended a few Vegas fights VIP style.

"You got this," Zulu said to Jaron.

Jaron nodded. Even though Nacho was once the light heavyweight champion, he was assured of himself. Both opponents stood on opposite sides of the ring, their adrenaline running, egos ready to clash. They sized each other up, and though this was only a sparring match, it nearly felt like the real thing. There were some heavy hitters in attendance. Everyone was hustling bets. The action was heavier than both fighters' weights combined.

A shot caller from Brooklyn named Leon Knight shouted to Zulu, "Should I bet the fight don't go the distance? Your boy feeling strong, Zulu? He up against the best. That's a five-time national champion."

"A hundred grand. Put your money where your mouth is," Zulu countered.

Leon smiled and nodded.

Zulu gave Jaron a pep talk to make his protégé feel courageous and animalistic. Jaron listened intently, knowing Zulu was once a great boxer himself.

"Listen, you win this for me, and I'll give you ten percent of my winnings. That's forty grand. You want that money, muthafucka?" Zulu exclaimed zealously.

Jaron fervently nodded and clobbered his gloves together. "I want it!"

Zulu grinned. "Then earn it, muthafucka. Make that money and get you some pussy tonight."

Jaron smiled widely, bouncing, looking relaxed and focused.

Zulu climbed out of the ring. The bell rang, and Jaron made the sign of the cross and then hurried to the center of the ring. The fighters quickly engaged in battle. Everyone's undivided attention was on the fight. Jaron threw the first punch, a stiff jab. Nacho blocked it and sent one back. Jaron ducked it and caught Nacho clean with two counters.

Zulu shouted, "Nice! Nice!"

Nacho quickly shook off the hits and grabbed Jaron, surprised that he was in for a rude awakening. The young boy had speed and power. But Nacho would show him why he was once the five-time national champion. Jaron bounced in on Nacho, sending out a couple of jabs, and Nacho blocked them and sent a couple back at Jaron. Jaron ducked the first few and tried to counter with a left jab. But Nacho slipped it and was able to get Jaron into the corner. Then he began sending shot after shot at Jaron. Jaron dodged a few of them and tried to make a hard slip to the right when blam!

Jaron was caught flush in the side of the head by a left hook from Nacho. Jaron became wobbled by this. The crowd exploded. Nacho was ready to finish him off.

Zulu shouted, "Jaron, tie him up and bang him on the ropes!"

Jaron did what he was told.

"Show me that you want to make some money today," Zulu added.

Jaron jabbed three times to work his way in. First, Nacho threw a big right, but Jaron slipped it beautifully, and then he drove a hard wide left hook into Nacho's ribs. Nacho grunted in pain. He was hurt and spun out, and Jaron threw a five-punch combo as the bell rang.

It was an entertaining first round.

***

Detective Acosta's gold Camry turned into the gravel parking lot to Jackson's Boxing Gym in Hollis, Queens. He hopped out of the car and walked toward the gym with a purpose. A batch of luxury vehicles was parked outside the gym, but the detective charged into the gym like the Terminator.

He stormed inside, where a sparring match happened between Nacho Cruiz and Jaron Ortiz, and Zulu was standing ringside like some training coach instead of a drug kingpin. One of Zulu's goons tried to prevent the detective from entering the gym. He came in front of the detective and exclaimed, "Yo, the gym is closed for now."

Detective Acosta responded with a hard right to the man's jaw, and then he pushed past another man and continued forward. The commotion at the doorway caught everyone's attention, with the sparring match ending, and Acosta was fortunate he wasn't shot right away.

He glared at Zulu and shouted, "What did she do? Huh? What did she do to deserve to die like that?"

Zulu and everyone else were baffled by the detective's rant. Detective Acosta continued to push toward Zulu heatedly but was prevented from approaching by a wall of men ready to beat him to a pulp.

"This is the wrong time for your foolishness, Detective," Zulu growled. "Now is not the time."

"Fuck you! You killed that girl for what?" Acosta heatedly shouted.

Zulu stared back at the detective with confusion.

"Oh, Cynthia's body washed up on Jamaica Bay early this morning. Whoever you hired to get rid of the body, they failed at it," Acosta vehemently roared.

"I don't know what you're talking about, Detective."

"You killed that girl. I know it was you, and I'm going to hunt you down and lock you up, and I pray someday soon they'll put that fuckin' needle in your arm," Acosta hollered.

Zulu scowled. The detective was embarrassing him inside of the gym he owned. Everyone was watching and listening. Detective Acosta continued to tussle with a few of Zulu's henchmen.

"You're going to burn in hell, Zulu. I swear you are! And I'm not going to stop until you're either dead or locked inside a prison cell twenty-four seven," Acosta continued to rant.

Molten anger rolled through Zulu, and he charged toward Acosta with his fists clenched, ready to brawl with the cop. But Zodiac immediately came in between the men. He pushed Zulu back and uttered, "No. Not here, not now. Don't let him bait you."

Zulu resisted, but Zodiac was adamant, seething. Zodiac then spun around and shouted at the henchmen, "Get him the fuck out of here! Now!"

The detective wrestled with the henchmen as they struggled to remove him from the gym. Zulu wanted to brutally tear into the detective, not caring whether he was a veteran cop. He couldn't believe the audacity of him storming into his place of business, insinuating that he had the mother of his children murdered and dumped into the ocean.

"I'm going to put you in handcuffs myself!" Acosta shouted.

Everyone in the gym watched as the henchmen roughly ejected Acosta from the premises. With the cop gone, things were far from going back to normal. Zulu continued to seethe. Jaron and Nacho stood in the ring in awe. Zulu pivoted and marched into the gym's office with Zodiac following him.

Zodiac closed the office door for their privacy. Zulu threw an aggressive tantrum inside the office. He angrily swiped everything off the desk with one sweeping motion, toppling everything to the floor. He then glared at Zodiac and exclaimed, “I want a fuckin’ contract out on that muthafucka cop right now.”

“You think that would be wise, Zulu?”

“I don’t give a fuck what you think it is. He fuckin’ embarrassed me in there! I want him dead,” Zulu retorted.

“And he’s a decorated detective who cracked some high-profile cases. So if you have him killed, the only thing you’re going to do is bring the full weight of the NYPD and the Feds down on us,” Zodiac explained.

“So I’m supposed to let some fuckin’ cop continue to harass and embarrass me?” Zulu countered. “No. He needs to go. I want it done, Zodiac. Soon!”

Zodiac huffed. It felt like there was no reasoning with Zulu.

“And how the fuck did Cynthia’s body resurface? I told them I didn’t want her found. How did they fuck that up? Now I got heat on me because of niggers’ incompetence. They need to go too, Zodiac. With this muthafucka cop having a hard-on for me, I can’t afford any loose ends. So make it happen,” Zulu proclaimed.

Zulu then stormed from the office, leaving Zodiac behind to plot the unthinkable—the murder of an NYPD detective.

Chapter Fourteen

It was a cool October night with the faces of poverty, despair, and addiction on full display on the impoverished Queens street. The red-light district, an eight-block industrial stretch in Jamaica, Queens, was bustling with activity. The South Road area had been notorious for its prostitution industry since the 1980s. It was well after midnight, and a few scantily clad women walked mid-block, their heels click-clacking on the asphalt, some moving from car to car, leaning into car windows to entice the driver for a date. It was an open-air sex market with a few pimps pulling the strings from the shadows.

Lou cruised the area in his dark green Pathfinder. He took a pull from his cigarette and set his eyes on a few ladies working tonight, some young and some old. He was familiar with the area and a few working girls. A few waved his way, but Lou smiled and continued cruising through the site. This was his world. He loved the streets, the prostitutes, the drugs, the gunplay, and the hustle and bustle—survival of the fittest. It was what he lived for. Lou was a colorful character with a deep love for family.

He continued to cruise through the neighborhood in search of someone, and though other ladies wanted Lou's attention, he had one particular girl in mind. He soon found her when he turned onto 157th Street and saw an older prostitute named Lexi strutting down the dim street in a pair of red heels, a short skirt, and a loose-fitting top underneath a black jacket. Lexi walked parallel to an empty lot. Lou maneuvered the Jeep to the curb and rolled down the driver's window. He slightly leaned out of it and hollered, "Hey there, beautiful."

Lexi turned to see Lou, and she smiled. "You lookin' for a date tonight?" she asked him.

"Of course," Lou responded right away.

Lexi strutted toward the Pathfinder with zeal. Lou was one of her regulars, and seeing her, Lou was all smiles. He stared at her with anticipation. Lexi was 36 years old, and she was a veteran on the streets. Prostitution was her livelihood, and crack cocaine was her party favor, but her drug use didn't affect her looks and curves—not yet, anyway. She was dark-skinned. Long lashes framed her eyes, and she wore bright emerald green contacts.

She climbed into the passenger seat and immediately kissed Lou on his cheek. "How have you been, hon?" she asked him. "I haven't seen you around lately."

"I've been good. Been busy," Lou responded.

"Too busy to come see me lately, I see."

Lou chuckled. "Nah, never that."

"Well, it's good to see you."

"Ditto."

"And what are you looking for?" she asked him.

"I've been stressed. Lately, a lot's been goin' on. Need some of that old-school head right now," he said.

Lexi smiled. "I got you. Find us a spot."

Lexi wasn't any spring chicken, but something about her kept Lou coming back to her for years even though she was ten years his senior, and though she worked the streets and had a drug habit, Lexi had an infectious smile and a catching personality.

Lou pulled away and glanced at her thick thighs peeking from underneath her short skirt. He soon parked at a dead-end, desolate location a few blocks from where he picked up Lexi. Then he handed her $100 when she only charged her clients $50. He liked her, and he knew she had it rough.

"You always lookin' out for me, hon. I appreciate it," Lexi said.

"No doubt. You're worth it."

He unbuckled his jeans and removed his erection. He was thick and average. Lexi smiled, ready to please him and take him to the moon. Lou reclined in his seat, keeping his gun close just in case, and Lexi bent into his lap and quickly took him into her mouth. Lou groaned with the sudden jolt of pleasure, feeling the suction from her lips. She leaned farther to take more of his dick into her mouth, moaning, sending a touch of vibration down his shaft and into his balls. Lexi continued to shove his dick down her throat.

"Damn, girl. Oh, fuck," Lou moaned.

She bobbed her head up and down in the front seat with Lou's hand on the back of her head. Then, just like that, it was over. He shuddered from the orgasm and groaned above her while she swallowed strange, bitter semen.

With Lou spent and satisfied, Lexi arose, wiped the remnants of sucking dick from her mouth, and smiled at Lou.

"Damn, you definitely know how to make me relax," said Lou.

"That's what I'm here for, hon," Lexi replied politely.

Lou began to collect himself. He arose in his seat and fastened his jeans. Then he started the Jeep and drove off.

"You got a cigarette?" Lexi asked him.

While driving, he removed his pack of Newports and handed it to her. Lexi pulled two cigarettes and quickly lit one. She took a needed drag. It had been a long night, and the nicotine was another stress reliever.

Lou arrived at the same area where he picked up Lexi. But she wasn't in any rush to get out of the Jeep. They soon noticed a young, curvy girl climb out of a blue Accord across the street, indicating she'd just finished with a date. The car drove off as the girl pulled down her skirt and made her way toward an idling Cadillac Escalade. It was her apparent pimp keeping watch from his flashy vehicle idling on the stretch. The girl walked to the driver's side and handed the driver something. She then pivoted and went back to work.

Lexi frowned and rolled her eyes. It was obvious she was displeased with what was happening.

"You know that nigga?" asked Lou.

"That's Earth," she uttered.

"Earth?" Lou replied, surprised by the unique name.

"He runs most of these girls around here. He even tried to get at me a few times, but I kept reminding him that I'm independent. I see he's in his Escalade tonight."

"He's getting money like that?"

Lexi nodded. "Some days, he's in a black Mercedes or a Lexus. I can't stand him. He thinks he's God's gift to these bitches. He beats his girls and keeps them living off of scraps."

"Oh, word, that's a foul nigga."

"He is," Lexi concurred. "But it's been fun, Lou. Don't wait too long to see me again."

"I won't." Lou smiled.

She smiled back, gave him another kiss on the cheek, and exited his Jeep. Lou watched Lexi strut up the block heading back into the life she knew best. He would always have a special place in his heart for her—long ago, she was his high school teacher who taught art. But unfortunately, a few bad decisions and an abusive boyfriend altered her life completely.

Lou lingered in the area, slyly parked, and watched the pimp's every movement like a hawk. He observed a stable of pretty young girls go back and forth to the Escalade, dropping off money. Earth sat comfortably on the block, sporting a Rolex and a diamond ring. His mere presence was enough to maintain a general sense of business-like order in the flesh trade.

Lou lit a cigarette and began to plot against Earth. He'd decided that he would rob Earth of everything he had.

Lou placed a Smith & Wesson 457 and Mossberg 500 shotgun on the kitchen table and proclaimed, "It's time for us to get paid, cuzzo. You've been home long enough."

Nasir remained quiet and stared at the artillery on the table.

"I got the guns ready and got a nigga ready to get got. He's making too much money on the streets, and we need to take some of that. Nah, we need to take all of it," Lou added.

Nasir stared at his animated cousin, somewhat dumbfounded.

"What the fuck are you giving me that look for?" Lou asked.

"So we're stick-up kids now?" Nasir replied.

"How the fuck else you think we gon' get paid, muthafucka? This is what I do, cuzzo. You know that. It's time to get your name ringing on these streets again. We gon' get this money, and we gon' flip that paper and do us," Lou proclaimed vibrantly.

"And who's the target?"

"I've been watching this pimp nigga named Earth for a few days get money pimping these bitches. This ho put me on to him. He's pushing an Escalade, a Lexus, and a fuckin' Benz. He be on the track flossing, cuzzo. I'm talkin' about Rolexes and diamonds, nigga. He out there solo, thinkin' he can't get got. This is our chance," Lou stated.

"You know where he rests his head?" asked Nasir.

"I'm gonna find out, believe that shit. But it's time for you to stop playing house with this bitch and do you again, cuzzo," said Lou.

"Don't call her a bitch," Nasir replied.

Lou chuckled. "Look, cuzzo, I'm not trying to disrespect shorty, but I want you to get back on your A game, and you can't do that being deep in some pussy every night."

While Lou and Nasir discussed the robbery, Denise came out of the bedroom clad in one of Nasir's T-shirts and entered the kitchen. She had been staying with them since the bar fight, and every night, the two had been having porn-style sex.

"You in here talking about me, Lou?" asked Denise.

"Yeah! I am," Lou responded frankly.

"What, are you jealous? You wanna fuck me too?" Denise said.

Lou chuckled. "Nah, you ain't my speed, Denise. Besides, you're like family."

Denise stepped closer to Lou and placed her hand against his chest, displaying an awkward but intimate moment. Then she locked eyes with Lou and replied, "That's good to hear because I'm a one-man woman."

"Well, you need to tell your man that it's time to start goin' out there to make this money again," said Lou.

"And what do you have planned?" Denise asked.

She stepped toward the table with the guns and picked up the Smith & Wesson 457. She held the gun in her hands with familiarity.

"You know what you're doin' with that? It isn't a toy, you know," said Lou.

Denise coolly removed the clip to the handgun, then cocked back the chamber, and a bullet ejected from it.

She caught it into her hand, and the clip was fully loaded. Lou was impressed.

"My brother taught me about guns, and he taught me how to shoot. He wanted me to know how to defend myself," she replied.

"Okay. I respect that," Lou uttered.

Nasir grinned. He was impressed too.

"So what's going on? Who are y'all going to war with?" she questioned, eyeing them both. "This is some grown-man business," said Lou.

"Then why are you in the room?" Denise countered.

Nasir laughed.

"Oh, you got jokes, I see," Lou responded.

"Don't treat me like I'm some brittle, naive bitch who don't know shit about the streets. You know what the streets took from me, Lou," Denise vehemently proclaimed.

The look in Denise's eyes said it all. She was down for whatever. Lou nodded and replied, "Okay. Then you can be of some use to us."

"Y'all get money, we get money together," she announced.

"Then let's get this money," Lou exclaimed.

Denise took a seat on Nasir's lap at the kitchen table. Nasir warmly placed his arms around her, squeezing her close.

"Ah, aren't y'all two looking all cute? Now don't be having my cousin overdosing on some pussy," Lou joked.

Denise smirked and flipped him the middle finger with a polite, "Fuck you!"

"But anyway, as I was saying to cuzzo, I got put on to this pimp named Earth. He's making too much money out there, and I want it."

"So what's the plan?" Denise asked him.

"Reconnaissance first. I'm watching this fool every night. He got about eight girls working for him, and each girl is bringing in, on average, about a thousand dollars a night."

"Damn!" Nasir uttered.

"Yeah, cuzzo, this fool is bringing in nearly ten grand a night pimping, selling pussy. Muthafuckas is really horny out there like y'all two," Lou pointed out.

Denise rolled her eyes at the comment, then sighed.

"But I ain't gonna front. This nigga got some badass bitches in his stable."

"Did you fuck one of his bitches, Lou?" asked Denise.

Lou smiled. "No lie, yeah, I fucked a few. Earth's bitches are hitting niggas in the head for a hundred dollars a pop. But he's smart. He moves around a lot. A few nights, he's in Brooklyn, then the Bronx, Harlem, New Jersey, shit, even Staten Island."

"So what's the plan then?" Nasir inquired.

"Two options. We kidnap one of his bitches and force her to give up the spot, or two, we kidnap one of his bitches and force her to give up the spot," said Lou seriously.

Denise chuckled dubiously. "That's it? Are you serious? His hoes might be loyal, and what makes you so sure they'll give up that information?"

"That's why you find the weakest link, and fortunately for us, I already found the bitch. I came out of my pockets to fuck the bitch a few times and got her to like me. But we can work her. I vetted this bitch, and she got kids and a grandma looking after them," Lou proclaimed. "We use that against her, threaten this bitch's kids and family, and she'll give it up."

Nasir and Denise were impressed.

"So when are we going to execute this shit?" Denise asked.

"In a few days," Lou said. "Y'all ready to get this money?"

Nasir and Denise shared a glance, then replied, "Let's do this."

Chapter Fifteen

"Attract what you expect. Reflect on what you desire. Become what you respect. Mirror what you admire," Cook Gamble preached proudly to the young boys and girls in the classroom of the youth center, with them hanging on every word coming from him.

Cook addressed the adolescents looking sharper than ever in an Arthur Black classic-fit blue plaid three-piece wool suit and polished wingtip shoes. He paced back and forth with confidence and posture in front of the youths. He was the epitome of Black success and excellence to everyone inside the room.

"A successful man can lay a firm foundation with the bricks that others throw at him," Cook continued. "I've worked hard to get where I am, and for every young, fresh face in this room today, you can get where I'm today. But it takes determination, focus, drive, and a plan."

The youthful faces staring back at Cook were dreamers from ages 14 to 19. It was a packed classroom, and the adult ladies were all smiles, and they listened attentively. Cook Gamble was fashionable, handsome, successful, and black, and their attraction to him was palpable. Cook relished the admiration he received. He talked about himself and his businesses and preached about his past. Cook was a product from the streets of Jamaica, Queens—an orphaned boy who never knew his parents. He grew up in a heap of foster homes, joined a gang when he was 12 years old, and had been arrested for everything from shoplifting to drug possession. By the time he was 17, he was a fierce adversary of law enforcement. By the time Cook turned 21, he'd changed his life completely and had become a different man with focus and a plan.

So it appeared.

Cook glanced at the time on his Cartier watch. It was after 6:00 p.m., and it was time for him to wind things down. He had some business to take care of.

"Any questions for me?" Cook asked.

A young girl raised her hand and stood. She smiled at Cook and asked, "I love your clothes. But I want to know, is your clothing store hiring?"

Cook smiled. "Come in anytime and apply. I'll see what I can do."

More students began asking him a few questions, and Cook coolly answered them the best he could.

One 16-year-old male asked him, "How can I dress fly like you? I know you get all the ladies."

The room laughed. Cook too. Then he responded with, "'Fashion is not necessarily about labels. It's about something else that comes from within you.' A quote from Ralph Lauren, one of my favorite designers."

It was deep, and everyone nodded approvingly.

The speaking engagement ended, and Cook did some small talk with a few ladies interested in him. It was flattering. But with his bright, golden-boy smile, he said to them, "Excuse me, ladies, but I must leave soon for a subsequent engagement."

"We understand, and we enjoyed your time and company," said Maria, the center director. "And we would love to have you back."

"And I would love to come back and continue to enlighten these kids about my success and Black excellence," he said.

Cook pivoted and made his exit from the room and, soon, the building. He marched toward his prized Mercedes-Benz, deactivated the alarm, and climbed inside. He brought the vehicle to life and drove off, heading to his next destination.

It was a beautiful night, warm night. Cook threw the moonroof back and let some music play as he cruised through the streets of Queens. Business was good. The community loved and respected him. He was also a rich but greedy man, always looking for new opportunities to make more money and create a stronger influence on the streets. It was about money, power, and respect. Nothing less.

Cook lit a cigarette and jumped onto the Belt Parkway going toward Brooklyn. He soon arrived in Coney Island, Brooklyn. He parked his Benz in the parking lot near the boardwalk and the Parachute Jump, a now-defunct amusement ride and landmark in the city. It was later in the night, and the amusement park was closed. The entire area was still, sparse of any activity, and sketchy. Coney Island was known for its gangs, drugs, and violence. However, Cook felt comfortable climbing out of his Benz in his expensive suit and pricey watch. He lit a cigarette and looked around.

Soon, a black Yukon arrived where Cook stood waiting. The headlights were bright on him as Cook peered unflinchingly at the vehicle. He took a final pull from the cigarette and flicked it away. The doors to the Yukon opened, and two men climbed out, Ricky and Tony, two young Brooklyn hustlers with ambition.

Ricky smiled at Cook and sized him up.

"Answer me something, Cook. Will I ever see you in some jeans and Timberlands, nigga? You always meet us looking like you're coming from fuckin' Wall Street," said Ricky.

Cook laughed. "What can I say? Clothes do make the man."

"Well, point a nigga like me to your tailor. I might need an upgrade myself and be fashionable as you," Ricky replied.

"I don't do fashion. I am fashion, nigga," Cook coolly responded. "But did we come out here to talk about clothes or do some business?"

Ricky and Tony smiled.

"You got that for us?" asked Tony.

Cook opened the trunk to his Benz and removed a small black duffle bag filled with five kilograms of cocaine.

"Five kilos. What you asked for," said Cook.

Ricky gave Tony a nod, and Tony retrieved the duffle bag from Cook in exchange for the cash.

"These deals ain't gonna come back on us, right?" Ricky asked.

"Why would they?" replied Cook.

"You're jumping off the rail, Cook. You think we don't know?" said Ricky.

"Know what?"

"You're in business with the Hispanics in Washington Heights, going behind Zulu's back," Ricky uttered. "I mean, business is business, and I like to make money. But the last thing I need is to be on Zulu's radar on some fuckboy shit."

"As you said, business is business, and you still showed up despite what you know, right? So you get your product. I get my money. Don't complicate it. You're not that stupid," Cook replied.

"Yeah, well, we're always gonna be good on our end. You know? We just don't want whatever stink that might land on you to stain us," said Ricky.

Cook grinned, then did a fashionable spin and replied, "Look at me, nigga. Do I look like a nigga who gets shit tossed on him?"

Ricky and Tony laughed. Cook was charismatic.

Their transaction seemed to be over, and Ricky and Tony headed toward the Yukon. But Ricky spun back around with an afterthought.

"Yo, Cook, I'm also gonna need some of those party favors you be offering," said Ricky.

Cook looked clueless.

Ricky chuckled. Then he added, "Let's just say I know a guy you did some business with. Pussy, right? You're a jack-of-all-trades on these streets. Too bad the right people ain't seeing you."

"I don't know what you're talking about," Cook responded nonchalantly.

"Think about it," said Ricky.

"I already have, and there's nothing to think about," Cook replied with finality.

Cook pivoted and marched back to his vehicle. Ricky smirked and retreated to the Yukon with Tony, and they went their separate ways.

Cook tried to keep a low profile, but the streets did talk. It slightly bothered him that Ricky knew about his sex-trafficking operation. However, it was something he and Winter kept hushed, and they moved clandestinely through the internet. The extra money coming from moving girls went to buying coke and dope from the Hispanics in Washington Heights. It was a risky move, but Cook had grown tired of being subservient to Zulu's money laundering and distribution. It was time for him to expand.

He jumped back onto the Belt Parkway and headed back to Queens. What Ricky said to him was on his mind, but he tried not to let it trouble him. It would be a busy night, and he had other matters to deal with.

Chapter Sixteen

It was a few hours before dawn. Cook's Mercedes-Benz arrived at a seedy motel in Far Rockaway, Queens. He exited the vehicle and walked to the lobby of the motel. When he entered, there was an old black man with masses of wrinkles around his eyes and uncountable frown lines across his forehead behind the thick partition. His name was Smitty. The older man's dull brown wrinkled skin creased into a smile when he saw Cook.

"You're back so soon?" asked Smitty.

"Business doesn't stop for me," Cook responded. "Has it been quiet?"

"Not a sound from her room."

"Cool. Thanks for looking out," said Cook.

"Anything you need, Mr. Cook. You always look out," replied Smitty.

Cook reached into his pocket and removed a wad of cash. He peeled off a few hundred dollars and slid it underneath the glass partition.

"A little something extra for you, Smitty."

Smitty took the cash and grinned. "The money and perks working here. Best job I ever had," he proclaimed.

Cook grinned, knowing what perks the old clerk was talking about.

He made his way up the steps toward the motel's second floor. The place had seen better days. The medley of characters and personalities hanging around the motel was intriguing. There were many black faces, young and old, primarily prostitutes turning tricks out of the rooms and drug addicts. It was a haven for lots of unsavory activities.

Cook moved down the narrow hallway, and while doing so, he could hear the sounds of debauchery and specific sleazy actions. Sexual commotion echoed from certain rooms. A room door opened, and Cook caught a glimpse of a sexy but abused-looking model strutting around the room in some performance for a businessman. He laughed.

A real buzz of perverted energy permeated the entire place.

Finally, Cook arrived at the designated room and used his keycard to enter. Immediately, he smiled at Anna. She was still up, lying on one of the twin beds watching TV.

“Did you eat anything today?” he asked her.

“Some pizza,” she said.

He unbuttoned his suit jacket and placed it around the back of the chair. The motel room was subpar. The bathroom had peeling paint and black mold on the walls. The carpet was stained, and you could write your name on the top of the microwave. However, the offensive decor of the room didn’t bother Cook.

Anna was clad in a T-shirt and jeans. It’d been nearly twenty-four hours since he’d rescued her from her pimp. Now Cook had a decision to make. He wrestled with the idea of pimping her himself or putting Anna up for sale on the black market. She was easy to persuade and manipulate. She was young, not from New York, and naive. The only thing Cook needed to do was show her some concern and friendliness. But what he was doing was bringing Anna into a situation of dependency both financially and emotionally. In her eyes, the cheap room was a five-star place compared to other dire situations. Young, shapely white girls weren’t a dime a dozen.

The one thing Cook liked to do was sample the goods himself. His natural animalistic and primitive instincts took over. Cook knew he needed to fuck her soon. He had ways to manipulate young girls to engage in various forms of commercial sex with paying customers, either by force, fraud, or coercion. Fortunately for him, Anna had already been broken in by her previous pimp. It showed in her docile eyes and her meek actions. But now, it was time for him to add his seasoning to her distress.

"You are beautiful," said Cook.

She smiled while he maneuvered closer to her.

"I want to take care of you," he said while laying her back on the bed and pressing his body into hers. "You want me to take care of you?"

Anna nodded. "Yes."

He began whispering in her ear, "I want you. I need you."

Cook then took her hand and directed it toward his crotch, which was desperate to break free from its confines. She started to massage his genitalia, and then she marveled at the length and thickness of his erection. Cook was big, and he became hard. She opened her mouth wide, relaxed her throat, and soon took him into her mouth. Cook groaned as Anna took him as deeply as she could into her mouth, with the urge to gag.

"Damn, girl," Cook moaned.

Anna bobbed her head up and down, and then Cook placed his hand on her head, shoving his dick into her mouth. She gagged but kept going with her hand stroking him, too.

Cook quickly undressed her until she was completely naked on the bed. Her nude olive skin glowed. He took every delicious inch of her body in, savoring her with his eyes. Cook stood at the foot of the bed and lowered his remaining garments, standing firm, hard, and ready in every possible way. Climbing on the bed, he crawled between Anna's legs and spread them. She felt exposed and vulnerable. She knew what was in store for her, knowing that she was ready and wanted to please him. She wanted this. Cook had his entire weight pressed deeply into her. He lined up the head of his dick with her wet slit and rubbed it up and down. His fingers gripped her flesh tightly, taking careful aim, and he rammed himself inside her. The heat was intense, and he'd shoved himself into her in one full stroke.

Cook began pounding Anna like he was a man driven by lust. It was clear he was treating her like a fuck doll. Anna's breathing was labored. Her chest heaved up and down, showing her arousal. The harder Cook pounded, the more she screamed. Her cries were primal, carnal even.

"Fuck! Fuck!" she cried out.

Cook's colossal length and girth left no room for her to breathe, and Anna had to brace herself for the ride of a lifetime. He cocked her legs and contorted her like a pretzel, taking full advantage. She was 19. He was in his early thirties. Cook knew the mind games to implement given her petite stature and youthfulness.

Nevertheless, Anna loved every second of the rough treatment. The more she was about to come, the harder he fucked her. Finally, the pounding became intense, and it soon drove her crazy, giving her a string of multiple orgasms.

"Ooh fuck," Anna hollered and squirmed underneath him.

He rammed, fucked, and pounded her without mercy.

Cook pulled his dick out, and he watched as Anna's body reacted by going into convulsions. Then without warning, he shoved himself back inside of her slippery, wet folds, ready to repeat the act. This time, he fucked her slowly, intentionally, hitting hard the right spots, making Anna beg for more. Her body became covered in sweat as she released moans and groans, with the buildup becoming too much for her to bear. She used the muscles of her pussy to squeeze and stroke Cook's giant erection inside her. If she had any control left, it was in how her tight pussy massaged him. He fucked her, and she fucked him back. Soon, Anna hollered uncontrollably, and her body went limp with her having the mother of all orgasms. Cook refused to give in, and he kept fucking her with all his might.

When Cook was about to come, he pulled out with her wet, foamy juices on his dick and began jerking off over Anna's stomach. Then he released his seed on her flesh. Anna collapsed on her side, exhausted and drained of energy from such a strenuous experience. There was no intimacy or cuddling afterward. It was about control for Cook. He smiled at his work. Anna had been fucked into absolute submission.

As Cook began dressing, he said to her, "You're a phenomenal fuck with some really good pussy. Damn, I'm still trying to figure out what to do with you."

It was a bold statement that Anna wholly ignored. She had been dickmatized. Her young white flesh continued to glow with delight.

"I have to make moves. Continue to make yourself comfortable. If you need anything, contact the front clerk, and he'll get it for you. Everything's on me," said Cook.

Anna smiled.

Cook was now fully dressed back into his business armor, transitioning from a lust-crazed deviant to looking like a man who was a pillar of the community. He looked at Anna as she lay naked on the bed, childlike.

"Stay put. I'll be back soon," said Cook before exiting the room.

She nodded.

He made his way to the lobby, where Smitty was behind the glass partition watching television. Cook went up to him and said, "Keep an eye out for her, okay? I might make her a long stay here."

Smitty nodded. Then he replied, "Well, can I hit that too?"

"Just do your job, nigga. That's what I'm paying you for. Besides, this one's special," Cook snapped.

Smitty understood.

Cook turned and made his exit from the motel, and he climbed into his dark blue E-Class a proud man. Business was good. He felt he had the best of both worlds. But before pulling away from the seedy motel, he lit a cigarette and took a needed drag.

He was a deceitful man instead of being a pillar of the community. He laundered drug money and clandestinely moved kilos for his benefit, unbeknownst to his superiors. He trafficked, abused, kidnapped, and pimped young girls for profits and desires. Cook was a monster, a wolf in sheep's skin.

Chapter Seventeen

The gray light of morning in the urban jungle descended onto the derelict Queens street, gradually shining daylight onto areas where debauchery and sexual activity once took place. The prostitutes, tricks, and drug dealers were fading from the site or busy with a final customer. A few pillars of the community—doctors, lawyers, accountants, businesspeople, and married men—were regulars in the daily sex trade. The night on the track had its own cadence to which its participants would dance.

Daybreak began to percolate into the silver BMW. A married accountant with three children was hard as a rock as he fucked Iris's mouth. She was one of the last girls still working the track. Her trick was losing control as Iris gave him the sloppiest, wettest blowjob he'd ever gotten. She sucked him like a vacuum, pulling him in with her full lips. The intensity of her suction and pulling lips had the middle-aged accountant out of his mind.

"I'm going to come!" he announced.

Iris continued sucking his dick until he exploded like Mount Saint Helens into the condom. As he orgasmed, he jolted violently like a car moving on a rocky road, moaning, and groaning. Then his body went limp in the seat. Iris arose with a grin, knowing her services were exceptional. It took her trick a moment to collect himself. She wiped her mouth as he removed the filled condom to discard it onto the street.

"Whoa, now that was something else," her trick said.

"You had fun?" she asked him, already knowing the answer.

"Oh, yeah, a blast. We need to do that again."

"You know where to find me," she said.

He nodded.

The man pulled up his pants and fastened his belt. Now it was time for him to head home to his wife and kids. Iris noticed the car seat and toys in the back seat. She didn't judge. A man needed his nut, and she was there to provide with no judgment. He started the Beemer and pulled away from the curb.

Iris got dropped off on the corner of Sutphin Boulevard and Archer Avenue. She climbed out of the silver Beemer, and the man headed home. The Queens intersection gradually began to buzz with morning traffic as the day ascended. Before crossing the busy hub, Iris noticed the idling Ford Explorer parked across the street near the Long Island Rail Road. The occupants of the vehicle were watching her every move. She held the driver's stare for a moment, then proceeded toward the Crown Fried Chicken & Pizza fast-food dive that was open twenty-four hours. Inside the dingy eatery, she met up with her coworkers and sisters in prostitution lounging at one of the hard tables and benches, drinking tea or coffee and munching on stale breakfast. It had been a long night for them.

The girls were instructed to meet at the chicken eatery at a specific time and wait for their pimp, Earth, to come to pick them up. He had several girls spread out in different locations across the tristate area.

Iris ordered a cup of coffee and took a seat at the table. While they waited, the girls began to share stories about their encounters with tricks. They shared ideas and particular horrors, chuckled, and waited. Iris sat there sipping her coffee and remained aloof from their conversation. She seemed troubled by something.

Soon, Earth arrived in his Cadillac Escalade. The moment his SUV pulled to the curb outside of the eatery, the girls didn't hesitate to get up and greet him outside. They all piled into the back seat of the truck. Iris was the last to exit the place.

Earth glared at her and growled, "Bitch, hurry the fuck up before you get me upset."

Iris put some pep into her step and was the last one to climb into the Escalade. Earth then drove off. Unbeknownst to him, he was being followed.

The Escalade arrived at an area called Bricktown, a neighborhood in South Jamaica named for its row housing. The Escalade pulled into the narrow driveway to a run-down two-family brick row house on the inner-city block. Earth and several girls exited the Escalade and entered the residence through the back door.

Meanwhile, the Ford Explorer had followed them to the location, and Lou, Nasir, and Denise observed the activity from a short distance.

"It doesn't look like much," Nasir said.

"Believe me, that's our payday inside that place," said Lou.

"And you trust this bitch?" Denise asked him.

"I trust her fear and dislike of her pimp," Lou replied. "Like I told y'all, I know everything about this nigga, been watching him for two weeks. He looks like a threat, but he's not. He thinks he's cautious and feared, but he's sloppy with it. His brother, Rondo, now he's the wolf. This pimp nigga moves the way he moves because of his brother's reputation."

"What's his brother into?" Nasir asked.

"Drugs and dropping bodies out in Brooklyn. The nigga is from Brownsville and runs a crew out there. Earth pimps the girls. His brother runs drugs," Lou informed them.

"So what's the plan?" Denise asked him.

"Tomorrow night, we hit them hard. They're not gonna see us coming. That bitch already gave me the layout of everything, and I promised her a ten percent cut."

"Ten percent?" Nasir questioned.

"It doesn't go smoothly without her involvement," said Lou.

"And what's her fuckin' involvement besides feeding you information?" Nasir uttered.

Lou looked back at Denise in the back seat and grinned. "You're our Trojan horse," he mentioned. "Look, this nigga Earth lost three girls to arrest for drugs and prostitution the other day. They got caught up in some vice sting. So he's always looking for some new pussy to pimp. He'll see you, and shit, he'll let his guard down, I guarantee. Iris is already in his ear about you. You come knocking, and then we'll come in right behind you."

Denise and Nasir didn't look too sure about this plan.

Lou picked up on their dubious stares and said, "It's gonna work. I did my homework on this fool. He's not that smart. He's predictable, and he likes nothing better than new pussy to pimp and fuck. Earth being down three girls will give us the advantage. Desperate situations will make a nigga do desperate things."

Nasir and Denise shared a look. Unfortunately, Denise would be the one placed in harm's way.

"Are you good with this?" Nasir asked her.

Denise nodded. "I am. Let's do this."

Lou grinned, lit a cigarette, and replied, "That's what I'm talkin' about. She's ride or die, for real, nigga."

2Pac's album *All Eyez on Me* blared through the living room of the three-bedroom home in Bricktown. Though the place didn't look like much on the outside, it was a completely different aura inside. The row house was outfitted with expensive, modern furniture, most of it from an ultra-slick, upscale home store, Huff Furniture and Design. Then there was the somewhat-eccentric assortment of Afrocentric art in the living room and a state-of-the-art entertainment system. The walls of the main bedroom were hung with three framed photographs of Al Pacino lifted from various scenes in *Scarface,* two photos of infamous Gambino family mob boss John Gotti, a portrait of slain rapper Tupac Shakur, and, rounding out the collection, a photo of Tupac's archnemesis, fellow deceased rapper Christopher "Notorious B.I.G." Wallace.

Five girls, including Iris, were getting dressed and ready for tonight's action on the track. First, they walked around the place topless, nude, or in their panties, bantering and chatting. Then like vampires, they slept most of the day and became active at night.

Earth had just finished showering, and he toweled off in the bathroom. He was a tall man, well over six feet and probably over 250 pounds, but neat and well put together for his size. Tattoos covered his physique, and his hair was braided into long cornrows. He was a handsome man with smooth dark skin.

Earth knotted the towel around his waist and walked into the fashionable main bedroom. He could hear the rap music playing and the banter from his hoes in the next rooms. He glanced at the time on the wall. It was nearly 9:00 p.m. He liked to have his hoes on the tracks no later than eleven. He took a seat at the edge of the king-size bed. He brooded on the loss of three of his hoes in jail for drugs and soliciting. The judge had set each ho's bail at $25,000 because they had multiple priors. Each night his bitches sat in jail lost him a profit of over $3,000, and to bail them out via a bondsman would cost him roughly ten grand. His bitches benefited from their arrangement because Earth provided them with free clothing, food, housing, medical and legal assistance, and protection. But unfortunately, he had to bail them out soon.

Fuck! Earth cursed to himself. He sighed. Then he stood up and walked to the bedroom threshold and called out, "Iris, get in here, bitch."

Iris hurried toward the bedroom in her panties and bra. She smiled at Earth and asked, "You need something from me, daddy?"

Earth stared at her stoically. "Where this bitch at you keep putting into my ear? What's her name again?"

"Skyla," Iris answered.

"And you saying this bitch trying to get this money?"

Iris nodded. "She needs it. Like me, she got her kids and obligations."

"And how you meet this bitch? You know you ain't got time to be out there socializing. You supposed to be out there getting my fuckin' money, bitch."

"You're always telling us to recruit bitches for you, right, daddy? I went to high school with her. She saw me working the track and came at me. She's beautiful."

"This bitch knows making this money is full-time, right? I don't want any part-time hoes in my stable. She's either with it or not. She becomes a problem, bitch gonna get fucked up and learn the hard way what the game is about," Earth proclaimed.

"She knows," Iris responded.

"A'ight, finish getting dressed, bitch. We gotta make this money tonight," said Earth.

Iris pivoted and removed herself from the bedroom. Earth walked to the bedroom mirror and stared at himself. He was great at pimping, and he loved it. Money, pussy, respect. Who would want to do anything besides pimp? He thought about this new bitch coming to him tonight. If she were anything like Iris described her, Earth would have the first crack at fucking her. He had to sample that pussy before she worked the tracks. It was one of the benefits of being him.

Earth spun and walked toward the closet to start to get dressed. The moment he opened the closet door, the doorbell chimed, indicating they had company. Earth didn't bother to put any clothes on. He figured it was Skyla. He grew excited. He marched out of the bedroom still in his towel, moved down the stairs into the living room, and approached the door. Iris was right behind him. When Earth took a look outside and saw a beautiful, petite young girl standing on the front steps, he lit up. No doubt, Iris was right. She was lovely. Earth opened the door with a charming smile and invited Skyla into his home.

"You must be my early birthday gift. You are gorgeous," Earth said smoothly.

Skyla smiled and stepped into the house. She wore a sexy seamless minidress featuring a low-cut front, short sleeves, and a low back with cut-out detailing underneath a chic leather jacket. Earth couldn't take his eyes off of Skyla. She had curves, beauty, long legs, and style.

"Damn. So you're ready to make some money for me?" Earth asked her.

"Iris told me about you. I really need to make some money. I have nowhere else to go," Skyla replied.

It was music to Earth's ears. He figured if he pushed this bitch hard, she probably could profit $1,500 a night. She was a new face humbled with desperation. Earth knew that desperation could force anyone to consider options they ordinarily wouldn't consider.

Iris stood behind Earth nervously, watching their interaction. Unfortunately, the pimp didn't deduce that it was a ruse because he was in awe of Skyla's appearance and situation. He quickly had let his guard down, excited to sample some new pussy and see how much money this bitch would profit him. If he had been paying attention to Iris, he would have noticed something was up.

"Tonight, you're about to become the life of the party in that fuckin' dress," Earth proclaimed.

Skyla smiled.

"But first, we need to talk business in the bedroom." Earth smiled.

"We do?" Skyla questioned with a raised eyebrow.

"Yeah, we do. You wanna start making this money tonight, then I gotta see what you working with, love."

Skyla knew she didn't have a choice. Earth was determined to bust her pussy open in the bedroom. So reluctantly, she followed Earth toward the bedroom. But as she passed Iris, Skyla shot her a threatening look, warning her with a glare, *"Don't fuck this up! Do it now."*

While Skyla followed Earth up the stairs, Iris went toward the back door to implement their plan.

Chapter Eighteen

After seeing Denise enter the row house, Nasir and Lou coolly removed themselves from the Ford Explorer. Clad in black and wearing ski masks, they stealthily moved toward the narrow driveway, armed. Lou gripped the Mossberg 500 shotgun, and Nasir was armed with a Smith & Wesson SW99. They covertly neared the back door and waited. Every second mattered. They needed Iris to open that back door. It was chancy to depend on a ho, but Lou was sure she wouldn't betray them. He had enough information on Iris to destroy her life and endanger her kids. Lou understood how important intel was in the streets. He used Iris's weakness to his benefit.

Fortunately for them, the backyard was small and cluttered with a run-down shed, and it was dark. In addition, the adjacent house was abandoned and boarded up, so they didn't have to worry about any nosy neighbors. But time was critical. If that back door didn't open up, then they would lose the element of surprise by forcing their way inside.

Nasir was worried about Denise. He knew she could take care of herself, but she was in there alone with Earth, and the last thing he wanted was for her to be raped by him. It was her decision. But on the other hand, he cared about her and didn't want to see anything happen to her.

As Lou predicted, Iris opened the back door to the residence in secret, and both men hurried into the house. Finally, their plan was coming to fruition. Iris nervously stepped aside. Lou gave her a stern look and said, "I knew you would play it smart."

Once inside the house, they were struck by the echo of voices and footsteps reverberating from the other rooms. Nasir looked at Iris and asked, "Where is she?"

"In the bedroom with Earth," Iris replied.

Nasir frowned. The thought of his woman alone in the bedroom with a pimp was disheartening. He didn't want to think about what Earth might be doing to his woman. He and Lou hurried deeper into the house with their guns drawn. Iris, afraid, remained in the kitchen, cowering in the dark.

Most of the activity was happening on the second floor. The girls were getting dressed for tonight, unaware that shit was about to hit the fan. Lou and Nasir moved toward the second level like trained police. Their arms were outstretched. They were cautious and ready to react when the time came. Nasir was determined to find Denise first, make sure she was safe, and begin the nightmare for everyone inside the house.

They quickly but stealthily moved toward the main bedroom. But unfortunately, interference hindered their element of surprise in the hallway. One of Earth's girls emerged topless from one of the bedrooms, and the moment she saw two masked shooters, she shrieked.

Lou rushed to her, shouting, "Shut the fuck up, bitch!" Then he slammed the butt of the shotgun into the side of her face. The stunning blow crushed her cheekbone and sent her colliding with the ground.

Nasir quickly went to the main bedroom and kicked open the door. Unfortunately, the moment he entered the bedroom, Earth reacted to the intruders. Panicking and naked, he hurried to retrieve his gun from nearby while Denise was damn near naked on the bed. Seeing this, Nasir responded and opened fire.

Bak! Bak! Bak!

Earth went down.

Shit!

The girls screamed. Denise leaped from the bed as Nasir tossed her a second gun. She grabbed it and helped Nasir take control of the room.

"You okay?" he asked her.

"I'm good," she responded.

Earth was sprawled on his back, and surprisingly, he was still alive. He'd been hit twice in his leg and once in the left side. He wasn't going anywhere. He was badly hurt and bleeding profusely. Lou forced four nearly naked girls into the bedroom. They were teary-eyed and terrified.

"Y'all bitches shut the fuck up and get down on your knees!" Lou ordered the girls.

They complied without resistance, lying face down on the floor. When Lou looked down at Earth shot and bleeding, he shot a puzzled look at Nasir and exclaimed, "What the fuck happened, nigga?"

"He reached, so I shot him," Nasir replied.

"Fuck! Fuck!"

"He's still alive, though," said Nasir.

Lou hurried and crouched near Earth, whose breathing was shallow. Yes, he was still alive, but for how long?

"Look, nigga, we can save your life, call 911. Maybe you'll live. But let us know where that money is at," Lou calmly said.

Earth didn't respond to Lou's levelheaded demand. Instead, he stared at Lou almost defiantly and mumbled, "Fuck you!"

"You for real, nigga? You leaking like a broken faucet. Are you ready to die for some money, muthafucka?" Lou growled.

Earth frowned. He couldn't move and was dying, but his last action was bold and rebellious.

"If you care about your bitches, nigga, you'll give it up," Lou continued, growing angry and desperate.

However, Earth remained stubborn. Finally, Lou stood up with a look of frustration that was palpable. He wasn't leaving without money or something valuable. He knew there was a safe somewhere inside the house because Iris had told him about it.

Lou angrily kicked Earth in his ribs as he lay there. "Don't die on me yet, nigga!" Lou hollered.

But it was too late. Earth was dead. *What now?* everyone thought. Lou cut his eyes at the four hostages he held at gunpoint. They were whimpering and crying. His plan had gone to shit, and he needed to salvage it somehow. He picked one girl to interrogate: Earth's bottom bitch named Comfort.

"Pick that bitch up," he instructed Nasir and Denise.

Nasir grabbed Comfort, a thick, big-booty redbone bitch wearing bright booty shorts and a bra. She whimpered as she stared down the barrel of a shotgun.

"You his bottom bitch, right?" Lou asked her. "Where does your pimp keep his safe at?"

"What safe?" she cried out.

"Bitch, don't play stupid with me. Iris already told me that fool got a safe in here somewhere. Where the fuck is it?" Lou hollered.

Then it came to him. *Shit*. Iris. They'd left her downstairs in the kitchen. Lou stared at Nasir and uttered, "We left that bitch downstairs."

Nasir was on it, and he pivoted and bolted from the bedroom while Denise and Lou remained behind. Lou shoved the shotgun closer to Comfort's face and glared at her. He was in no mood to hear any excuses.

Nasir charged back into the bedroom and uttered, "She's gone."

"Fuck!" Lou shouted, upset. "Fuck this. One of these bitches is gonna talk."

Lou glared at the girls lying face down in the bedroom, and a sinister look appeared on his face. He was determined to find this pimp's money by any means necessary. He looked at his two accomplices with malice, thinking, *there isn't any turning back tonight. Fuck it!*

"They know your face," Lou uttered to Denise.

Denise glanced at Nasir. Whatever Nasir decided, she would follow his lead. She didn't mean to fall in love with him. It simply happened. Nasir had seen her at her most vulnerable and lowest point. He showed that he was willing to protect her no matter what, and the sex was mind-blowing. Denise had surrendered her feelings to him and merged with Nasir the past month, becoming completely preoccupied with him to the point where he dominated her thoughts. Now she was headed down this road to perdition at full speed. Her emotions for Nasir were challenging to suppress, and now she was willing to do anything for her man.

They'd hog-tied the girls, and then Lou disappeared from the bedroom for a moment while Nasir and Denise continued to hold the girls at gunpoint. When Lou came back into the bedroom, he quickly tossed a clear plastic bag over Comfort's head, and she immediately started to asphyxiate. Comfort wildly squirmed and struggled to breathe. The other girls watched in horror.

Lou continued to taunt her, shouting, "Where's the fuckin' safe?"

She couldn't answer him. He removed the plastic from around her head, and she immediately gasped for air. Then she exclaimed, "I don't know."

Lou didn't want to hear that. Wrong answer. So he tossed the plastic bag back around Comfort's head so she could suffocate. Then he positioned himself behind the girl lying face down on the ground next to Comfort. Lou leveled the shotgun behind her head and fired.

Boom!

The gunshot echoed deafeningly in the confines of the bedroom, and the shotgun shell punched its way through the girl's neck, causing a gaping hole in its wake. A pool of blood immediately began forming around her as she choked to death on it and died right away.

"Lou, what the fuck, nigga!" Nasir shouted, shocked.

"I'm not playing with these bitches, cuzzo. Fuck that!" Lou griped.

Denise stood there deadpan, and there was no turning back now. Comfort was dead too. It took a while, but she'd suffocated. Two girls were left. They were absolutely beside themselves with fear and terror, and they couldn't move at all, being hog-tied, and they knew they were next to die.

Lou moved toward them, aimed the shotgun at their heads, and spewed, "Y'all bitches know I'm not fuckin' around. Look at y'all, two friends. Where that fuckin' money at?"

Their faces were coated with tears, fear, and agony. They had no idea, but they were scared to tell Lou that. So instead, they begged for their lives.

"Please, don't kill us. We'll help you find it," they dreadfully pleaded.

But Lou had no time to listen to their pleas or show them mercy. He had wasted too much time with them. It was time to move on and implement their contingency plan—ransack the place from top to bottom. As with Comfort, Lou and Nasir tossed clear plastic bags around the girls' faces and left them there to suffocate. Lou didn't want to fire off more rounds because the shotgun was loud, and as the last two victims lay hog-tied, facedown, asphyxiating, the trio began rummaging through the place. They went from room to room looking for the safe but collecting anything of value simultaneously.

Unfortunately, they didn't find any safe. Still, they collected jewelry, a wad of cash, and some devices like cell phones and a laptop. All three then hurried from the house and climbed back into the Ford Explorer under cover of night.

Once inside the vehicle, Nasir exclaimed, "What the fuck was that?"

"You shot him first, cuzzo, before I could get to him," Lou griped.

"I told you, he reached for his shit. You wanted me to get shot, nigga?" Nasir argued.

"I'm just sayin', we ain't come here to collect like some fuckin' crackheads on the block," Lou countered. "Five bodies, and we ain't got shit to show for it. Fuck me! And that bitch Iris is missing. We need to find that bitch."

The cousins argued as they sped away from the gruesome crime scene. Denise sat in the back seat, reflecting on what happened back there. What she witnessed would give anyone nightmares and make them cringe. But surprisingly, she remained calm over the bloodshed. In fact, it was nearly exciting for her.

Chapter Nineteen

Business was good. It was a few weeks until Halloween, and the holidays were right around the corner. With the weather changing and becoming cooler, the clothing changed—summer dresses, shorts, and T-shirts were replaced with nice-looking sweaters, stylish jackets, and leather boots. The boutique always kept up with the local and national trends in the fashion industry, and the cash was pouring in like a tidal wave.

Cook coolly placed his hand against the small of the back of the new hire, a beautiful girl named Tandy. It was her first day, and he was instructing her on how to work the cash register. She was a fast learner. Tandy was from the youth center, and she'd asked him if his store was hiring. Fortunately for her, a position had opened up, and she didn't hesitate to fill it. She was petite, with a caramel complexion.

"I've had this store for three years, and five things make a clothing store successful," Cook said to her.

Tandy gave him her undivided attention. She admired Cook, and him spewing his knowledge to her was like priceless gems coming out of his mouth.

"One, always keep a theme. Make sure customers know what to expect when they come into your store. Two, keep well-informed of the latest trends. This will give you some insight into what your customers' new preferences are likely to be," he proclaimed.

Tandy nodded. Cook removed himself from the cash register, and Tandy followed him. Like always, Cook was dressed stylishly in a charcoal suit and brown wingtips. The 19-year-old girl smiled widely, not being able to contain her excitement about working in the clothing store where she regularly shopped.

"Three, retain your customers," Cook continued. "A good way to retain your past and current customers is to offer them attractive discounts. Four, focus on quality. Your business will continue to thrive as long as it offers high-quality products and services."

Cook removed a floral silk dress from one of the racks and handed it to her.

"Feel the material and know your material. It would help if you always had a sharp eye for spotting knockoffs," he said. "That dress right there is a hundred percent silk, and it sells for a reasonable price. The moment you stop offering good quality starts your business's decline."

"It's a beautiful dress," said Tandy.

Cook didn't respond. Instead, he uttered, "And five, there's upselling. A good way to make more money from customers is to encourage them to buy other products they did not originally intend to buy. After making their purchases, customers should be shown items related to what they bought and given reasons to buy those items too. This strategy will help you generate more sales and record more profits."

Cook stared at his new employee. Her brown eyes glimmered with readiness, and she was dressed in curvy jeans and a rhinestone T-shirt.

"I won't let you down, Mr. Cook," she said confidently.

Cook smiled and replied, "I know you won't, Tandy. You're going to fit in just fine here, and you'll have the best team to support you."

Kyra and Danielle were working the floor today. Cook smiled at his young ladies. They were beautiful, bright, and sociable, and Tandy couldn't wait to be part of the team.

"Kyra will continue to train you today," said Cook. "And don't worry, you're in good hands with her."

Tandy smiled. She walked to where Kyra was behind the cash register, and Cook's eyes lingered on her backside. But he had to catch himself and politely turn away. But there was something about the young beauty that created fire and excitement in his groins. She had nice legs, natural beauty, and she somewhat favored Nia Long with her short hairstyle.

Cook silently argued with himself whether to keep things business or pleasure with his new, attractive employee. It looked like Kyra and Tandy were going to work well together.

It was mid-afternoon, and it seemed like it would be a typical day. Customers were flowing in and out of the store, and the line at the cash register was attractive. Cook stood in the center of his boutique and admired the progress he'd made. Then Zulu and Zodiac entered the store out of the blue, and everything changed. Both men had intimidation and authority written all over them, and all eyes were soon on them. Cook was entirely shocked by their sudden presence. Zulu rarely visited the clothing store. Cook perked up and hurried to greet the drug kingpin with the warmest smile.

"Zulu, I'm surprised to see you here. What's the reason for this visit?" Cook asked him coolly.

Zulu shot Cook a deadpan gaze and replied, "We need to talk in your office."

"Not a problem," said Cook. "This way."

Both men followed Cook toward the back of the store. Their presence spoke volumes, and Cook kept his cool.

They soon entered the quaint back office, where Cook shut the door for their privacy and took a seat behind his desk. Zulu and Zodiac chose to remain standing.

"So what's going on? What can I do for you fellows?" asked Cook.

"I see business is doing good, Cook," Zulu said.

"This store pretty much sells itself. I just manage things," Cook replied.

"We need to talk about a few things," Zulu uttered suddenly.

Zodiac placed a small duffle bag on Cook's desk. Cook unzipped it to reveal the cash inside, nearly $100,000.

"I'm going to need a cashier's check for a hundred thousand by Friday. Can Winter make that happen?" Zulu asked.

"I'm sure he can. He's good at what he does."

"Cool. Second, can you move half a million dollars through your clothing stores by month's end?" asked Zulu.

Cook sighed. *Shit!* "That's a tall order, Zulu. The books are level at the moment between turnovers, sales, and capital gain. Moving that much can raise some red flags with the wrong people. Yes, business is good right now, but moving half a million dollars, I don't know."

"It's not impossible, Cook. You and Winter are smart men. My business in the streets is growing, and I need my money to grow faster in legitimacy. Three years in business with you, and no problems yet. I respect that," Zulu said.

"It's always a pleasure to do business with you, Zulu. But the last thing we need is to become sloppy. Putting money through the business accounts extremely quickly and bypassing all the usual operating procedures could flag us right away," Cook proclaimed.

"I'm not asking. I need this done, and I can't trust anyone else to move this amount. You and Winter are my numbers guys, great with business and hiding transactions, and I respect that y'all are cautious."

Cook sighed heavily and leaned back in his chair, and he had to brainstorm. Zulu was persistent.

"The FBI, IRS, the State, shit, even ATF and the CIA are circling New York like vultures after 9/11, tapping phones, monitoring bank accounts . . . it will be difficult. What you need, Zulu, is a new hub, one that is off the radar of every law enforcement agency in the States. Something that is virgin territory and cash rich."

"And what do you have in mind?" asked Zulu.

"Restaurants, bars, nightclubs, liquor stores, and all-cash businesses are impossible to track."

"I already own those," Zulu responded.

"You do, but not in the right places. What about a franchise, a resort management company, or a marina? There's the Jersey Shore, Atlantic City, and Miami. Every summer, the population explodes in these places. There are tourists, white-collar, blue-collar, Midwesterners, folks with jobs and money to spend coming and going all summer," Cook proclaimed.

Zulu was listening.

"Look, the more straitlaced and benign the institutions seem, the longer they can fly under law enforcement's radar, especially out of New York City. So a half dozen clothing stores in different boroughs and a few other of your businesses probably won't cut it anymore," Cook added.

Zulu shared a glance with Zodiac. Then he slightly smiled and replied, "I like the way you think, Cook. That's the reason why you and Winter are my guys. Set it up, make it happen."

"I'm on it, Zulu," said Cook.

Believing it was the end of their business, Cook stood from his desk to usher them out of his store, but there was something else.

"One more thing," Zulu uttered.

"And what is that?" asked Cook.

"I'm having a problem with this cop, a detective actually, and I want you to green-light a hit on him."

Cook was taken aback by the demand. "What? That's not me, Zulu. I launder money, run these clothing stores, invest in stocks, and keep everything legitimate. So you want me to arrange to have a cop killed?"

Zulu stared at Cook. "I know you're still in contact with the Shower Posse."

"Yes, but vaguely," Cook responded.

"The thing is, this will be a high-profile job, and I can't have it linked back to me. That's the reason why I want it outsourced. This detective is respected and decorated, but he's becoming a pain and a threat to my business, and he's disrespectful," said Zulu.

Curious, Cook asked him, "Who is it?"

"Detective Michael Acosta."

Cook was familiar with the name. "The cop responsible for bringing down that serial killer four years ago. Wasn't he Mob Allah's older brother?"

"Who fuckin' cares? They're both dead. But I trust you with this as I trust you with handling my money and businesses. So get it done," Zulu replied.

Cook reluctantly nodded. "I'm on it."

Zulu and Zodiac pivoted and removed themselves from the quaint office. Cook didn't usher them out. Instead, he dumped himself into his chair and sighed heavily. Though he was no stranger to murder, killing a cop was bad for business—especially a respected detective in the NYPD. But the order had been given.

Cook grew tired of being subservient to Zulu and his organization. He didn't want to continue to be someone's puppet on strings. Therefore, he knew it was time to expedite his exit.

Chapter Twenty

It was a horrific crime scene. Five bodies were sprawled across the crimson-stained carpet. It was almost like a nightmare out of a horror movie. Throughout the bedroom, there were pools of blood that had turned into a goodly portion of brown dried blood. The victims had been dead for several hours, and it was evident to the detectives and everyone moving about the bedroom what had happened. The girls were nearly naked and hog-tied. Three of them had plastic bags over their heads. There wasn't much left of the fourth from the shoulders up. Her brains and flesh decorated the carpet. Their pimp was shot three times. One of the bullets had hit an artery in his leg. He bled to death.

Detectives Acosta and Emmerson were investigating the scene. One thing about being an NYPD detective—there was never a dull moment on the job, so they said. Acosta stared at the girls. He could see the fear in their faces. They were tortured and scared. But then an odd thought came to him. *They'll never see another sunrise.*

The flash explosion from the camera went off several times, capturing the dead. The crime scene photographer had his work cut out for him, and so did the detectives and forensics. The photographer twisted and turned his camera this way and that. He was freezing time—creating a supposedly incontestable record of the chaos inside the bedroom. He couldn't afford to leave out an essential piece of evidence or produce photographs that could be considered misleading in court.

The camera flash bothered Acosta. He turned to the photographer and asked, “Can you give us a minute here?”

The photographer held his stare for a moment. Then he stepped out of the room. Acosta took a seat at the edge of the bed and sighed heavily. It was a lot to take in.

“You okay, partner?” Detective Emmerson asked him.

“I’ll be fine,” Acosta replied.

“This isn’t your first rodeo. So I know it isn’t shock,” said Emmerson.

It wasn’t shock. It was fatigue. The girls were young. Detective Acosta guessed them to be in their early twenties or late teens, except for one, who looked in her early thirties.

“So what’s your take on this horror show?” Emmerson asked. “Home invasion went wrong? We know they were looking for something, money maybe. They killed the pimp first, then tortured the girls to get them to talk.”

“This had to be an inside job,” Acosta uttered.

“What makes you believe that?”

“They got hit while they were getting dressed. Either it was a coincidence or planned, and our male victim was rudely interrupted at a vulnerable time. He was naked for a reason. I assume maybe he was intimate with a young lady. Our suspects come charging in, caught him by surprise, and he went reaching for something. A gun,” Acosta proclaimed.

Earth’s body was located near the bed and nightstand. Detective Acosta walked toward the nightstand and slowly opened it to reveal a .357 Magnum inside, proving Acosta’s theory was correct.

“Maybe he should have kept it closer to him, underneath his pillow,” Emmerson joked lightly. “Reaction time is critical.”

Acosta didn't respond to him. Instead, he continued to walk around the bedroom, taking in the decor, the bodies again, and the framed photographs of Al Pacino, Biggie, Pac, and John Gotti.

"He was a fan of gangsters and gangster rappers. Live by the sword, die by the sword," said Emmerson.

"He was a pimp wannabe gangster," said Acosta.

Detective Acosta pulled back the window blinds and glanced outside. The block was lit up with police activity. The blaring blue and red lights disturbed the neighbors and indicated the worst of humanity. The neighbors and the lookie-loos were outside the house in droves, watching everything out of curiosity and gossiping. It was a drug-fueled and violent area.

The detective moved from the window and stared back at the bodies with a stoic look. They were being placed into body bags by the coroners, and he had seen enough. The coroners began carrying the body bags out of the house. Acosta followed behind them into the street. The crowd outside had seemed to grow from when he peered out the window. It had become a circus outside, along with the news media. News of the gruesome murders had traveled quickly throughout the area. Five young girls and their pimp were brutally murdered. It would become front-page news.

Acosta lingered on the short concrete steps and observed the controlled chaos. People wanted to know who had gotten killed. NY1 and NBC journalists were loitering nearby and hungry for information or access to the carnage inside. The murder of several people in a home invasion gone wrong was a juicy story. "If it bleeds, it leads," and several young prostitutes shot dead along with their pimp was prime-time news.

Sickened by everything, Acosta went to his car, ducking people and journalists. He was in no mood to answer questions or be harassed by the locals. He climbed into his Camry and exhaled behind the wheel. He sat there for a moment in silence. There was something on his mind. While he sat there inattentive, the sudden drumming on the driver's side window interrupted his thoughts. Acosta turned to see his partner telling him to roll down the window.

"You okay, Mike?" Detective Emmerson asked. The question was becoming redundant. "We'll need you on your A game for this one."

"I'm fine, Chris."

"Listen, let's get a drink somewhere, you and me, and talk," Emmerson suggested. "We deserve one."

Acosta thought about it for a moment, then relented. "Okay."

Emmerson walked away, and Acosta sighed.

The Beer Garden in Hempstead, Long Island, was popular for entertainment and drinks. The place was filled with an eclectic mix of people. An old couple was eating side by side, one glass of wine each. In their twenties, a group of young women collapsed with helpless giggles as a stern male patron drinking alone nearby looked on and frowned. Several businessmen in their dark suits were lighting up cigars. The noise level was high, the music came from a live band, and the attractive servers were pleasant.

Detectives Acosta and Emmerson sat at one of the dark walnut tables inside the place. They were drinking beers, still in their jacket and ties, with holstered guns on their hips. Emmerson took a swig from his beer and said to his partner, "What's been eating you lately?"

Acosta took a drink from his beer. His attention briefly diverted from his partner to the young ladies still collapsing with helpless giggles. It was beautiful to see a group of pretty girls smiling and laughing, still alive and enjoying their lives. Acosta then looked at Emmerson and held his stare.

"You know you can talk to me about anything, Mike. We're partners and family," said Emmerson.

Acosta took another drink, huffed, and started rambling, telling a story out of the blue. "I remember when I was riding with my FTO in the Bronx. I started the job in the mid-eighties when crack was becoming an epidemic. We get a call to a scene at some project apartments in the South Bronx. A ruthless and violent place in Castle Hill. I followed my FTO in the Castle Hill projects. We show up at this eighth-floor apartment, and immediately we hear this mother screaming her lungs out. I mean, she's screaming like some banshee. I never heard anything like it before. We entered the apartment. She cried her eyes out and fought her boyfriend simultaneously. He's high. Come to find out this monster tossed his girlfriend's newborn infant into the oven because he wouldn't stop crying after the boyfriend sexually violated the boy when changing his diaper."

"Fuck," Emmerson muttered, shocked.

"Yeah, it was that kind of reaction. This perp was both high and aggressive. Whatever drugs he was on seemed to dull the pain as we tried to subdue him for arrest. It took five cops to take him down. It was worse trying to remove him from the apartment and transport him to the car. Word quickly got out. Neighbors heard what he did. A lynch mob came for him, and they wanted to tear him apart. We had to fight to protect this monster from being beaten to death by an angry mob. There was a side of me that wanted to surrender him to this mob and have him pay for what he did to this baby. He cooked it inside an oven. But my FTO kept it together. He reminded me that it wasn't our job to judge or prosecute him. We were there to implement order and arrest him," Acosta proclaimed. It was a heavy story that weighed heavily on Acosta.

"I've had my fair share of horrors too, being a cop, and in a way, your FTO was right. There's always going to be monsters out there, Mike. Humans are the most violent animals on this planet. They're all capable of enormous levels of violence, given the proper motivation," Emmerson proclaimed. "We just got to make sure we don't become monsters ourselves."

Emmerson signaled for their server. She swayed toward them with the brightest smile and saucy blue eyes.

"Let me get two more beers," said Emmerson.

She nodded and walked away. Emmerson finished his beer. He soon went into his own story.

"My first case as a detective was in Bushwick, Brooklyn. It was simply open-and-shut," Emmerson started.

Acosta was listening.

"We were called to a murder scene. The paramedic was called not for the victim but for a female rookie cop who started vomiting and then became catatonic at the scene. A woman killed her husband with a blast from a shotgun. The husband was drunk and abusive, and he decided to fart in the wife's face at the dinner table. The wife's upset now. She gets the gun, shoves it into her husband's stomach, and fires. She blew the back half of his torso away—some crazy shit. But then it doesn't end there. After her husband is dead, the wife puts the shotgun in his mouth and blows his head off. It was some horrible shit to see. The female cop resigned from the force a few days later. This isn't a job everyone can do," Emmerson stated.

The two shared some of their darkest moments while being NYPD officers and homicide detectives. Then finally, the pretty server arrived with their beers, and she placed them on the dark walnut table and shared a polite smile with both men.

"Thank you, beautiful," Emmerson said.

"If you two need anything else, let me know," she replied.

"We will." Emmerson smiled.

She pivoted and marched off. Emmerson's eyes lingered on her backside for a moment. Then he said to Acosta, "I really do like this place."

Acosta sat there aloof from his friend's statement, brooding about something. Then he looked at Emmerson and uttered, "I need to tell you something. I need to get this off my chest."

"What is it? I know something's eating away at you. I'm here to help if I can. You've been a little cold to me lately," Emmerson replied.

Acosta heaved a sigh, and he was constantly inhaling. His throat felt like it was being sliced to pieces with every breath.

"You didn't kill anyone, right?" Emmerson joked, trying to alleviate whatever tension Acosta was feeling.

"Cynthia Blackwell." Acosta uttered her name out of the blue.

Emmerson grew confused. "What about her? And why are you bringing up a dead girl's name suddenly?"

"I had an affair with her a few years ago," Acosta confessed.

"Whoa! What?" Emmerson exclaimed.

"It happened the year after Janette left with the kids. I was in a vulnerable place. I met Cynthia at this bar. I didn't recognize her at first, but we hit it off, things happened, and we kept happening for about a year," Acosta explained.

"Oh, shit. Damn. You don't think she was killed because Zulu found out about y'all?"

"I don't believe so. We were always careful," Acosta replied.

"Still, it looks bad, Mike. You were romantically involved with a victim found dead in the water a few days ago. The last thing you need is for this to roll back on you. It would be best to tell the captain this," Emmerson said.

"He killed her. I know it," Acosta uttered.

"If so, it will be difficult to link him to her death," said Emmerson. "Now hearing about this . . ." Emmerson sighed heavily.

"I want him, Chris. He needs to pay for what he did to her. I can't allow her death to have happened in vain," Acosta said.

Acosta's eyebrows lowered and pulled closer together. Then tears started to pool in his eyes before a few streaked down his cheeks.

"Jesus, you were in love with her, weren't you?" Emmerson deduced.

"We couldn't continue the relationship. It became too dangerous and difficult," Acosta replied with the corners of his mouth drawing downward.

"I can't believe I didn't see it and that you didn't trust me to let me know what was going on," Emmerson griped. "I could have helped."

"And what would you have done?"

"I would have told you to end it, and that it was foolish for you to get involved with a drug kingpin's girl. It's suicide to your career, Mike," Emmerson chided.

"It's easy for you to say," Acosta protested. "You still have your family at home, someone to go home to. Me, I'm alone. My kids are in fuckin' Jersey living their best life with some wealthy prick, and us, we're out here chasing demons and monsters."

"I know it's rough—"

"Don't do that. Don't start to undercut my emotions," Acosta interrupted, looking at his partner contemptuously.

"You can't personally go after him, Mike. We have to do our jobs by the book, and you need to put your personal feelings for her aside. If not, it will destroy you. I see it happening now. You were already obsessed with capturing Zulu before her death. Now I fear you might go off the rails and become unhinged," Emmerson proclaimed.

"He had her dumped in the fucking ocean like she was trash to him," Acosta reminded him. "She didn't deserve to die like that."

It was getting late, and Detective Emmerson was prepared to leave. He signaled for the server, and then looked back at Acosta.

"I have one piece of advice for you, Mike. Take some time off for yourself and regroup. You need to. There's something my mother used to say to me, a quote from Nietzsche: 'Whoever fights monsters should see to it that in the process he does not become a monster. And if you gaze long enough into an abyss, the abyss will gaze back into you,'" Emmerson proclaimed.

Emmerson stood and removed himself from the table. He was leaving his partner there to ponder his words.

Chapter Twenty-one

Lou knew the easiest way to torch a car was to crack open a window, douse the interior with lighter fluid, and toss in a match. From experience, he knew if the windows weren't open or smashed, a car fire would burn itself out for lack of oxygen. The Ford Explorer's interior contained the easiest parts to ignite: carpets, seat foam, soft plastic, and even windshield washer fluid. So Lou ignited a single sheet of newspaper and tossed it into the Explorer.

Lou stood to the side and watched the Explorer go up in flames within a few minutes. First, the fire in the vehicle's interior spread quickly to the rear. Then it passed forward through the metal divider that protected the engine compartment. The fire had gone through the whole engine compartment, burning flammable fluids and melting plastic and metal components within ten minutes. He grinned. There was something special about how quickly a fire could destroy something and rapidly make anything unrecognizable.

With the car fully ablaze, the tires blew out, and the heat inside the vehicle caused the airbags to deploy suddenly and then melt into white goo. The cylinders that help pop open a hatchback or a hood heated up and exploded, sending rods flying dozens of feet from the vehicle. Yet Lou stood there undaunted. It almost seemed as if he was fascinated and dazzled by the blaze.

It wasn't like in the movies. Where a flaming car would blow up, Lou knew a vehicle's fuel tank would never create the kind of explosion that would send people flying off their feet. He wished it did, though. Now that would have been a sight to see. When that gas ignited, the fire would flare up, but it wouldn't burst with concussive force. He'd torched several cars over the years and watched them all burn, some with bodies inside.

A car horn blew in the distance, and Nasir yelled out, "C'mon, nigga! We gotta go."

Lou pivoted and coolly walked back to his idling dark green Pathfinder. He climbed into the passenger seat with Nasir behind the wheel and Denise quietly in the back seat. They left the vehicle burning on an abandoned strip in Far Rockaway, Queens.

Nasir drove back to the neighborhood. Everyone was quiet, especially Denise. What they did tonight was unspeakable. Things went from a robbery to mass murder, and he felt some kind of way about it. He didn't want to shoot Earth, but it happened so quickly that he reacted to save his own life. But the others were murdered in cold blood. They were young girls, and Nasir couldn't help but think of his daughter. But he assisted with suffocating the girls to protect Denise. Lou was right about one thing. They'd seen her face. Keeping them alive would have been a risk to them.

However, it tore him apart. That wasn't his style.

While crossing the small bridge toward Howard Beach, Nasir glanced at Denise through the rearview mirror. She remained quiet and calm, staring out of the window. He wondered what she was thinking. There was no coming back from what they'd done. Denise was in deep now, and she was an accomplice to five brutal homicides. Nasir wanted to protect her.

As they cleared the bridge and entered Howard Beach, Nasir noticed a marked NYPD squad car following them.

"Shit!" he uttered. "We got a fuckin' cop behind us."

Both Lou and Denise turned around and saw the cop car. Denise's eyes widened with concern. They were riding dirty, and if they were to get pulled over, it would most likely end in disastrous results.

"If he stays on us longer, we might have a problem," said Lou. "Fuckin' Howard Beach, racist-ass fuckin' place."

Nasir stopped at a red light with the cop car right behind them. While idling at the red light, Lou calmly removed a pistol from the glove compartment.

He glanced at Nasir and said, "We gonna do what we need to do if he pulls us over."

Nasir sighed. *Damn.* The last thing they needed was another homicide during the night. While idling at the red light, Nasir watched the cop's movement via the rear-view mirror. There was only one silhouette inside the cop car. That was the only good news for them.

Finally, the light changed green, and Nasir casually moved through the intersection with the cop still behind them. It became evident that the inevitable would happen, and Lou was willing to murder a cop tonight. There was no way it would be a routine traffic stop. The shotgun was in the back seat with Denise, along with a few stolen items from the robbery.

"I swear, I don't want to have to kill a muthafuckin' cop tonight. But I will," Lou exclaimed.

It was becoming tense. Nasir was about to bring the Jeep to a stop at another red light at another intersection. It looked like the cop car was about to come to another complete stop behind them again. But something miraculous happened. The cop's sirens sprang to life, and the vehicle sped past them through the red light and intersection and raced toward some incident. Nasir and Lou sighed with relief.

"Someone was praying for that fool, because I was gonna light his ass up if it came to that," said Lou.

The trio arrived home after midnight. Lou placed the bag of stolen items and the guns on the kitchen table. Denise looked at Nasir and said, "I'm exhausted. I'm going to bed. You coming?"

"Give me a minute," Nasir replied.

"Hurry up and lie with me, baby." Denise smiled.

Denise started to undress as she marched toward the bedroom. Lou and Nasir watched her, wondering if she would be okay. So far, she seemed undisturbed by what happened tonight. Maybe it was a façade. The last thing they needed was for her to start falling apart.

When Denise disappeared into the bedroom, Lou got straight to business with his cousin. "Look, cuzzo, shit went bad tonight, but we gonna be okay. We need to keep a low profile until our next hit. Give it about a week or two. But what we need to do is find that bitch Iris and handle that. I got the info on her people."

Nasir frowned. "What you mean, next hit?"

"Like I said, we gotta get this fuckin' money, cuzzo," Lou proclaimed unequivocally.

"We killed five people tonight," Nasir reminded him.

Lou looked impassive. "So what? It's the game, the life, cuzzo. You know that, nigga!"

Nasir seemed annoyed. He huffed, locked eyes with Lou, and disputed, "I'm not trying to get locked back up."

"Nigga, you ain't gonna get locked up. Don't start acting like you some bitch-ass nigga, cuzzo. Because you aren't that. I know it. Besides, it's too late to start having a muthafuckin' conscience. You and I both know you crossed that line a long time ago," Lou proclaimed.

"And you wanna continue to cross that line and kill Iris and go after her family?"

"Why the fuck do you care what happens to her? You don't know the bitch. She gotta go because she know all of our faces. If you don't wanna go back to jail, we gotta make that happen. We killed five people tonight, remember?" said Lou.

Nasir sighed. Then he muttered, "This isn't what I signed up for."

Hearing that statement infuriated Lou. What happened to his cousin?

"You must have fuckin' bumped your head and forgot where you came from, nigga," Lou griped. "Look where you're at, cuzzo. You're staying here with me with nothing to show for your life on the streets. You lost everything out there, and you ain't tryin' to do anything about it!"

"I am doin' something about it," Nasir refuted.

"Like what, cuzzo? Tell me your plan right now. Since you came home, the only thing you did was get between the legs of your best friend's little sister and fuck. But you know what I see? Sincere's name ringing like bells, muthafucka. He locked up and got more fuckin' respect than you ever had. When they killed his little brother, what he do? He went out there and made them niggas pay. He was ruthless, and he's still ruthless inside them prison walls. But you out here free like a bird, lookin' crazy with these streets forgetting about you. You fuckin' want that, cuzzo?" Lou proclaimed wholeheartedly.

Nasir frowned. He didn't want to admit that Lou was right. Sincere had always outshined him growing up. Sincere caught his first body during that robbery on Long Island. Then he fled to the military for four years. He came back to New York, and though it was for revenge, his best friend seemed to have picked up where he'd left off—murdering men and making money.

Lou stared intently at his cousin and uttered, "What's it gonna be, cuzzo? Are you gonna solidify your muthafuckin' name on these streets or fade away like some bitch out there? Because I don't want that for you, cuzzo. I got your back. You know that. But if you ain't tryin' to get this money out there like you used to, then I'm sorry, you can't stay here any longer."

Nasir frowned. "Are you serious?"

"Like a heart attack, cuzzo," Lou countered. "I know who the fuck I am. I take from niggas by violence and force. I'm a fuckin' leopard that can't change its spots. I've been homeless and hungry, cuzzo. You know what it was like for me growing up. You grew up the same way. Do you really wanna go back to that, being broke and desperate?"

Nasir didn't talk much about his upbringing. Lou was the only family member he had left besides his daughter.

"Shit, Sincere's little sister is acting more gangster about tonight than you are, cuzzo. "She's in the bedroom sleeping, don't give a fuck, not questioning me about shit. What's done is done. Fuck it, move on, and let's get this fuckin' money, cuzzo. You feel me?" said Lou.

Nasir frowned. Lou stepped closer to him, holding his cousin's stare.

"It's late, and you must be fuckin' tired, because you talkin' crazy right now. So get some sleep, and we'll talk in the morning. Then hopefully you'll be back to your senses. The Nasir I remember growing up with, that muthafucka getting money in these streets, he'll be the one with me tomorrow," Lou proclaimed.

Lou then turned from his cousin's stare and disappeared into his bedroom, slamming the door behind him. Nasir remained still for a moment, absorbing his cousin's words. He'd never been a cold-blooded killer. He killed only in self-defense. Before tonight, Nasir had murdered one man in his lifetime. Four years ago, when Zodiac and his goons accosted him outside his home, he'd killed the driver to escape their threat. The thoughts of looking weak to his cousin and his name and reputation fading or becoming a joke in the streets did bother him. He used to be somebody. Now he felt like a nobody, like a cool breeze in the summer, there for a moment, and then gone and forgotten.

There was another feeling Nasir endured. It was jealousy of his best friend, Sincere. Lou was right. Sincere always had more respect than him on the streets. So when Sincere needed his help to fight, Nasir left town, only to come back when the smoke had cleared, and instead of going to war with Zulu, Nasir decided to align himself with his organization to keep the peace. It was a lesser move, but Nasir believed it to be the smarter move at the time. But when push came to shove, Zulu completely abandoned him when he got locked up. Meanwhile, Sincere still held a grudge toward his enemies and was murdering them in prison, and Nasir continued to feel like he was a man without a country.

He groaned, then turned to join Denise in the bedroom. Nasir became surprised to see that she was still awake and lying naked on her stomach.

"I thought you would be asleep already," he said.

"No. I'm horny," she announced.

It was unexpected.

"You heard everything between me and my cousin?" he asked her.

She turned around to face him and replied, "I don't want to talk about that, especially my brother. What I want is to feel you inside of me right now."

Nasir grinned. It was odd that Denise was turned on after tonight's murders and wanted to fuck. She was different. He knew she was hiding something from him.

He believed she was finding some kind of relief from any pain through promiscuity and violence. Something happened in her past, and Denise refused to speak about it. She was becoming unpredictable and volatile.

"Come fuck me," Denise demanded.

The invitation had been made, and Nasir responded with eagerness. He unbuckled his jeans, quickly undressed, and climbed on top of her with her remaining face down in the bed. He took careful aim and rammed himself inside her from the back. Denise jerked and moaned. "Fuck me," she cried out.

Nasir began pounding her like he was a man driven by lust. The harder he pounded, the more she screamed for more. They both were in that mental space where their sexuality was in control. He intended to keep her like this for as long as possible until they broke with a relentless release. The more Nasir fucked her, the more her juices flowed.

"Please don't stop," Denise cried out with a glazed look in her eyes.

Lights danced behind Nasir's eyes. This was fucking like it was meant to be. Panting and breathing and juicy, squishing sex. He fucked her deep and slow and hard. He built up his pace, fucking her faster and harder, making her moan. He could feel her pussy grabbing him and start throbbing. Waves of pleasure consumed him with the sensation of her wet pussy surrounding him.

"Ooooh, shit," he cried out.

His heart was racing, and soon he and Denise were at the point of no return. They couldn't hold back any longer. An uncontrollable force drove Nasir to drive himself deep inside her. Then Denise screamed into the pillow as Nasir grabbed her hips and delivered his essence as they exploded together.

Nasir collapsed against her, breathless. "You good?" he asked, genuinely concerned for her well-being.

Denise nodded.

Nasir just wanted to lie there and feel protective of her. He gently pressed his lips to her forehead and whispered, "I love you," very softly.

Whoa!

Chapter Twenty-two

Impulse in Harlem on 125th Street was a charming bar and lounge restaurant with a stylish design. The place was built on having the best Southern comfort cuisine in Harlem. It was someplace special Nasir wanted to take Denise for the evening. Nasir and Denise sat at the sleek table enjoying their main courses. The food was so good that it felt like their tongues were having an orgasm.

Nasir wanted to do something special for Denise. What transpired a few days ago was tragic, so he figured the best way to try to forget about everything was to take his woman somewhere special. He'd heard about Impulse while incarcerated on Rikers Island. A few inmates had spoken highly of the place, and he wanted to check it out to see if the hype was real.

It was a brisk evening, and Denise stood out in a geometric-print zip-front long-sleeve jumpsuit that accentuated her curves and booty. It was her taste, sexy and daring. She'd decided to treat herself at the mall. Nasir kept things simple, wearing jeans, beige Timberlands, and a Coogi sweater.

Denise looked around the restaurant and smiled. "Thank you for this," she said to Nasir.

"You deserve something special," he replied.

"No one has ever done anything special for me or taken me anywhere. So I barely left Queens, except for when I stayed with Monica and her son in Long Island for a while," she said.

It was hard for Nasir to believe. "You mean to tell me no one ever done anything nice for you?"

She nodded. "Yes. It's a cold world out there, and men can be colder."

"Well, you know I'll always be around to warm things up," Nasir replied.

Denise smiled. Nasir stared at her like it was his first time seeing her. Then he wholeheartedly uttered, "You're beautiful."

She blushed. "You're trying to get some tonight, I see."

He chuckled. "It's not even about pussy. It's about you, letting you know that I love you."

Hearing those three words come from Nasir stirred some heavy emotions inside Denise. She had become a tough girl, but the waterworks in her eyes were inevitable. She loved him too.

"Do you really love me?"

"No doubt, with all my heart. I watched you grow up, and you're a survivor like your brothers. But we're in this together, no matter what. Whatever you wanna do, or wherever you wanna go, name it. We can go away and not come back," Nasir proclaimed.

She sighed heavily, then averted her attention from his profound gaze. Denise was a tortured creature.

"There's something you need to know about me," she uttered.

"I'm listening, baby."

"I was raped a few years back," she confessed.

It was stunning news to Nasir. He couldn't believe it. He immediately flew into protective mode and anger and asked, "By who?"

"I always felt that Sincere should have been around to protect me, but he was locked up and left me out here to defend myself. It's the reason why I became so angry with him and stopped visiting him. I lost my entire family within months and became alone and vulnerable. I was broke, too. I'd gotten this job at this clothing store on Jamaica Avenue, and the owner was charming and nice to me until that day he wasn't. He took advantage of me and raped me. He'd gotten me pregnant, and I couldn't have a baby. So I did what I needed to do. For a few nights, I danced and turned tricks to pay for an abortion," she admitted.

Nasir frowned. It made sense why she was so angry at Sincere. Given what she'd gone through, Nasir felt that he was the one who had let her down.

"What was his name?" Nasir asked her.

"Why does that even matter now? It happened a few years ago."

"Because he hurt you."

"And now you want to hurt him, or worse," she replied.

"Yeah, I do," Nasir admitted wholeheartedly. "And Sincere might not be around to protect you, but I'm here, and anybody who fucks with you, I'ma fuck 'em up and kill them for you."

It was flattering. "And that's one of the reasons why I love you too."

"So give me his name," Nasir demanded. "You deserve your revenge, baby. He can't keep breathing after what he did to you."

Denise sighed. "We used to call him Mr. Cook."

"Mr. Cook?"

"Cook Gamble, and he owned this clothing store named Urban Boutique," she said.

"And this Cook Gamble is a dead man walking. He raped you. I'ma kill him," Nasir quietly proclaimed to her.

Nasir was the behemoth she needed back then. Maybe Denise wouldn't have become this killer and promiscuous bitch involved in the street life if he had been around. But she couldn't change her past. There was only the future to look forward to, and she believed her future was with Nasir.

Nasir dropped a C-note onto the table for the meal, and the two left the restaurant. It was good to spend some quality time together. It was needed. They climbed into the back seat of a cab and left for Queens.

Denise was nestled against Nasir in the back seat of the cab. Their love was relentless. She wanted to melt in his arms and feel connected to him emotionally and physically. They shared similar energy along with a similar purpose. Denise believed they were soul mates. But Nasir couldn't stop thinking about what she'd told him. He had never heard of Cook, but he wanted to find him and kill him. Nasir felt he owed Denise that, knowing that if Sincere were home, then Cook would have already been a dead man.

Chapter Twenty-three

Cook sat naked in the rickety armchair, glistening with sweat as Anna lay buck naked on the motel bed. They'd fucked several times, and now she was asleep. He watched her sleep and admired her smooth olive skin, long, straight hair, and angelic face. Anna had become his beautiful young snowflake with a pussy wetter than melting ice, and she had become his whore. Cook decided not to sell her to anyone but to keep her for himself and profit. The motel room had become a place for her to turn tricks. Anna had gone from a young, violent pimp to a manipulative and dangerous man who'd gained unscrupulous control over her situation and mind. The price for a date with Anna was $150, and the moment Cook put her services up for sale, the clientele came pouring in.

He lit a cigarette and took a needed drag. Cook had a lot on his mind. Zulu wanted the hit on the detective to be green-lighted right away. He had to meet with a member of the Shower Posse soon to arrange everything. It was nerve-racking, and Cook didn't want to be involved, but he didn't have a choice. Zulu put him in charge of it, and he made it clear: "Don't fuck it up." Cook sighed at the task and continued to smoke.

The motel phone rang and Cook answered it. "Yeah?"

It was Smitty. "Sorry to bother you, but she has a date waiting in the lobby. What you want me to do?"

"Tell him to wait ten minutes, and then send him to the room," Cook replied.

"Will do," Smitty said and hung up.

Cook ground the cigarette into the ashtray. He stood up. He proceeded to get dressed. He had placed his suit neatly inside the closet. Though Anna had business waiting for her, Cook was in no rush to get dressed. Instead, he put himself back together steadily, pants, shirt, jacket, shoes. He maneuvered to the mirror to inspect his attire and was pleased. Then he went to the bed to stir Anna awake from her slumber. He nudged her a few times and then slapped her face twice.

"You have company coming to you soon. Get yourself right. Don't make him wait," said Cook.

Anna lifted from her side, looking a bit groggy. She was taking too long to collect herself. So Cook pulled her to her feet and uttered, "Let's get right, now. I don't have time for you to be sluggish. This nigga will be knocking on that door soon. I want you at your best for him."

Anna nodded. She disappeared into the bathroom to freshen up. Cook gathered the rest of his things and inspected the room. Anna was a mess, and cleaning wasn't her forte. But she wasn't there to clean the place. She was there to sell pussy. But Cook knew having a clean room to make customers feel comfortable was important.

"I'm going to get housekeeping to clean up this fuckin' room," Cook announced.

He heard the faucet running. Then there was a knock at the room door. Knowing it was a customer, Cook pivoted and went to answer the door. When he opened it, a middle-aged black male was standing in front of him. Seeing Cook, the man was taken aback. He didn't expect a suited man to answer the door.

"Sorry. Is this the wrong room?" the man asked.

"Nah, you're in the right place. She's in the bathroom freshening up," said Cook.

Cook stepped to the side to allow him into the room. He quickly sized him up and figured the man to be in his late forties. He had a spick-and-span appearance in black slacks and a button-down with a pencil-thin mustache and a goatee.

When Anna exited the bathroom completely naked, the man's face lit up, and excitement immediately swelled throughout him. It was palpable that he liked the merchandise. She greeted him with an intimate hug as if she knew him personally. Cook watched Anna naturally intermingle with the trick from the threshold to the room, and he was impressed with how she worked him. Anna knew how to soothe his ego with inviting touches and soothing speech. The erection manifesting in his pants indicated how good she was. The man reached into his pocket right away and removed the payment necessary for her to continue with her treats.

Cook smiled. *Yeah, she's a keeper*.

He closed the door on his way out to let her work her magic on him. Cook took the stairs to the lobby, where Smitty watched TV behind the partition. The man rarely left the place. This was his home.

"You're leaving, Mr. Cook?" Smitty asked.

Cook nodded. "I'll be back soon."

Smitty nodded. Then he said, "That young snowflake you got up there, she brings in good business. She must be something special. I see it every night. These fools keep coming back for more like it's crack."

Cook grinned. "I know."

"We need more like her," said Smitty.

Cook curtailed their conversation with, "I need to go. If you need me, call my phone."

"Yes, sir, Mr. Cook."

Cook exited the lobby and walked toward his parked Benz. He removed his car keys and deactivated the alarm. Chirp! Chirp! He slid into the driver's seat of the sleek Benz. He huffed, knowing what he needed to do next. It was late, with mild weather for late October in New York. He started the ignition, lit another cigarette, and drove away from the sleazy motel.

The Mercedes-Benz arrived at a Brooklyn pier that had a view of the Brooklyn Bridge stretching over the East River. The Benz moved over the cobblestone street toward a dead-end street and parked near the East River. Cook sat and waited. It wasn't a long wait. Minutes later, a dark blue van rounded the corner with its headlights shining in his rearview mirror and slowly approached him from behind. Cook coolly removed the .45 he kept underneath his seat and concealed it underneath his left thigh. It was a precaution.

Cook observed from the rearview mirror the passenger door of the van opening, and a young man named Dante, who was in his late twenties, climbed out. The driver remained inside the van. The man approaching his Benz was somewhat ripped with a shaved head, wearing a sleeveless shirt, despite it being October, and jeans. He looked like an average guy, but Cook knew what he belonged to.

The Shower Posse was a violent Jamaican gang involved with drug and arms smuggling and murder for hire.

Dante opened the passenger door to the Benz and slid inside.

"Wah gwaan?" Dante greeted Cook with his thick accent. "Mi brethren! Mi nuh see yuh inna long time!"

"I know," Cook replied.

"Yuh uncle says hello. Yuh need ti see him," said Dante.

"I will."

"So who yuh need mash-up, hey?" asked Dante.

"A cop."

Dante looked surprised by this. "Waah Babylon bwoy a cum fo yuh?"

"Nothing personal, this is business. Coming from Zulu," Cook explained.

"Zulu want a cop mash up, hey? It's gon' be expensive, yuh know?"

"We know," said Cook. "But it's not my call. I'm just following orders."

Cook handed him a stuffed envelope filled with cash. Dante took it and opened it to see $25,000 inside.

"Half of it now, and the other half when it's done," Cook said.

"Yuh start getting ya'self involve inna bai badman ting, huh?" Dante joked and chuckled.

"It is what it is, right? The life we live."

"Yuh, smart, Cook. Always been. But me, mi a shotta inna di streets. Mi a real gangalee," Dante proclaimed.

Cook laughed.

"Yuh si singting funny?" Dante responded.

"No. I don't. No disrespect to you, Dante. But you don't know shit about me. It's been a long time," Cook replied.

"So you say yuh different now?" Dante asked.

"I'm not that scared little boy from Jamaica anymore," Cook replied.

Dante laughed. "Big up. Respect."

Cook handed Dante another package: a big brown envelope. Dante opened it to find a picture of Detective Michael Acosta inside and some needed information. He stared at the image of the cop as if studying him.

"Fuck di cops," Dante uttered. "Mi wi git eh dun."

Cook nodded.

"Nuff love," Dante said to Cook. Then he made his exit from the Benz.

Cook exhaled. He glanced nervously at the rearview mirror to observe Dante getting back into the van. He'd just placed a hit on an NYPD detective. There was a combination of anxiety, dread, and excitement.

The van made a U-turn and left the premises while Cook remained seated inside his Benz. It was a nice night. So instead of leaving right away, Cook exited his car and went for a walk around the area. He took in the sprawling Brooklyn Bridge.

Across the East River was Manhattan with a picturesque skyline. Cook stood at the edge of the East River, staring at the city. He was a lost and scared immigrant from Kingston, Jamaica, when he came to America. He grew up in one of the roughest areas in Kingston, where there were high levels of crime and violence. Cook went to the States with his grandmother when he was 10 years old. It was a culture shock to him to be in New York City, where he felt confused, unsure, and uncomfortable.

For so long, Cook lived in poverty-stricken places and remembered eating corn dogs almost every day for lunch, little pizzas for snacks, and sugary cereals for breakfast. Though everything had changed, including his immediate support system of family and friends, he'd gone from one dangerous environment to the next in the US and had experienced sadness. But he soon learned to adapt to his atmosphere, got with the program, as some said, pulled himself up by his bootstraps, and made something of himself in the US.

Instead of being scared of monsters, he'd become one of them.

Chapter Twenty-four

Nasir took a pull from the cigarette and gawked at the clothing store named Urban Boutique. He stood across the street from it and watched the traffic of women, young and old, black and white come in and out of the store. It was a busy place. Jamaica Avenue was a bustling mecca for shopping, food, and diversity. However, Nasir wasn't there to shop. He had a purpose. What Denise had told him a few days ago bothered him, and he wanted to do something about it. The fact that Cook Gamble raped and assaulted the woman he loved meant a death sentence in his eyes.

It didn't take much for Nasir to find out who Cook Gamble was. He still had his connections in the streets and took advantage of that. Cook was a money launderer for Zulu, and he was a critical piece of Zulu's organization. Therefore, Nasir knew if he killed Cook Gamble, then there would be some heated backlash from Zulu and Zodiac. However, Nasir was determined to right what was done wrong to Denise.

While Nasir continued to stand across the street from the clothing store, blending into the crowd of shoppers, he noticed a showy white Benz pull up to the store and come to a stop. The driver's side door opened, and a well-dressed man climbed out. He wore a brightly colored tailored suit with a contrasting shirt. Nasir immediately knew he was staring at Cook Gamble, and everything about the man spoke established and well organized.

Cook disappeared into the clothing store. Nasir took a final pull from the Newport and extinguished it underneath his boot. He then marched toward the clothing store to look closely at everything.

Once inside, he looked for Cook Gamble, with a gun tucked and concealed in his waistband. The place was for the ladies, having stylish garments displayed everywhere. It was busy with customers and the young female staff, and Nasir played it cool and walked around.

"Hello, can I help you with something, sir?" one of the young ladies asked him.

Nasir smiled and replied, "I'm just looking around, shopping for my girl."

"Well, if you need help, I'm here. I was told that I have excellent taste."

Nasir continued to smile and replied, "I will."

She turned and walked away. He continued to walk around the store and pretended he was browsing. Nasir inspected the store and deduced it was a front, used for money laundering for Zulu's drug empire. Zulu was on top of the world, while Nasir was back to becoming a stick-up kid.

Cook entered the sales floor of the store from a back room, and immediately Nasir scowled. He watched as Cook interacted with his female employees and a few shoppers. He was charismatic, flirtatious, and friendly. Nasir noticed that Cook wasn't shy in touching the young ladies and some pretty shoppers. Nasir saw behind his polite and professional mask and knew what Cook was: a predator. He preyed on young girls and took advantage of them. The thought of this monster assaulting and raping Denise, the woman he loved, and getting her pregnant enraged him. He wanted to kill this muthafucka where he stood, right there in his own place of business. It would have been that simple.

Nasir watched Cook work the store like an expert, and he reached for the gun tucked in his waistband. He tried to remain inconspicuous but was a black male in a female clothing store. Suddenly, Nasir's cell phone rang, and it was Lou calling.

"What up?"

"Where you at, cuzzo?" Lou asked.

"I'm handling something," Nasir replied.

"Well, make it quick. We need to meet up."

"I'll be back at the place in about an hour," said Nasir.

Surprisingly, when Nasir ended the call, Cook was standing right before him. Nasir was somewhat taken aback. He wondered if Cook knew about him or deduced that he was there to harm him. But instead, Cook smiled and said, "Let me guess, you're shopping for your wife?"

"I'm not married," Nasir replied dryly.

Cook kept his smile and guessed again, "Girlfriend then."

"You can say that," Nasir said.

"Well, I know women, and I know style, a benefit I have," Cook joked. "And for what you leave this store with today, you'll be thanking me tomorrow."

Nasir didn't laugh.

"Does your girlfriend have a particular style she likes?" asked Cook.

"I never paid too much attention to it."

"You must be a busy man, I guess," Cook uttered.

"You can say that," Nasir replied.

Nasir wanted to smash his head in and beat him to a pulp, but he kept his composure and allowed Cook to believe he was there shopping for his girlfriend. But while Cook talked, two male customers entered the store and immediately captured Cook's attention. He eyed them with importance, and then said to Nasir, "Will you excuse me for a moment?"

Nasir recognized the two men. They were goons working for Zulu. Cook greeted them, and then the three moved to the back of the store and disappeared into a different room. Nasir wanted to kill him, but then he thought it would be better to rob, torture, then kill him when the time came. He would consult with Lou about it, believing he'd secured their next victim. The only problem was Denise. Though he was a potential payday, Cook was a nightmare she wanted to forget.

It was one of the colder nights of the month, forty degrees and windy. Lou navigated his dark green Pathfinder back onto the Queens track. Surprisingly it was slow tonight. There were barely any girls working tonight. News had gotten around about Earth and his stable of girls. The killers hadn't been caught or identified yet, and Iris was missing. Lou and Nasir had come up empty on that lick, and things got ugly. But Lou wasn't about to let this setback deter him from his come-up. *Shit happens.*

Lou steered his Jeep through the urban area, searching for Lexi. He pulled from the Newport and slowly went from block to block. He lit a Newport and continued to drive around the area until he finally spotted Lexi climbing out of a black Toyota. He smiled. Even in the cold, Lexi looked sexy in a short miniskirt and boots. She wore an old jacket and kept a smile at work. Lou steered his Jeep toward her and rolled down his window.

"Hey, beautiful," he called out.

Lexi saw Lou and huffed. She wasn't too thrilled to see him tonight. However, Lou immediately picked up on her attitude.

"Lexi, what's up with you? Why you actin' brand new to me?" he uttered.

"Not tonight, Lou," Lexi replied.

Lou was stunned. "What? What you mean not tonight?"

"I mean, I'm not in the mood to see you," Lexi barked.

Lou frowned. *What the fuck is her problem?* Lexi pivoted and walked opposite him, but Lou wasn't taking no for an answer. Instead, he killed the engine and leaped from his Jeep with arrogance.

"Lexi," he shouted. "What the fuck is your problem tonight?"

"I just wanna be left alone," Lexi hollered back.

But that wasn't happening. Lou strutted her way and quickly caught up to her. He grabbed her by the arm and pulled her close to him.

"Yo, don't be walkin' away from me like that," Lou hollered.

"Lou, please, not tonight," Lexi protested.

"Why? You know I always got you, Lexi. What the fuck is your problem?"

Lexi looked concerned and upset at the same time. She locked eyes with the young killer, knowing what he was capable of doing. When she heard the news about Earth and his girls, it triggered anger, fright, and guilt inside of her.

"Why did you kill them?" Lexi hollered.

"What?"

"Lou, don't stand there and act like you don't know what the fuck I'm talkin' about. I was friends with some of those dead girls Earth pimped. I heard what happened the other night. I heard what you did to them," Lexi proclaimed.

Lou stared at her stoically. He didn't deny it or confess it. Instead, he kept a tight grip on her arm and huffed. Of course, the streets were going to hear about the killings. But he didn't want to incriminate himself. But also, he felt Lexi deserved an explanation. He didn't want to lose her, as strange as it was.

"Shit happens, Lexi. It went bad. What the fuck you want me to say?" he replied.

"What? They were young girls, Lou."

"And this is the life, the streets, Lexi. Them bitches knew what they were getting into, and Earth came at us first. We just reacted," Lou explained.

But Lexi didn't believe him. She didn't care about Earth but about the girls, the youngest 17.

"I heard they were tortured, suffocated, and blown apart!" Lexi griped. "You didn't have to do them like that!" Lexi glared at Lou. There was no way she was sucking his dick tonight. She saw him as some monster.

"What, now you wanna grow a fuckin' conscience, bitch? You helped set that up, remember? You put me on to Earth, and you know what I'm about—gettin' this money. Shit went left. That's the game. You know how it's played," Lou uttered.

"And how much did y'all get?" Lexi asked.

Lou smiled. "Oh, I see where this is going. What, you want your cut? Well, I'm sorry to say we came up empty-handed."

Lexi didn't believe him. "Huh?"

"You think I'm lying to you? We came out there with nothing, zero, with our dicks in our hands."

"So Comfort and them girls were murdered for nothing."

"Unfortunately," said Lou.

Lexi definitely couldn't believe it, and Lou felt he had already said too much. But there was one more thing he needed to mention.

"Yo, you seen Iris around?" he asked.

"Iris? Why?"

"We just need to talk to her, that's all," Lou said.

But Lexi was no fool. "No. I haven't, and if I did, I wouldn't tell you anything. Why, so you can hunt her down and finish what you started?"

"It ain't even like that," Lou lied.

"Then what is it like, Lou?"

Lou sighed. He only wanted a blowjob from her, not to be interrogated. Lou looked Lexi up and down. His groin was flaring. He didn't come here to talk. But Lexi was adamant she didn't want to see him tonight.

"You really doin' this shit, Lexi?"

"Doing what?"

"How long have we known each other, huh? You know why I'm here. Shit, I'll pay you double tonight," said Lou.

He went into his pocket and removed a small wad of cash. Lexi eyed it.

"One and fifty for your time," Lou uttered, enticing her. "You a crack fiend, bitch, Lexi. So don't stand there and act like you got a conscience about some dead bitches you barely knew, and I ain't leaving until I get what I want from you."

Lexi sighed. Sadly, she knew Lou was right. She craved the extra cash, and they both had an addiction. She loved getting high and working the streets, and Lou was addicted to her for some strange reason. He stared at her intently, waiting for her answer, knowing what it would be. Finally, she relented and walked back to his idling Jeep nearby. Lou grinned. "That's my bitch."

Lexi and Lou climbed into his Jeep, and he drove off.

Money over everything, he thought. Lexi contradicted herself when she slid Lou's hard dick into her mouth, consuming him entirely. As was routine, Lou reclined in his seat and enjoyed the show. When he finally exploded into her mouth, Lou smiled and collected himself. Lexi was the fix he needed. Before she climbed out of the Jeep, Lou gripped her forearm and said to her, "Listen, if you see Iris around, holler at me. I just wanna talk to her, that's all."

Lexi remained quiet.

Lou passed her an extra $20 and added, “I’ll make it worth your time.”

Lexi didn’t respond to his request but quietly took the cash and left.

Chapter Twenty-five

Lou let them know that their next hit needed to be big. There was no way they were going to come up empty-handed again. He felt it was embarrassing. Nasir wanted to bring up Cook, but he knew Denise wouldn't be for it. She'd warned him to forget about the ordeal. However, once again, Denise would be the bait that would lure the target into her web of deceit. But Nasir felt reluctant to keep placing her in harm's way, but Denise was with Lou, adamant about getting this money by any means necessary, to Nasir's chagrin.

It was a wet night. It had been drizzling for an hour with the steady patter of water against the pavement and the windshield of the Chevy Cutlass. Nasir and Lou sat quietly in the front seat, watching a specific residence's front door. This lick took a week of planning, but Lou was confident that everything would execute smoothly. Surprisingly, Denise was good at this shit, picking out the correct targets to entice, seduce, and set up. Because of who her brothers were, especially Marcus, niggas didn't see her as a threat. Instead, they were attracted to her and would make it clear what they wanted, some pussy, and because of her attractiveness and background, she became that honey trap. The trio had committed three violent armed robberies without a hitch, but it wasn't the payday they expected. Instead, they came up with a $7,000 total on all three scores, leaving one man dead.

But this next one came with a sizable payday but a considerable risk. The three had their eyes set on Daquan, a minor lieutenant in Zulu's organization. Daquan wasn't that dangerous but was linked to a ruthless and violent organization, and Lou knew that sticking up and misleading him would lead them to a pot of gold.

Daquan's weakness was pussy. He had a wandering eye and walked around with a perpetual erection, and Denise became the perfect decoy of legs, beauty, and promiscuity. She'd caught Daquan's eyes at the club wearing a basic tube chemise, a strapless style, and a curve-hugging skirt. If you got it, flaunt it. It was inevitable. She had caught Daquan's attention. He approached Denise at the bar with that cliché pickup line, "Can I buy you a drink, beautiful?"

At first, Denise played hard to get. She couldn't make it too easy for him, but eventually, she caved in at his advance, and they seemed inseparable. That was a week ago.

"What's taking them so long?" Nasir griped.

"Relax, cuzzo, Denise got this. They'll be here soon," Lou responded. "Look, this could be a big payday for us, so put your feelings aside, cuzzo, and let's get this money. I need you right on this one. I need this, and you need this. Don't forget."

"I am right," Nasir replied.

Lou chuckled. "Yeah, but Denise has been having your minds in the clouds. That pussy got you beaming up to the stars like Scotty."

Nasir frowned. "I told you, I'm good, and I don't need you talking 'bout my sex life."

Lou continued to chuckle and replied, "You see that you in your feelings, nigga. We don't need that. I need you to be sharp like a knife, ready to cut the muthafucka. Opportunity! We are planning and scheming and goin' for the glory."

They sat parked outside a residential Queens home with the rain falling. It felt like it would never be dry again. Shortly after, a white SUV arrived and parked in front of the house. Lou and Nasir perked up.

"Here we go. They here. Let's get this money," said Lou, cocking back his 9 mm Beretta.

They watched Daquan and Denise climb out of the white Denali. But a third person came with them, most likely muscle. Denise followed Daquan, wearing tight jeans, heels, and a trendy jacket. They entered the home while Lou and Nasir remained seated in the car watching the place like a hawk.

"We wait for her signal," said Lou.

Nasir gripped a .45 and tried to remain calm. His woman was inside that house alone and unprotected, but he knew she could handle herself, and they were right outside, ready to react. The plan was for Denise to pretend that she had forgotten her clutch handbag in the SUV, giving her a reason to exit the premises briefly. It would allow Lou and Nasir to come in behind her and take control of the place. Daquan wasn't the sharpest knife in the drawer or the most polished coin. He was a lieutenant in Zulu's organization because of nepotism.

Ten minutes passed with it still drizzling outside. For Nasir, it was ten minutes too long. He wanted to break into the home with their guns blazing. The two smoked a Newport with anticipation. Then suddenly, there was life at the front door. Denise hurried from the threshold toward the SUV to retrieve her clutch from the vehicle. Before she pivoted to go back inside, she glanced at the silver Cutlass parked across the street, subtly acknowledging Lou and Nasir.

"Here we go," said Lou.

Both men quickly exited the car while Denise headed back inside. They were clad in black hoodies and gloves and hurriedly approached the residence before Denise was fully inside. They instantly piggybacked behind her into the house with their guns cocked and ready, and right away, chaos ensued. Lou shoved Denise to the side and charged into the home, screaming, "Everyone, get the fuck on the ground!"

Daquan and a second man, named Conner, were taken aback. But to Lou and Nasir's shock, they had company. A young girl and a male teenager were inside the living room. Everyone became wide-eyed with fear. Lou and Nasir quickly took control of the room, making everyone lie face down on the ground except for Daquan.

"Everybody just be chill," said Daquan coolly.

Lou scowled his way. "What the fuck you say, nigga?" Lou exclaimed.

Daquan locked eyes with the hooded intruder and uttered, "Just be chill, a'ight?"

Lou immediately smashed the butt of the gun across Daquan's head, which was a painful and crippling blow. Daquan dropped to his knees in agony while Lou thrust the barrel of the 9 mm into his face. It looked like he was staring down the Holland Tunnel and prepared to die.

"You don't say shit or run shit, nigga!" Lou hollered. "I'm running this ship, muthafucka! I'm the captain now."

Daquan's head throbbed with a blaze of pain. He glanced at Denise, and he knew she'd set him up. He'd been caught slipping, and this was the consequence. Everyone in the living room cringed in fear. It was happening. They were being robbed. Lou did most of the talking while Nasir and Denise kept everyone submissive at gunpoint.

"Listen carefully, Daquan, because I don't like to repeat myself. Where everything at?" Lou asked him.

"There's nothing here," Daquan responded.

"What the fuck you mean ain't shit here?" Lou barked impatiently. "You think I'm stupid, nigga? You are a drug dealer, so I expect to see drugs and money here, and if I don't get that, why keep you alive then?" Lou threatened.

The color drained from Lou's face.

"I only have ten stacks on me," Daquan shouted.

"What, that's it? We ain't come here for ten stacks," Lou griped.

Lou glanced at Nasir, who stood over Conner and the young boy. Denise also had a 9 mm Beretta, and she scowled at the victims.

"I know who's holding that kind of weight and cash right now," Daquan exclaimed.

"Who?" asked Lou.

"Tyrone," Daquan quickly replied. "I know he's holding a lot of weight and cash right now."

"Where does he live at?"

"He's not too far from here," said Daquan.

Lou was contemplating the idea of heading there, but Nasir uttered, "It's too risky. How do we know he's telling the truth?"

It was a smart question. Lou looked at Nasir and returned, "You know I ain't come here for no pennies, nigga. So we gon' do this shit."

There was no turning back now. Lou wanted it all, no matter how risky it became.

"This is what we gonna do. We gonna tie these fools up, and then Denise and I are gonna go take Daquan on this journey," said Lou.

Right away, Nasir was against it. "You and Denise? Nah."

"Cuzzo, what I tell you about being into your feelings when we tryin' to get this money?" Lou reminded him.

Nasir remained reluctant to follow this plan, but he was outnumbered. Denise and Lou were going that extra mile. They came too far.

"This is happening, cuzzo. You stay back and keep our guest company," said Lou. "You got this?"

Nasir nodded. "I got it."

Lou smiled. "Cool. This gonna be fun."

Everyone was hog-tied and left face down on the ground except for Daquan. They took him hostage, leaving Nasir behind to babysit.

Chapter Twenty-six

Daquan directed Lou and Denise to Springfield, Queens. It was overall a quiet suburb. However, the site was a known area in New York and could be both enjoyable and dangerous.

Denise drove while Lou sat in the back seat with Daquan sticking the gun into his side. If Daquan sneezed wrong, Lou would blow his right side out. The night was still young and on the edge of becoming eventful.

"Turn left here," Daquan instructed.

Denise made the left onto a quiet street, and it was passive with lovely homes and appealing cars parked in the driveway. Denise brought the white Denali near an old-fashioned house with a chain fence around it.

"This is it, Tyrone's place," Daquan said.

"A'ight, this is what we gonna do. We gonna keep it tight together like Legos. How many usually be inside?" Lou asked him.

"I'm not sure," Daquan replied.

Lou jaggedly nudged the gun into his side and replied, "Don't lie to me nigga. Who in there?"

"Maybe Joseph and Lamont."

"And who they?"

"One is his brother, and the other is his cousin," Daquan returned.

"They be strapped?"

Daquan nodded. "Yeah."

Lou stared at the house. There was a camera aimed at the front door, motion lights in the backyard, and a Lexus ES300 in the driveway. It wasn't impossible or impenetrable.

"How we gonna do this?" Denise asked Lou.

Lou grinned and replied, "We gonna go knock and walk right in the front door."

Denise thought he was kidding, but he wasn't.

"C'mon, nigga, you gonna introduce us to your friends," said Lou teasingly.

Daquan and Denise walked arm in arm to the front door. Daquan took a deep breath, glanced at Denise, who stood by his side, and then he knocked politely on the front door. Fear trickled down his spine, as he knew tonight would most likely end badly for him.

"Yo, who the fuck is it?" a voice boomed from the other side of the door.

"Ty, it's me, Daquan," Daquan coolly replied.

The main door opened, and a six-foot thug clad in a wife beater and black sweatpants loomed into their view. His body was sculpted from hours of hard work in the gym. There was an iron screen door between them. Tyrone glared at Daquan and Denise.

"Daquan, what the fuck do you want?" Tyrone barked. "And who's your lady friend?"

His voice was deep and brooding.

"This is Latoya," he lied. "And I came to get that work like you promised."

"Muthafucka, I told you to come Saturday. You two days early, nigga," Tyrone griped.

"I know, but the thing is . . ." Daquan uttered nervously.

"The thing is what, Daquan? Why the fuck you here with this bitch?" Tyrone exclaimed.

"Look, I can't wait until Saturday," Daquan replied.

Tyrone frowned. "What? Why the fuck not, nigga?"

What they needed was for Tyrone to unlock that iron screen door. Unbeknownst to Tyrone, Lou was nearby, hiding in the cut. He was concealed in the shadows, out of sight from Tyrone and the cameras. When the iron screen door opened, Lou planned on seizing the moment. It was a narrow window for him, but he was poised discreetly with the hoodie pulled over his head and his 9 mm ready for anything.

But Daquan was fumbling the ball near the goal line and about to screw things up and cost them the game. Lou was perched by the side of the house, watching this nightmare unfold. Daquan was weak and scared, and there wasn't much he could do without giving away his location.

"He can't Saturday because we got plans, nigga," Denise intervened.

Tyrone was stunned by her response. "Bitch, what? Who the fuck are you talking to?"

"You stupid. You a stupid nigga, or deaf, which one?" Denise retorted. "I'm talking to you, you fuckin' clown!"

Tyrone couldn't believe what he was hearing. The bitch was bold. Tyrone clenched his fists and glared at Denise heatedly, and if looks could kill, her blood and guts would have been sprayed everywhere on his front steps. But Denise continued with her insults.

"You know what, baby? I don't even know why you deal with this clown-ass nigga. You definitely was right about him. He ain't nobody. Just an asshole living on borrowed time," Denise continued.

Tyrone became a bull seeing red. For him, becoming mad was an understatement. He became enraged. Then without thinking, he reacted. Tyrone finally unlocked the iron gate, pushed it open, and became that bull charging out of the gate, ready to pierce Daquan with his horns. Denise's plan had worked. She'd poked the bear, and

Tyrone's temper gave them their opportunity. Tyrone angrily grabbed Daquan and tried to attack him, and while that was happening, Lou rushed from his hiding spot and banged the butt of his gun into Tyrone's head.

The sudden blow was staggering, and before Tyrone could react with his own act of violence, he was staring down the barrel of Lou's pistol. The ruse had worked.

"Do it, nigga! 'Cause I ain't got no problem squeezing death at you," Lou warned him.

Tyrone scowled. Before the occupants inside had any inclination of what was happening at the front door, Tyrone was forced back inside at gunpoint. Lou knew it was time to get this party started. But Lou and Denise had one surprise for them after another. Tyrone's cousin was there as expected, but another man named Big Joe was sitting on the couch instead of Tyrone's brother. He was a high-ranking lieutenant and someone close to Zulu's circle. Daquan's eyes grew wide with fear and shock when he saw Big Joe.

Fuck! Fuck! Fuck!

"What the fuck is this?" Big Joe growled at the intruders.

Lou wasn't a bit intimidated by him or the others. He was the one with the gun and the authority at the moment. However, Big Joe scowled at the intruders and stood up.

"You know who the fuck I am, who I'm with? Y'all making a fuckin' mistake," Big Joe warned them.

"Ain't no mistake, muthafucka. I know who you are and what you are about," Lou retorted with a smirk. "But guess what, nigga, you ain't shit to me. So now come off that watch and come out the pockets."

Lou aimed his gun at Big Joe's head while Daquan, Tyrone, and his cousin stood frozen nearby. The tension inside the room was thick like a brick wall. Lou knew the odds were against him but remained undaunted and ambitious.

Big Joe glared at Daquan and uttered, "Friends of yours, Daquan?"

"I ain't got shit to do with this, Big Joe. Believe me," Daquan responded.

"Everyone shut the fuck up!" Lou shouted. "Too much fuckin' talking in this fuckin' room!"

Lou trained his pistol on Tyrone and exclaimed, "We here for a reason, and I swear to God, I'll drop every muthafucka in this room right now if y'all move wrong and don't comply. Now where it at, nigga?"

Tyrone remained stubborn and bitter. He locked eyes with Lou defiantly. But of course, it wasn't happening because the last thing he feared was answering to Zulu about any loss of product or cash.

"Fuck you!" Tyrone cursed.

Lou huffed. *Okay, they wanna make things hard.* So to prove to them that he wasn't bluffing, Lou aimed the gun at the cousin's head and didn't hesitate and squeezed the trigger.

Bam!

Tyrone's cousin dropped dead near his feet. "Muthafucka!" Tyrone exclaimed.

"Now let's do this again," Lou taunted.

Tyrone and Big Joe stood there fuming, and Lou and Denise were becoming impatient, and Daquan wanted to disappear.

Big Joe stepped closer to the two intruders and said, "Okay, man, y'all got this." He looked at Tyrone and added, "Get them what they came here for."

Tyrone frowned and became reluctant. "What?"

Big Joe continued stepping forward to Lou, and as he did, he swept his left hand up in a blur and grasped the barrel of Lou's pistol in a tight grip. Lou was surprised, and Big Joe directed the weapon down and right, moving it farther away from himself. A struggle ensued, and

Tyrone saw his opportunity to strike too. He charged toward Denise. However, she reacted by letting off two shots.

Tyrone immediately went down, but he was still alive. Denise shot him in his right leg, and then she quickly pivoted in Daquan's direction and was ready to kill him. But Daquan immediately threw his hands up and shouted, "Please, don't kill me. We good, right?"

Denise frowned. She glanced at Lou struggling with Big Joe as the two wrestled for control of the gun. She tried not to panic and kept her gun trained on Daquan, hoping Lou took control of the fight.

"I'ma kill y'all!" Big Lou screamed.

Big Joe was fierce and strong, but Lou was crazy and relentless. Tonight wasn't his night to die. He summoned the strength like the Hulk, kicked Big Joe in the knee, then twisted the gun back a quarter of a turn and yanked the gun out of Joe's hand. Then he stepped back with the gun pointed at Big Joe and shot him three times in the chest. Big Joe went down like the Twin Towers.

"This stupid muthafucka!" Lou shouted, angry. He glared down at the body and added, "Look at you now. I told you not to fuck with me!"

Now it was only Tyrone and Daquan alive. Lou was becoming an unhinged and impatient maniac, a lethal combination. Finally, he wheeled the .45 in Daquan's direction and shouted, "I'm tired of playing fuckin' games with you stupid niggas!"

He then pointed his attention to a crippled Tyrone on the ground who was clutching his leg, squirming, and bleeding heavily.

"This bitch shot me. You muthafucka! I swear you are dead," Tyrone hollered. "I ain't telling you niggas shit."

"If she hit an artery, then you're fucked, nigga," said Lou. "Maybe we'll call 911, and maybe we won't. Or maybe we watch you die slow, then next we go after your family, your son first, then your daughter, following with your baby mamas, and we wipe out your entire bloodline."

Tyrone believed he was bluffing.

"Louis, Alexis, Shaniqua, and Lisa." Lou uttered the names of his kids and baby mamas. "I know their names, and believe me, it will just be a matter of time before I know their addresses, too. So if you want their blood on your hands, continue to be stubborn and make me wait, and I promise you, I'm gonna take my time torturing then killing them."

"You touch them, and I'll—"

"You'll do what? You ain't in the position to spew threats at me, nigga. Listen, nigga, coke, pussy, and money you can always get back. Plenty to go around. But a life, your family's life, you can't get that back," Lou proclaimed chillingly.

Tyrone knew he was right. The position he was in was between a brick wall and a dead end. So Tyrone relented and decided to play ball finally. But Lou held the cards, and he didn't have a choice. Thinking about his kids, he spewed, "Everything's in the basement. There's a safe inside the wall behind a tool storage cabinet."

Lou grinned. Finally, there was progress. He looked at Denise and said, "Watch them."

Lou entered the basement, turned on the lights, and immediately saw the tool cabinet. It was a decoy. He slid the cabinet to the side to reveal the safe embedded into the wall. When he opened it, the look on Lou's face was priceless. *Jackpot.* There were bundles of cash and a few kilos of cocaine stored inside. This is what he came for, a huge payday, and it finally had arrived.

Lou ascended from the basement carrying his newfound goodies in a small black duffle bag. Tyrone was still on the floor, bleeding profusely, and Daquan was lying face down with Denise watching him like a hawk. Lou was smiling the moment he came back into the living room.

"Are we good?" she asked him.

"Oh, we're good," he responded.

Lou stood over Tyrone and said, "Good news: your family is gonna be okay. But unfortunately, it won't be the same for you. Shit happens, right? That's the game."

Lou aimed and fired his weapon, killing Tyrone with a gunshot to his head. Next, he focused on Daquan crying and cringing while facing down on the floor. Finally, Lou looked at Denise and said, "Do you wanna do the honors?"

Denise took a deep breath and squeezed the handle of the .45 in her hand. She was apprehensive initially. She'd never killed anyone before, especially in cold blood. But this was new and exciting. Lou was waiting for her to pop her cherry.

"You got this, Denise. Just aim and squeeze. The bullet will do the rest," said Lou coolly.

Daquan begged for his life. "Please, don't do this. I don't wanna die."

But his pleas would fall on deaf ears. Denise stood over Daquan and aimed the barrel at the back of his head. Lou continued to give her encouragement. "We ain't got all day, Denise, and he knows your name."

"C'mon, don't do this," Daquan cried out. "I won't mention this to anyone. I swear."

Suddenly, a switch went off inside Denise, and she thought about her brother Marcus and her mother. There was this rapid and unexpected anger that developed inside of her, like a volcano that was soon to erupt. The streets had taken everything from her, and she couldn't be weak, and Nasir was her family now. She scowled down at Daquan and did what needed to be done.

She put three bullets into the back of his head and neck and then exhaled. It seemed like a sudden weight had been lifted from her shoulders. She was a killer now. Lou grinned and replied, "I knew you had it in you."

They hurried from the house, climbed into Daquan's white Denali, and fled the scene. While Lou drove back to the first residence where Nasir was inside, he made a phone call to him. Nasir answered right away.

"How we looking?" asked Nasir.

"Look, it's done," said Lou. "We'll be there soon. After that, it's time to clean house."

Chapter Twenty-seven

Cook opened the trunk to his Benz and removed the duffle bag inside. So his late-night meeting with Ricky and Tony in Coney Island, Brooklyn, was right on time, and Cook didn't disappoint them with his fashion statement, stunting in a gray outfit and a tweed overcoat with a red statement tie for a terrific signature look.

Ricky smiled at Cook's fashion and said, "You need your own fuckin' runway show, Cook. Sometimes I don't know if I'm coming to a drug deal or a fashion show."

Ricky laughed. Cook didn't find him funny.

"What, I'm not funny enough for you?" Ricky uttered, grinning.

"I'm a busy man, Ricky. I have a lot on my plate," Cook responded.

"Damn, who took a piss in your coffee? Usually, you're more fun than this," said Ricky.

"I got a lot on my mind," Cook replied.

"We all do. It's the world we live in, right?" added Ricky.

Cook handed him the small duffle bag containing five kilos of cocaine, and Ricky gave him the carrier bag of cash. Cook glanced inside, and the money, money, money brought a slight smile to his face. It was always great doing business with Ricky.

Noticing Cook's minor smile, Ricky uttered, "Yeah, that will always bring a smile to a nigga's face."

No doubt.

Cook was ready to part ways with Ricky. But of course, Ricky had something else to bring up to him. He smiled Cook's way and said, "Yo, Cook, you never did hook me up with those party favors. What's good, you don't like a nigga?"

Cook looked at Ricky.

"I'm no faggot or anything, but you're a handsome guy. Why are you so interested in buying pussy?" asked Cook.

"Look, I want the best of both worlds like you. What's the point of making all this money if I can't invest and celebrate with it?" Ricky answered.

"That's what strip clubs are for."

"I don't want to flirt and fuck with strippers. I want control," Ricky replied seriously.

"Control?" Cook chuckled. "What do you want control of? Huh?"

Ricky held Cook's stare. Then suddenly, there was something different about him—something ominous. His gregarious personality seemed to diminish, and he became a man who wouldn't take no for an answer.

"How do you know about my business anyway? You and I deal with one thing, not the other. Have you ever heard the phrase 'stay in your own lane'?" Cook uttered.

Ricky smirked. "You're a businessman, Cook. I understand that. So let me speak your language."

Ricky nodded to his partner, Tony. Tony turned and walked back to their black Yukon. Cook remained alert, watching their every move. It was the middle of the night, and they were in a rough neighborhood, and anything could go wrong in a heartbeat. Therefore, Cook kept his pistol close. Tony returned and tossed Cook a large package. He took a peek inside, and there was more money.

"That's twenty-five grand," said Ricky. "I want my party favors because I like to party. I mean, who doesn't, right?"

"Question: how the fuck you know about my business in the first place?" asked Cook seriously.

"How do you think? The streets talk."

"Nah, not about this," Cook replied incredulously.

That statement worried Cook. *"The streets talk."* The last thing he wanted was anyone to know about anything he did, especially when pimping, kidnapping, and trafficking young girls for profits. But to everyone, he was a businessman, a pillar of the community, someone people could look up to and respect. He ran several clothing stores and was a profitable investor and broker.

But Cook recognized something in Ricky that he saw in himself. He was a sexual predator and borderline sadist. So it made sense to Cook.

"I'm willing to pay you five thousand dollars for each young girl," Ricky said.

"And what do you plan on doing with them?" asked Cook.

"Why is that your business? Do you want to make some extra money or what?"

Cook sighed. It seemed unreal. There was that old saying, "Do not let your left hand know what your right hand is doing." He only wanted to deal with Ricky when it came to selling cocaine. Mixing businesses with him was probably a bad idea. The more Cook studied Ricky, the more he understood why Ricky needed his help. Ricky was a young thug with an appetite he couldn't control. It made sense to him. Cook was a gentleman but a wolf in sheep's skin. Cook could fake sincerity and create emotional displays to influence, intimidate, charm, and seduce young girls. He was a predator who developed a relationship with his victims and used manipulation to coerce young girls into doing something they didn't want to. He would interfere with his victim's relationship with others, especially if he felt threatened. Cook would become controlling, and sexual intimacy was a way to assert dominance.

Ricky wasn't Cook.

"You haven't answered my question. How do you know about my other exploits?" Cook asked him.

Ricky held his intense stare. Tony stood behind him patiently.

"How else? Your partner in crime," Ricky answered.

Cook was taken aback. "Winter?"

But it didn't make sense to Cook. Winter wasn't one to run his mouth, especially about what they did. So Cook figured Ricky was lying about his information. Nah, something was wrong. Suddenly, this drug deal seemed too suspicious to him. So he subtly sized up Ricky and Tony and thought, *they look and speak the part, but who are they?*

"You talked to Winter?" asked Cook.

"Let's just say I ran into the nigga a few times," said Ricky.

"Ran into him where?"

Ricky smiled, "Damn, nigga, what's up with the 411?"

"We're just talking, right?" said Cook.

"Yeah."

"So let's talk."

Cook glanced at Tony and wondered why Ricky did most of the talking while Tony was the silent one. Once again, he felt something wasn't right. However, it was too late to turn back around because he'd already done business with them.

"Tony, why are you always so quiet?" Cook asked him.

"Because I don't like to run my mouth," Tony replied.

Cook chuckled.

"Yo, Cook, what's up with you?" Ricky chimed.

"Every time we meet, you always in my business about these girls," said Cook.

"Because I want to make some money," Ricky responded.

"We already making money."

"Well, I want more money and pussy," Ricky laughed.

Cook kept a stoic gaze and replied, "You know what they say about greed."

"What they say, nigga?"

"'Greed makes man blind and foolish, and makes him an easy prey for death,'" Cook stated, quoting Rumi.

"Well, I ain't blind or foolish, and I ain't dying anytime soon," Ricky replied.

Right away, Cook knew he was dealing with a fool. But he was a hypocrite himself, being blinded by money and pussy. Staring at Ricky, it felt like he was staring at himself. He was in too deep and taking too many risks. Zulu had him place a hit on a cop. There were the young girls, the drugs, the money laundering. Now it felt like Ricky and Tony were setting him up for something.

"Yo, listen, I ain't tryin' to pressure you, Cook. We ain't no snitches or cops. I'm an entrepreneur like yourself, always looking for the next great investment, and you're that. I respect you, real talk. How long have we been doing business together? A few months now, right?" Ricky proclaimed.

But there was something about them that Cook didn't see before, and it was with Tony. Some people could easily vouch for Ricky, but it was Tony whose background was a mystery. *Where did he come from?* Cook had been so distracted with making money, climbing the ladder, and removing himself from underneath Zulu's thumb that he had never gotten the chance to vet these two appropriately, especially Tony. There were red flags with Ricky continually asking him about girls.

Cook grew nervous and quickly became paranoid. Instead of seeing them as business partners, he saw them as a threat to his freedom and livelihood. He feared Ricky was a snitch and Tony was an undercover cop. Somehow, they'd gotten Ricky to become an informant, and Cook felt he became their mark.

"Let's make this money, Cook," Ricky uttered.

"We'll talk," Cook replied with a halfhearted smile.

Cook was in too deep now, with them, with Zulu, and with Winter. He went to his car and climbed inside. From his rearview mirror, he watched Ricky and Tony get inside their black Yukon. He removed a SIG P228 from the glove compartment. He checked the clip, which was fully loaded, and then he stared in the rearview mirror again. Cook thought about doing the unthinkable. With his eyes fixed on Ricky and Tony through the rearview mirror, he sighed heavily and slowly stepped out of his Benz with the concealed gun. What he wanted to do was kill them both right there. Cook felt it was necessary to protect himself.

"Hey, Ricky," Cook called out.

Ricky stepped out of the Yukon. "What's up? You good?"

Cook approached him and was ready to draw the pistol. He'd never taken someone's life before, but he had to start somewhere.

"You changed your mind about that business with the girls?" Ricky asked.

Tony remained seated in the Yukon. Cook locked eyes with Ricky and told himself, *just do it*. He felt everything was at stake, feeling he was in the crosshairs of either cops or snitches. But he couldn't do it. If Tony was undercover and Ricky was an informant, then killing them right now would be a mistake. There had to be another way.

"Let's have drinks and talk elsewhere soon," said Cook.

"Drinks? You wanna go out for drinks?" Ricky replied incredulously.

"Yes. Let's you and me have a lengthy talk. Get to know each other better."

Ricky chuckled. Then he replied, "A'ight, I'm cool with that. As long as you bring some bitches with you."

Cook smiled. "Okay. We'll talk."

The two pivoted from each other and walked away. Cook climbed back into his Benz and exhaled. Yeah, he was sure that something was off with Ricky and Tony. But the question was, was it too late for him to do anything about it?

Chapter Twenty-eight

Billie's was a fancy and beautiful restaurant in lower Manhattan. It was lavishly decorated with soft lighting, tasteful artwork, and classical music that offered a very romantic theme. There were linen tablecloths and candlelight. Billie's was where couples, businesspeople, and vacationers came to enjoy a piece of New York's best from an establishment that had been around since Prohibition.

Zulu was dining among the pretentious crowd of capitalists, entrepreneurs, and the elite. He was clad in a spicey buttoned-down shirt, black slacks, and high-priced wingtip shoes. A Paul Newman Rolex Daytona flashed around his wrist with a diamond pinky ring. Sitting across from Zulu was Tammy, his date for the night. She was eloquently dressed in a femme fatale black dress with a V-neckline, thick shoulder strap, scalloped eyelash lace trim, and a high front slit. She was a beautiful woman reflected brightly in her ebony skin and long raven black hair. A half-empty bottle of Château Lafite Rothschild sat on the table near their unfinished meals.

A smile appeared on Zulu's face as he lifted his wineglass in Tammy's direction and said, "To prosperity, love, and health. Also, to us on this beautiful night."

Tammy did the same, and the two clinked glasses and downed the rest of their wine. Zulu was out on a lovely date with a charming woman. Tammy was a self-described around-the-way girl who left the neighborhood, went to college, and became an investment banker. They'd dated when they were teenagers, but regrettably, they'd lost contact with each other over the years. Tammy had shown up to Cynthia's funeral to pay her respects and reunited with Zulu. Soon, old feelings began to rise, and they wanted to explore them.

"You are beautiful, Tammy, and you haven't aged a day," Zulu complimented her.

Tammy blushed. "Thank you, and I see Father Time has been good to you too. But look at us. We're both successful and living out our dreams."

"I always knew you would be successful. You were always smart. I'm not shocked that you became an investment banker. You were always great with math and numbers," Zulu said.

Tammy continued to smile and blush. Then she suddenly changed the subject by saying, "I was so saddened to hear about Cynthia. It is so tragic and hard to believe she was killed. I knew you loved her and y'all were close."

Zulu had a fleeting moment of sadness and nostalgia. He did love his baby mama, but she had to go for her transgressions against him.

"Zulu, anything you need from me, ask, and I'm there," Tammy mentioned. "To lose the mother of your children, I can only imagine."

"Listen, enough talk about death and past relationships, Tammy. I don't want this night with us to become a bore," Zulu interrupted.

"I understand," she replied.

"But it's so great to see you again."

She smiled. "And it is great to see you too."

They continued to eat and enjoy the pricey wine, the rich decor, and each other. Around Tammy, he wasn't a murderous drug kingpin. Instead, he was a well-dressed man infatuated with a beautiful woman he'd known for years.

"Damn. I believe I'm sitting here having dinner with the next Warren Buffett, a future billionaire in the making," said Zulu. "Do you have any hot stock picks for me?"

Tammy laughed. "Invest astutely. But like you need my advice, Zulu. You're doing quite well for yourself right now."

Zulu sighed then replied, "What's having the keys to a kingdom when you don't have a queen by your side to share it with. I always loved you, Tammy."

"But Cynthia . . ." she brought up.

"Cynthia wasn't you. When you went away to college, I wanted to fill that void you left behind. When you left New York to further your education, something left me too. Yeah, I loved Cynthia, but I was in love with you, Tammy," Zulu proclaimed wholeheartedly.

Tammy seemed smitten by his words. She couldn't take her eyes off Zulu. He was a handsome and powerful man, but dangerous, too. This aura to him was magnetic and resilient, and their chemistry was passionate.

"The way you're talking, it feels like you're ready to propose to me," Tammy joked.

"Hey, anything is possible," said Zulu.

Tammy chuckled. "Well, don't. We may have known each other for years, but we're now getting to know each other again, and besides, you just lost Cynthia, and I don't want to piggyback onto a relationship right after her death."

"I understand that, and I respect it," Zulu responded. "So what was it like living in California?"

"Expensive," Tammy joked.

"I bet it is."

"But it was cool, different, a culture shock to me at first. Not used to it being seventy degrees in January, and then there's the risks of natural disasters and the heavy tax burden," Tammy mentioned.

"Me personally, I can't live in an area where the ground can shake underneath my feet," Zulu joked.

"Well, contrary to popular belief, earthquakes aren't that bad in California. Of course, they happen, but most times they can be so small it hardly interrupts everyday life."

"I'll take your word for it, then," said Zulu.

They dined on their meals and continued to consume the best wine. Everything was going as planned. It was becoming the perfect night for Zulu. But in his line of business, there was no such thing as the perfect night. There were always going to be hiccups and challenges, and danger, and while Zulu sat there in awe of an old flame, one of his henchmen was reluctantly approaching him with some bad news.

When Zulu saw Tommy approaching, he quietly frowned, knowing it wouldn't be good. Tommy knew not to interrupt his dinner with Tammy unless it was necessary. Zulu's attention shifted from Tammy to Tommy. Tommy leaned into his ear and whispered something into his ear. Then he left, leaving Zulu sitting there with a deadpan expression.

"Is everything okay?" Tammy asked him.

Zulu smiled slightly and replied, "Yes, everything's okay. But unfortunately, I have to leave and take care of something important, Tammy."

"Oh. Nothing too serious, I hope."

"When you wear the crown in my line of business, sometimes it is true, heavy's the head," Zulu stated.

He rose from the table, removed a wad of cash from his pocket, and dropped nearly a stack of bills onto the table, including a sizable tip.

"Of course, dinner is on me, and I had a nice time with you, Tammy. I definitely want to continue this soon," said Zulu politely.

"I understand. Go handle your business. I'll be in town for a few more weeks," she replied.

It was good news to him. That put a smile on Zulu's face after the news he heard from Tommy. "I'm looking forward to it, Tammy."

The two hugged and shared a quick kiss, then Zulu calmly left the restaurant with the new love of his life on his mind. Tommy was waiting for him outside, standing next to an idling Lincoln Navigator. Zulu climbed into the passenger seat of the truck. The moment his butt was planted into the leather interior, Zulu shouted, "What the fuck is going on? Tell me something, Tommy."

"As I said, one of our spots got hit tonight, and it's bad," Tommy replied.

"How? And by who?"

"We don't know yet," Tommy said.

"Tommy, stop this double-talking and lay everything on me because I just left having dinner with a beautiful woman I haven't seen in years, and I was hoping to get some pussy tonight until this shit," Zulu griped.

Tommy exhaled. "Big Joe is dead."

"What the fuck!"

"They hit two of our locations in Queens and killed everyone in both places," Tommy explained.

"And what's the damage?"

"Ten kilos gone, and nearly a hundred thousand dollars in cash," said Tommy.

Zulu seethed. *Fuck!* The loss wouldn't dent his organization, which made millions of dollars and moved hundreds of kilos a month. But it was the audacity and the principle behind this attack.

"Do you believe it was an inside job?" Tommy asked him.

Zulu didn't answer him right away. Instead, he sat there brooding in the passenger seat, trying to connect the dots. It was too early to say what happened and to know who was behind it. It had been a while since some crew was bold enough to come at them and take from them. The last time that happened, every last man and woman involved was decimated entirely, and they were still finding pieces of everyone two years later. Zulu's name was cemented in the streets. Since he'd taken over the reins from Mob Allah, he became the law and boogeyman in the streets of New York.

Zulu sighed heavily. "I need to make a call."

Tommy nodded and passed him a cell phone. "It's clean."

Zulu dialed a number, and it rang a few times before someone answered. "Who's this?"

"It's me. We need to meet and talk," said Zulu.

"Where?"

"Meet me at the usual location in about an hour," said Zulu.

He ended the call and released another frustrated sigh.

"If it ain't one thing, then it's fuckin' another," Zulu exclaimed.

Detectives Acosta and Emmerson climbed out of the Crown Vic like two men looking to head into another battle. Instead, they'd arrived at another crime scene in Queens. It was a residential house in a quiet neighborhood where the outside was swarming with cops. Some people's way of life had been foully erupted by death. It was a breezy night when they stepped into the front yard of the quaint house guarded by uniformed officers. Both men wondered what horrific treat awaited them inside.

Immediately, the detectives were hit with that familiar smell of death and madness when they stepped foot into the house. The place's interior was equivalent to the outside, with cops everywhere, including a few other detectives. Immediately, Acosta and Emmerson began taking in the scene with their skilled eyes. Four bodies had been bound with zip ties and executed by a single gunshot to the back of their heads. There were pools of blood throughout the house and blood on the furniture and walls of the living room and a back bedroom.

"This borough never keeps it boring," Emmerson uttered.

Time was of the essence, and CSI had already arrived to process the scene, and it was hard keeping up with the murders. They were happening rapidly.

"We got four down," said another detective, named Julius.

"Another home invasion?" Acosta asked.

"It appears to be. No forced entry. So they knew their killers, I assume," Julius said.

"I count three bodies in the living room. Where's the fourth?" asked Emmerson.

"Inside the main bedroom."

Detective Acosta and Emmerson walked into the main bedroom to find the fourth victim. It was an older woman in her underwear. She was sprawled across the king-size bed facedown and had been shot in the back of the head.

"We believe she tried to hide in the closet when it happened, they found her, and they didn't want to leave behind any witnesses," said Julius.

The crime scene emulated the one they'd picked up in Bricktown a few weeks back: a home invasion, everyone executed, no survivors. Detective Acosta stared at the woman for a moment and imagined the horror she probably went through, what they all went through. It was horrendous. Life was cheap to anyone who did this, and it was sad to say, but it was becoming the same cliché.

For a moment, Acosta stood over the body in silence, taking in every inch of the bedroom/crime scene. The entire home had been ransacked. The culprits were looking for something, and he assumed it was drugs and cash. What else?

"What are you thinking?" Emmerson asked him.

"This wasn't a random act. This was probably planned out," Acosta responded.

"You think it's the same crew from Bricktown?" asked Emmerson.

"Maybe. The same pattern, I believe. They gain access inside somehow, have the element of surprise, and then have no problem killing everyone. But if so, they're quick, violent, and methodical," said Acosta.

"Methodical?" another detective, named Jose, uttered. "Fuckin' savages. They do this and have us come behind to clean up their fuckin' mess."

There were five homicide detectives at the scene, and each had seen their fair share of murders throughout the years. Each area of the house had been bombarded with detectives, officers, and CSI processing everything meticulously. Police radios crackled, and then the news came in. A uniformed cop approached Julius and whispered something into his ear. He nodded and uttered, "Damn."

"What's up?" Emmerson questioned. "Something's wrong?"

Julius stared at Emmerson and Acosta. Then he revealed to them, "There's been another home invasion in Springfield, same motive with four dead, a few heavy hitters, I'm hearing."

"Who?" Acosta wanted to know.

"Big Joe and a player named Tyrone."

Acosta and Emmerson shared a look. They both knew Big Joe was connected to Zulu's organization. Their minds started to spin. Was this a takeover, an inside job, or payback? Acosta knew that both crime scenes were connected somehow. Along with the other detectives, he gathered information from the police officers and knew the victims' names.

"The place belongs to a Daquan Mitchel, and he's not here," said another detective.

"Dequan?" Detective Acosta repeated.

"You know the man?"

"He's a low-level player in Zulu's organization. Vice and DEA had him under surveillance a year back, I believe. Big mouth, flashy, but stupid," said Acosta.

"Who isn't in their line of work?" Julius joked.

A few detectives and officers laughed at the joke. But not Acosta. He remained focused on the scene, trying to deduce what happened. He was passionate about justice, having a thick-enough skin to endure the toxic nature of his work environment. Throughout the years, he'd been exposed to violence, drugs, sex, broken families, and some of the saddest stories.

Chapter Twenty-nine

It was a party like New Year's Eve 1999 inside the Manhattan strip club called the Velvet Room. The place was located in Midtown, and it was an upscale gentlemen's club. There were three floors with a unique ambiance, beautiful, sexy dancers, four stages with up-close seating, large-screen TVs on all floors, bottle service, and an outdoor terrace. The Velvet Room was where men could relax and be themselves, without any doubt. There were amazing girls of all ethnicities with phenomenal moves making men, even ladies, feel like they were on top of the world.

Lou, Nasir, and Denise were having the time of their lives, acting like there would be no tomorrow. They were celebrating in style. They had money to burn and wanted a good time outside the hood. A Manhattan strip club was the safest place to be where they wouldn't attract too much attention—because at the Velvet Room, balling out was common. The trio was lounging in VIP and had premium bottle service. They preferred Moët and Dom Pérignon, some of the best that money could buy. They also had a personal host, a sexy, voluptuous, long-legged blonde with more curves than the letter S. She had Lou's attention.

"Damn, I wanna fuck that bitch," Lou uttered for her to hear.

She smiled his way but kept things professional and stimulating. Denise, however, rolled her eyes and thought the bitch wasn't all that. She sat close to her man with a glass of champagne and clutched a fistful of cash in one hand.

Lou decided to play the stage close, and beside him was a stack of money so high it could create a blizzard of about two inches. Lou smiled brightly. He was happy and well-off for the moment. That last score was definitely a come-up for them. It was a dream come true. They'd stolen ten kilos and nearly $100,000 in cash. Among the three, they'd split the money at $33,000 apiece—not bad. But the drugs were where they came up. Lou and Nasir knew they could make between ten to fifteen cents on the dollar for each kilo. Nasir had an old connection out of town in Philly that he used to do business with. So they planned on moving the kilos there. The last thing they wanted was for word to get back to Zulu and the streets to make the connections about who would be dumb enough to steal from the drug organization.

Every step they took had to be careful. News of the murders and robbery had spread like a California wildfire, and people kept their ears close to the streets. Zulu had put a bounty on the culprits' heads, $50,000 for any information, and Zulu's goons were flooding the street, breaking arms and legs, fucking shit up, and creating havoc like a biblical plague. There was no way Zulu was about to let this pass. It was embarrassing but not crushing. The organization wanted to make an example out of these thieves like Mob Allah did to the three men four years ago.

Lou tossed a handful of cash at a young stripper named Sweet Dreams. She was a thick, curvy redbone woman with long, sensuous black hair and a girl-next-door look about her. She got buck naked on stage for Lou but stood tall in a pair of six-inch stiletto heels. He couldn't take his eyes off her. She was beautiful.

While Lou was distracted by Sweet Dreams, Nasir and Denise enjoyed the luxuries of VIP. Denise was down-to-earth, generously tipping the strippers better than the men. She knew the job well. It wasn't too long ago when she used to dance herself. Denise understood the perks and the occupational hazards of the job. Now she put herself at another risk with the streets. She was making more money with Lou and Nasir than she ever had before.

Denise downed the last of her champagne and poured another glassful. With her share of the money, she'd treated herself to a shopping spree, buying clothes, shoes, jewelry, and diamonds. So naturally, Denise wanted to look like a million dollars, and she did. Clad in a pair of tight-fitting jeans that accentuated her luscious curves, a stylish schoolgirl top, a diamond choker, and red bottoms, Denise was all smiles and horny.

"You good, baby?" Nasir asked her.

"I'm fine." Denise grinned. "Seeing all this tits and ass, the champagne, and having this money is making me horny."

Nasir laughed. "Say what?"

"I'm happy, Nasir," she expressed.

"Happy?" Nasir smiled.

"Yeah, happy. I got you," she said.

"Oh, word, you got me, huh?"

"Yes. You, and with you, I feel I have, or we have, a purpose," Denise proclaimed wholeheartedly.

She snuggled closer to him and placed her hand on his thigh. The way Denise looked at Nasir, there was no denying it. She was in love with him. She believed she was a different woman, a better woman with Nasir, and the sex was terrific.

"Let's have some fun," Denise said.

"What kind of fun?"

"The type of fun I know you'll like," she added.

Denise glanced at a big-booty ebony dancer nearby. She was cute and sexy.

"Oh, that type of fun," Nasir chuckled.

Denise stood up to approach the dancer with a proposition. Nasir sat back and watched his girl work her magic. He admired her. She was a remarkable woman, strong, smart, loyal, sexy, and surprisingly, she was about that life. Nasir worried about her, though. Denise was digging herself deeper in the game, and he knew something terrible had transpired at Tyrone's house. *What did my cousin make her do?* he wondered. *Did she kill someone?* Whatever he thought, Denise wasn't talking about it. Instead, she returned to him, excited and horny, and they fucked their brains out that night.

The champagne room was where the magic happened for top-notch customers. For $1,000 an hour, a man or woman had the luxury of a very private dance with any lovely dancer of their choice. Tonight, Denise and Nasir chose a dancer named Sasha to entertain them secretly. The room was dim, but the decor was classy, with cushioned red sofas and plush carpeting. Sasha closed the curtains tight while Denise and Nasir sat on the couch with another bottle of champagne to consume. Then Sasha began to entertain them in a red vinyl countdown bodysuit, and she had an ass so phat, it could have its own zip code. She teased them with a dance while Denise nestled next to Nasir. When Sasha removed her outfit and became naked, things became interesting. With no windows and tucked-in clandestineness, the champagne room was designed to make you forget what time it was, and the women were there to entertain customers in nirvana.

Meanwhile, Lou cluttered the stage with money, drowning Sweet Dreams with prosperity. She'd become his favorite for the night. Lou took a swig of champagne and lit up the place like Times Square, attracting unwanted attention to himself. Sweet Dreams was topless in front of Lou, smiling and flirting with the cash cow in her presence. However, Lou felt that balling in a Manhattan strip club away from the hood would be safe and secure. He figured word wouldn't get back to anyone in Queens about his sudden and unexpected come-up. But there was no guarantee about that.

While Lou kept his eyes on Sweet Dreams, a familiar face from the hood spotted Lou. His name was Dame, and he was a local crack dealer with minor status in Queens. Dame saw the money and the flash and found it odd. Lou was dangerous, a well-known stick-up kid in Queens, but the way he was throwing money around was an anomaly.

Lou grinned and drank. Being around pussy was pleasurable and entertaining, and he felt nothing could ruin his mood. But then he saw Dame staring his way, and suddenly all that changed. Lou knew who Dame was because he'd robbed him a few times. Lou thought, *what the fuck is he doing here?* The Velvet Room was supposed to be a secure location, away from ground zero. However, nothing was concrete. Lou and Dame stared at each other briefly, and then Dame turned and decided to leave.

"Fuck," Lou muttered to himself.

Although Dame was a nobody, Lou considered him a threat. Dame had seen the money, the champagne, the flashy wardrobe, and there was a possibility that he might go off and start running his mouth around town, and if word of his flashy escapade got back to the wrong people, there would be, no doubt, a large bounty placed on his head. Lou knew that they might have a slight problem.

Nasir gawked at Sasha as she danced seductively in front of him, naked. Denise tossed a handful of cash at her and continued to snuggle up against her man. The floor became littered with money while Sasha moved hypnotically in their presence. But they didn't just want to watch her dance. Denise wanted to make her man come on the spot. So she unbuttoned his jeans calmly and pulled out his dick. Nasir sat slumped with his jeans down and dick out as Denise wrapped her hand around his hard dick. She grabbed it like she meant it. She gave it an authentic tug and squeeze. Then she started with slower and subsequently longer strokes. Nasir moaned while Sasha rolled around naked near their feet.

"Oh, shit. Oh, fuck," he groaned.

While Denise gave him a pleasing hand job in the champagne room, he continued to stare at Sasha performing for them. It was forbidden to solicit sex in the champagne room. Still, anything went for the right amount of cash, and a stack temporarily allowed security to look the other way. Denise cupped his balls in her hands and began to caress them using her fingertips. She locked eyes with him while trying to bring him to absolute eruption.

Sasha's naked body was radiant, a sexual stimulation for them. Nasir huffed and squirmed. Denise's hands roamed like a nomad. She reached out and gave some love to the rest of his body. She played with his chest, his balls, and the area just behind his balls.

"Fuck. Shit, I'm 'bout to come," Nasir cried out.

Sasha flashed pussy, ass, and tits while Denise tried to bring her man into a euphoric release. Nasir was locked into Sasha's tantalizing performance while Denise's strokes sped up. Then Nasir closed his eyes, feeling the fascinating rhythm of her wrist movement. After that, there was no turning back.

"I'm gonna come, baby!" Nasir cried out again.

"Go ahead, baby, I got you. I got you," Denise cooed into his ear.

As Denise was going to work on his dick, she would occasionally reach down and touch herself with her other hand, and Sasha began to touch herself too. Finally, a light threesome began in the champagne room with Nasir close to sexual liberation.

And then it happened. Nasir couldn't control it any longer, and he released like a geyser spraying with his hard dick still gripped in Denise's fist. It was so explosive that his semen nearly touched the ceiling. He kept going and going until there was nothing left, and then he became spent and deflated like a balloon.

"Damn!" Sasha uttered, laughing.

Denise grinned. "You like that?"

Nasir was stunned and at a loss for words. But of course he liked it. His breathing became labored, and he sat there momentarily, trying to collect himself.

"That was fun," said Sasha.

It was a win-win for everyone.

Denise and Nasir exited the champagne room feeling like they were on top of the world. The experience was mind-blowing. But their smiles were short-lived when they saw the frown on Lou's face.

"What's going on, Lou?" Nasir asked.

"We might have a problem," Lou responded.

"What kind of problem?"

"I think I've been spotted in here."

"By who?" Denise asked.

"This local dealer named Dame."

Nasir wasn't familiar with the name.

"He's not a threat, but he could become one," said Lou.

"You sure it was someone from the neighborhood?" Denise asked him.

"I'm sure of it. The way he looked at me, I'm confident he recognized me in here. I robbed that nigga a few times," said Lou.

Nasir sighed.

"Dammit, Lou," Denise griped.

"Zulu put a fifty-thousand-dollar price out there for any information, and greed talks," Lou said. "Reason why we need to unload these kilos in a hurry. You heard back from your peoples in Philly?"

"Not yet," Nasir replied.

"Why don't we just leave town for a while?" Denise suggested.

"That wouldn't be wise. We go missing right after a heist like that, and someone gonna take notice of our sudden absence and most likely pinpoint us to everything," Nasir replied. "We just gotta keep a low profile. It was stupid coming out to this and spending that kind of money. Might as well put a target on our backs."

"It wasn't a stupid move a moment ago in the champagne room with Sasha," Denise fussed. "I just wanted to have some fun with you, baby."

"I know, but we need to be careful. Everyone's watching and listening," said Nasir.

Lou groaned. "Fuck that. We need to move this weight and find a steady connection. It's our time, cuzzo."

"And what about Dame?" Nasir asked.

"I'll take care of that nigga. The last thing we need is for him to start running his mouth," Lou replied.

Chapter Thirty

When the cell doors opened, several correctional guards were stationed on three separate tiered racks. Inmates of all races stepped out and walked down the stairwell to the middle of the building, where there were twelve stainless-steel tables with four stools to each table. Inmates quickly occupied each table. The first five tables belonged to the blacks. The Mexicans and Chicanos shared the next four, and the last three were for whites. White inmates, the Aryan Brotherhood, were the minority in state prisons. The loud chatter of over a hundred men's conversation quickly took over the dayroom. Most inmates came out of their cells for social interaction, to play cards, dominos, pinochle, or chess.

Sincere walked into the dayroom like he owned the place. In a way, you could say he did. His reputation proceeded him. Killing Rafe elevated his status inside the state prison, and Sincere gradually became a powerful man. The respect he carried was heavy. He'd become a changed man since his return from the army four years ago. Prisoners moved out of his way like the Red Sea was parting. Sincere coolly marched toward one of the stainless-steel tables where a chess game was set up. An older man named Gent was sitting at the table waiting for Sincere to join him for a game or two.

"Rise up, my brother," Gent said to Sincere.

Sincere grinned and replied, "Rise up."

"Sit, let's play," said Gent, referring to the chess game on the table.

Gent was doing life for a double homicide. He was in his early sixties and was once a prominent member of the Black Guerrilla Family, a Black power prison and street gang. Gent was an intelligent, retired gangster who minded his business and loved playing chess.

Sincere took a seat at the table across from Gent. The older man was looking forward to another game of chess with Sincere. The two were the best players inside Elmira Correctional Facility. Once they started playing, nothing else mattered.

"You ready for me, old man?" Sincere teased.

Gent smiled. "Bring it on."

"Another day, another lesson," said Gent.

"What you got for me today?" Sincere asked.

"Take it slow and easy. Playing naturally is always the best way," said Gent.

Sincere nodded. He was ready for another intense game with Gent. Although they were in a room filled with dozens of inmates, no one bothered them during their games. The conversations may have been loud, but these two men could tune everything out and focus on the game. Sometimes it felt they were the only two men in the dayroom.

Sincere made the first move on the board by moving his middle pawn. He opened with the Scotch Game. The opening's main benefit was that it quickly gave white plenty of space, particularly for the two bishops, who were both given open diagonals. Gent nodded and respected the opening move. He opened with the bishop on B5 instead of C5. It was a solid opening as white had reasonable control of the center with their pawn and knight and could castle with their next turn. The two men began to battle it out on the board.

"Chess is everything: art, science, and sport," Gent said.

Gent was full of knowledge. One of the things he would say was, "If you see a good move, look for a better one." He would also say, "Leaders who inspire play chess, not checkers."

Sincere soaked in everything Gent said. The man had seen everything imaginable and been through hell and back. He accepted his fate, receiving a life sentence knowing he would never see the outside of prison.

A few inmates stood around the table to watch the chess game, taking notes. Gent and Sincere didn't mind it. Teaching the younger generation was great.

"Checkmate," Gent announced.

Sincere didn't see it coming, but it was well played and a challenging game between the two men.

"One of these days, I'm going to take your king," said Sincere.

"And I'll always be here to protect it," Gent replied with a smile.

Sincere nodded. Respect. Sincere removed himself from the stainless-steel table and exited the dayroom. If it weren't for his regular chess game with Gent, he had no reason to spend time inside the dayroom. Most of the more intellectual inmates from all races stayed in their cells during evening dayrooms, occupied by other more constructive activities.

Sincere stepped into his jail cell and took a seat on the cot. His environment now was a stainless-steel toilet, a small sink, a small desk, and a cot that contained one blanket and one pillow. There was nothing else besides books, letters, and a few selected items allowed in the jail cell. The new warden wanted a lack of items within prison cells to prevent vandalism and disable the prisoners from making weapons.

For a moment, Sincere sat in silence and stared at the wall plastered with pictures of his family, from his kids to his sister, Monica, and old photos of his deceased mother and younger brother. He missed everyone. Monica and Denise had stopped visiting him a year ago. It seemed like his family had fallen off the face of the earth. Without them, Sincere felt he had nothing. Despite his reputation in the state prison, he often felt like a nobody. It was hard to imagine he was a step away from going into the police academy to a shot caller inside a state prison.

While Sincere took some personal and alone time in his cell drowning in nostalgia, he began to hear sudden chatter nearby. Several inmates were talking about the recent activities they'd heard happening on the streets.

"Big Joe is dead," said one inmate.

"What? Get the fuck outta here. How?" another inmate responded.

"I heard the nigga got gunned down in a home invasion. There's a crew out there getting niggas crazy right now and gettin' that money."

"Shit, they got a bitch wit' them, too, honey trapping niggas for that bread."

"And Zulu put a price on these fools' heads, and it's gon' be a wrap for them once the streets find out who these clowns are."

"Man, fuckin' with Zulu's money is suicidal."

Sincere started eavesdropping. For some strange reason, what they were talking about caught his attention. He stood up from his cot, walked onto the tier, and looked at the three inmates gossiping like bitches. When they saw Sincere, their conversation became muted, and the three men looked uneasy.

"What's up, Sincere?" one of the men uttered.

Sincere looked at them and asked, "What y'all niggas talking about?"

"Huh?" one of the inmates replied.

"What y'all were gossiping about caught my ear," said Sincere.

"It's nothin', just some talk about the streets. You know how it be."

"I heard y'all talking about some crew robbing Zulu's stash houses," Sincere reminded them.

"It's not just Zulu's shit. This crew hit a few other places, and they are dropping bodies like crazy," an inmate named Tate said.

"They hit five spots already, killed this pimp, and tortured his bitches out in Bricktown. It was like some nightmare on Elm Street at the place," an inmate named Chuck chimed.

For some reason, Sincere's intuition told him he probably knew someone who could connect to this. He knew Nasir recently came home from Rikers after doing a bullet. He'd lost contact with Nasir two years ago. But the street did talk, and it was known that Nasir returned home to nothing. He'd lost everything.

Then there was Denise. At the beginning of his sentence, the two remained close. Denise would write him and would come to visit him sometimes. However, it had been a year since he heard from her, Monica too.

"I'm tellin' you, it's like the Wild West out there," Tate uttered.

Sincere wasn't interested in hearing their gossip anymore. He pivoted and went back into his cell. But his mind was still on what he'd heard. He had no idea why he thought about Nasir, but his gut continued to churn like it was making milk into butter, and then he began to worry about Denise. Not hearing from her in a year was drastic. He had no idea what she was up to. Sincere didn't want to think about the worst. He'd suffered enough tragedies since his return from the military. If he lost Denise too, then it would be devastating. Besides his kids, she was all he had left in the world.

Chapter Thirty-one

Cook felt that he had the weight of the world on his shoulders right now, and he needed a timeout from the world. So he walked into his luxurious three-bedroom high-rise condo in LeFrak, Queens, and poured himself a needed drink, some bourbon whisky. He downed that in a heartbeat and poured himself another. Then he stepped out onto the terrace overlooking Queens from the fifteenth floor. It was a picturesque view of the neighborhood that someone could get lost in, especially at night. Cook consumed his second drink and stood on the terrace in a slight trance.

"They are cops," he assumed. "They're asking too many fucking questions."

He couldn't stop thinking about Ricky and Tony. He couldn't escape the gnawing feeling that he fucked up. He had gotten greedy and likely had gone into business with a pair of undercover officers, and if it was true, Cook knew he was a dead man. He'd met with the two men three times in the past four months. He'd gotten greedy, they wanted to buy some weight, and the money was good, and he had ambition. Ricky was questioning him about girls. It didn't make sense to him.

Then there was the hit he had placed on an NYPD detective at the behest of Zulu. Everything had been set into motion, and Dante was the man to get the job done. It was inevitable. This detective, Acosta, was a dead man walking. Cook sighed so heavily that his stomach started to churn. It felt like he was going to be sick.

"Okay, get right. Get right," Cook said to himself.

He was a respected entrepreneur and a pillar of the community. If his secret got out, he would be ruined. Cook didn't want that. He felt he needed to get ahead of everything. *But how?* First, he needed to contact Winter and warn him about a pending raid that he wasn't so sure about. They needed to clean the house immediately if they were coming for him. Cook Gamble was becoming paranoid. He stared at a sprawling Queens from his high-rise terrace, and there was that sense to jump, end it all right now. But nah, he wasn't crazy. It was a long drop, and he could only imagine what the fall or that drop would do to his body. Instead, Cook pivoted and marched back into his condo with a purpose—to survive.

Immediately, he dialed Winter's cell phone number, but unfortunately, his call went straight to voicemail. Second, he dialed the house number in Valley Stream, figuring Winter would answer that call, but he didn't answer that phone either. Now Cook started to worry. Winter always responded to his calls. *What is going on?* he griped. Cook paced around the room for a moment, trying to think. They had one young girl held hostage in the basement who they weren't able to sell off yet, and they needed to get rid of her, and they had nearly fifty kilos from cocaine to heroin and millions in cash, along with criminal documentation. That house in Valley Stream was a hotbed for a criminal indictment if the police or Feds were to raid it, and if that happened, bloodshed in the streets was sure to follow. Cook needed Winter to answer his damn phone.

"Fuck me!" Cook cursed.

Cook went to his makeshift bar and poured himself another drink. The wheels started to turn in his head. He thought about the repercussions of an indictment, arrests, prosecution, et cetera. But on the other hand, Cook was at the top of the food chain in Zulu's organization. Therefore, he would be a healthy meal for the Feds to consume. Good for him. His place in LeFrak was clean. But everywhere else was not.

Cook's cell phone rang, and he thought Winter was calling him right back. But it wasn't. It was Smitty. So he answered the phone by saying, "Now is not a good time for me, Smitty."

"We have a problem, Mr. Cook," Smitty said.

"What kind of problem?"

"Some pimp is here asking about Anna," said Smitty.

"What pimp?"

"I don't know. But he says he isn't leaving until she leaves with him," Smitty said.

Cook sighed. *If it isn't one thing, then it's another.* "I'll be right there," Cook replied.

He'd forgotten about Anna being at the motel. Cook left his condo right away. That gut feeling continued to wrench strongly inside of his stomach. He hurried to his Benz, started the ignition, and raced toward the motel. While driving there, he tried to call Winter again, and his phone went straight to voicemail.

"Goddamn it!" Cook shouted.

Cook arrived at the seedy Far Rockaway motel. He killed the engine, tucked the SIG 228 into his waistband, and hurried from the car toward the motel with a sense of urgency. Cook remembered the pimp. He was trouble at his clothing store on Jamaica Avenue, and he wondered how he found Anna. But none of that mattered now. What mattered was that Cook remove the nigga from the motel right away.

When Cook stepped into the lobby, he saw the pimp standing at the glass partition cursing at Smitty.

"Where that bitch at?" he shouted.

He was clad in a dark hoodie and still decorated himself with loud, gaudy jewelry. He banged his fist against the partition and frightened Smitty.

"You need to leave this place right now," Cook shouted.

The young pimp turned in Cook's direction and glared at him. "Yeah, muthafucka, I told you I'd be back," he exclaimed.

"How did you find her?" Cook asked him.

"Nigga, I keep track of all my hoes, muthafucka! And Anna is special. I know you know, nigga. You fucked her, didn't you? Yeah, you did. you got a whiff of how good that pussy is. It'll melt in your mouth, and she'll have you coming like a geyser," the young pimp proclaimed.

Cook was guilty as charged.

"It doesn't matter. She's not yours anymore. So go, before I make you leave myself," Cook threatened him.

The pimp chuckled. He was alone, but he wasn't afraid of Cook. He was tall, but Cook matched his height. Smitty remained behind the glass partition, being afraid to intervene. The two men glared at each other, not scared.

"Like I said, I ain't leaving here until Anna comes with me."

"Then we are going to have a problem," Cook replied.

"Nigga, we already have a fuckin' problem," the pimp chided him.

The pimp removed a large jackknife from his person and became a bigger threat to Cook. "Now what room is my bitch in? And I ain't gonna keep asking you."

Cook smirked. The boy brought a knife to a gunfight.

"You come for her with that?" Cook laughed.

The young pimp grew agitated and stepped heatedly closer toward Cook. But Cook remained undaunted, and before the young pimp could attack him with the knife, Cook pulled out the SIG 228 he carried and aimed it directly at the boy's head, stopping him dead in his tracks.

"Tell me why I shouldn't put a fucking bullet in your head right now," Cook shouted.

"Okay," the pimp uttered, knowing he was outmatched. "You got that?"

"You have me coming down here tonight to deal with this shit! I told you, she doesn't belong to you anymore. Y'all young niggas are fucking hardheaded!" Cook exclaimed.

Cook kept the gun trained on the pimp. He wanted to shoot the nigga just for creating unnecessary trouble. Smitty remained behind the partition with apprehension.

"You know how old she is, nigga?" the pimp questioned. "I bet she told you that she was nineteen."

Cook listened.

"Nigga, she's sixteen," the pimp revealed. "And how old is you, nigga? What, in your thirties or something? That's statutory rape, muthafucka."

Cook was taken aback by the news. The hole kept becoming deeper.

"Just get the fuck out of here," Cook shouted.

The pimp placed the jackknife back into his pocket. He was defeated again and forced to leave. Cook had too much on his plate to worry about Anna's age and her young pimp. This issue had put a delay on his plans. He was supposed to be on the highway headed toward Valley Stream. While Cook was holding the pimp back at gunpoint, his cell phone rang. It was Winter calling him back. *Perfect timing*.

He answered, "Where are you?"

"I'm heading to the spot. What's up?" Winter asked.

"We need to clean house now," Cook uttered urgently.

"Why? What's going on?"

"I don't know. But I got this gut feeling we need to move everything out of that place right now."

"You know how long that will take? And what about the girl?"

"She's got to go. She's a liability," said Cook.

Winter huffed. "Zulu knows something?"

"Winter, stop with the questions and just do it. Zulu doesn't know anything yet, but I got this gut feeling something's wrong, and something's going to go down," Cook exclaimed.

"You got a gut feeling?" Winter questioned dubiously.

"I'll be there in twenty minutes!"

Cook ended the call. He shot an angry look at the pimp and shouted, "If you come looking for her again, I'll kill you."

The pimp huffed and retreated from the motel. Cook went to Smitty when he was gone and said, "If he comes back again, you either shoot that muthafucka, or call me."

Smitty nodded. "And what about Anna?" Smitty asked.

"She's done for the night. No more clients, and change her room to be safe," Cook instructed him.

Cook hurried from the motel and climbed into his Benz. He then sped toward Valley Stream to the stash house. He knew there wasn't much time, hoping it wasn't too late.

When Cook arrived at the main stash house, everything seemed quiet. It was too quiet, but it was the suburbs of Long Island, and it was always still and peaceful. He maneuvered his car into the driveway and climbed out. Strangely, Cook's car was the only one there. Winter hadn't arrived yet.

Why not?

"Where is this nigga?" Cook asked himself while sitting inside his Benz, contemplating what to do next. He needed Winter's help with moving everything covertly and quickly. Hopefully, he was wrong about this gut-wrenching feeling, but it was better to be safe than sorry.

Cook climbed out of his Benz and walked toward the front entrance. He entered the house, and it was dark, still, and unprotected. Winter's life was this main stash house, nothing else. However, something felt odd out of the blue. He shook off the feeling and went into the basement. Everything was off immediately. Bundles of cash were missing, nearly a million dollars and a few kilos of cocaine had been taken. Using the remote IR signal, Cook unlocked the secret door behind the bookshelf leading to the hidden room and disappeared into the small corridor. He checked the underground chamber where the last girl was being held, and she was gone too.

"What the fuck is going on?" he asked himself.

It dawned on him that Winter wasn't trying to dispose of anything. He was fleeing the scene and most likely looking out for himself. Cook deduced Winter knew something, maybe the Feds turned him earlier, or perhaps he got spooked and decided to run off with the money, some drugs, and the girl.

When Cook emerged from the secret room, he heard the commotion. Bang! Bang! *What the fuck?* He ran toward the security cameras, and his worst nightmare was coming true. The FBI was coming into the house.

Fuck me!

An assault vehicle had slammed through the fence and stopped in the yard. Two doors swung open, and an army of individuals, SWAT, dressed for battle, rifles at the ready, came charging toward the residence. They reached the front door, a shotgun blasted the hinges, and the door fell like a drawbridge. SWAT officers rushed in, screaming, "FBI! FBI!"

Cook witnessed everything from the security camera, and there was no escaping them. They were everywhere. He had to think quickly. He scrambled like a fly buzzing around the room and grabbed cash and the drugs, and desperately tried to conceal what he could inside the room. But the agents swarmed through the house so fast he couldn't dispose of it all. Instead, he had to conceal the room again, and then he dropped to his knees and placed his hands behind his head, awaiting his fate.

Armed agents poured into the basement and spotted Cook surrendering peacefully.

"Bingo!" one of the agents shouted.

Cook Gamble was immediately arrested.

Chapter Thirty-two

Lou sat in an old white Chevy Cutlass, parked on the corner of Sutphin and Foch Boulevards, and observed Dame hanging out with his crew in front of the local bodega. His target was playing a dice game. Dame looked at home.

Word started to spread around the hood about a violent stick-up crew targeting drug dealers, pimps, and rival forces. It was expected. They'd robbed five places within a few weeks and left behind a string of bodies. But the death of Big Joe became a hot topic on the streets. He was somebody important, and a vicious retaliation from Zulu was expected to happen soon. The streets knew about this crew, but they had no idea who made up the crew. The only thing the streets were sure of was that it was a three-person crew, and there was a woman with them helping to honey trap their victims. But not only were the streets searching for them, but the cops were also.

Lou knew they had to remain on the down-low when their crimes had made the headlines several times, and the media was all over their crime scenes. Lou continued to watch Dame with a Glock 19 close. It had been a week since they saw each other at the Velvet Room, and that week was too long for Dame to still be alive. Lou feared that he'd already run his mouth to everyone he met, telling them what he had seen inside the Manhattan strip club. Now some people may have attributed it to Dame having a big mouth, random talk, and dismissed what he was saying. But then there would be that individual who might pay extra attention to his words, take heed to what he was saying, and probably put two and two together.

Dame had to go.

But Lou couldn't kill him now. There were too many witnesses around. So he had to sit, plot, and wait for the perfect moment like a lion crouched and hidden in the tall grass waiting for its prey to make a mistake.

While Lou waited for the opportunity to strike, his cell phone rang. It was Nasir calling him.

"Cuzzo, what's good? Good news, I hope," Lou answered.

"I finally got back with my people in Philly. They're willing to meet and talk," Nasir said.

"Cool. When?"

"Tomorrow evening," Nasir responded.

"The sooner we can unload everything, the better," Lou said. "You trust them?"

"Do we have a choice?"

"I just want this deal to go smoothly. The last thing we need is more trouble. We make this money in Philly and lie low there for a moment, allow for everything to cool down," Lou said.

Nasir ended the call.

Lou went back to focusing on Dame and his activity. His attention was on a swivel while he stalked Dame. Lou knew he needed to remain alert and on standby for anything. It was a dangerous area with shootings, and the last thing he needed was someone to sneak up on him while he was trying to sneak up on someone else.

Lou was a patient man. He waited and watched Dame for over an hour playing dice on the corner. At one point, Dame was on a winning streak. He clutched a fistful of dollars, downed a forty-ounce beer, and talked shit to the other players. But then his luck changed. He lost everything and cursed everyone around him.

"Fuck y'all niggas!"

Broke and upset, Dame staggered away from the corner and walked down Foch Boulevard. Lou saw his chance, started the car, and subtly followed his mark. It was dark, getting late, and there weren't too many folks around. Lou felt this was the perfect chance to kill the nigga and speed away. He wouldn't see it coming.

Dame crossed 155th Street and headed toward Baisley Pond Park. Lou continued to follow him in the Cutlass. While Dame walked parallel to the basketball courts, Lou decided it was the right moment to strike. He gripped the Glock 19, threw the vehicle into park, and opened the door coolly. Dame continued to walk and made the mistake of not paying attention to his surroundings. But he had no reason to believe his life was in danger. Seeing Lou that night at the Velvet Room was simply a coincidence. But unfortunately, it marked his fate.

It was a quiet fall night. The courts were empty, and Dame was going to see his girlfriend. He was broke, drunk, and horny and felt some pussy might do him good. He was going to cross through the park and come out on the other side, at 122nd Avenue near where his girlfriend lived.

Lou followed him with the Glock gripped and down by his side. He watched him like a hawk, and the moment Dame was about to pass the basketball courts and cut through the park, Lou decided to strike. He raised the gun and shouted, "Yo, Dame!"

Hearing his name, Dame turned around to see who was calling for him. But unfortunately, he stared down the barrel of the Glock. It was as if he were gazing down a dark tunnel. Dame was caught entirely off guard and like a deer staring into bright headlights.

Lou didn't hesitate.

Dame flew back into the tall chain-link fence that circled the courts. He took three shots to his chest, but he was still alive, barely. Lou stood over Dame and fired the fatal shot.

This one struck Dame between the eyes, and he was finally dead. The gunshots were loud and definitely would stir the neighbors' attention. Lou ran back to the idling Chevy Cutlass, threw the vehicle into drive, and sped away from the scene. He sighed with relief, believing he had taken care of the problem. But little did he know there was an eyewitness to the shooting.

Nasir, Lou, and Denise cruised on the New Jersey Turnpike headed toward Philadelphia. Nasir was behind the wheel of Lou's dark green Pathfinder. Denise was in the passenger seat, and Lou lounged in the back seat. Lou felt it would be safer if Denise rode up front so as not to raise suspicion of two black men in a Jeep. The last thing they needed was to be pulled over because of racial profiling. It had been a long twenty-four hours for them. With several kilos of cocaine in the back of the Jeep, Nasir made sure to do the speed limit on the turnpike.

"I took care of that problem yesterday," Lou mentioned out of the blue.

Nasir and Denise didn't respond to him. Instead, they immediately knew what problem he was talking about. A man died because of their reckless spending at an infamous gentlemen's club. Lou didn't lose any sleep over it. He would do it again if he had to. He was a cold-blooded killer.

"How many keys do you think he'll buy from us?" Lou asked Nasir.

"Not sure," Nasir responded.

"What you mean you ain't sure? Cuzzo, we're riding into a North Philly neighborhood with ten kilos in the back. How well do you know this fool?"

"We did some business in the past," said Nasir.

"And how long ago was that?"

"About three years ago," Nasir responded.

"What the fuck? Are you kidding me?"

"Look, we need to unload this shit, right? And he's the only nigga I know who's still around and willing to help us out."

"How you know he ain't planning to set us up once we get there? We gonna be looking like idiots and sitting ducks," Lou griped.

"What the fuck you want from me, Lou? Huh? I'm doin' my best. We can't move it in New York, especially in Queens. Zulu's gonna be all over us if we do. This is our only option. I've known Pike for a long time now," Nasir proclaimed.

"But do you trust him?" Lou questioned him.

Nasir sighed. In the game, you could never trust anybody, and Nasir wasn't dumb enough to roll into a rough North Philly neighborhood with ten kilos of cocaine to meet a man he hadn't seen or spoken to in three years. It would be suicidal.

The trio arrived in North Philadelphia early that evening and decided to check into a Days Inn. The plan was for Denise to stay at the motel with most of the coke and be armed with a pistol. Lou and Nasir would meet with Pike in Hunting Park, a not-so-charming section in North Philly, just south of Roosevelt Boulevard. The area was known to have a lot of gang activity. The area's crime stemmed from local neighborhood-based street gangs and the drug trade. Organized gangs such as the Black Mafia, Latin Kings, and various motorcycle gangs also operated in the area. Nasir was familiar with Hunting Park, so he and Lou came prepared with guns and wits.

"If we're not back within the hour, head back to New York," said Lou.

"No. I'm coming with you, and I'm not leaving you here, Nasir," Denise protested.

"Listen to me. I'm sure we'll be fine, but if anything happens, it wouldn't be safe for you here. So leave us," Nasir replied.

"I'm not doing that," she continued to protest.

"I don't want any harm coming to you. Your brother would kill me," said Nasir.

"And my brother isn't here."

"Denise, we need someone to watch the product while we're gone," Lou chimed. "We're coming back. I'm not trying to die out here in Philly. I got my cousin's back."

Denise sighed heavily, then nodded, believing Lou. "You better not let anything happen to him," Denise said to Lou.

"I won't."

The two were becoming Bonnie and Clyde, and if anything happened to Nasir, it would happen to Denise too, or first. She loved him, and she would do anything for him. They were living in a dangerous world, committing acts of violence against dodgy individuals, and the chance of one of them not surviving was high.

Before Nasir left Denise's side, the two shared a passionate kiss. Then Nasir had to pull himself away from her and leave. Denise stared at him lovingly and proclaimed, "Be careful."

Nasir and Lou left the motel and climbed into the Pathfinder, carrying a kilo of cocaine and armed with semiautomatic pistols. Nasir decided to drive while Lou rode shotgun. Lou lit a cigarette to calm his nerves. He wished it were a joint, but he needed his senses to be sharp. He was eager to make this deal happen.

They soon arrived at a mechanic shop called Philly's Auto on West Erie Avenue. It was a quaint brick building nestled in the middle of the block. The front entrance was cluttered with mostly stripped vehicles and people. Lou stared at the place and thought it was the wrong address.

"This is it?" asked Lou.

Nasir nodded. "It's the address he gave me."

They stared at the location for a moment, then climbed out of the Jeep. Lou carried the bag concealing the kilo, and they coolly approached the garage with the sky gray and gloomy and the sun nowhere to be found. Nasir hoped the weather wasn't a sign of trouble. Pike had always been a businessman before anything else.

Nasir walked toward one of the men lingering outside the mechanic shop and said, "We're here to see Pike."

The two were quickly sized up by the three shady-looking men lingering outside of the mechanic shop.

"Who y'all niggas?" one of the men asked.

"Tell him Nasir is here. He knows me."

One of the men turned and went into the mechanic garage while Lou and Nasir waited outside. It didn't take him long to return and give Nasir and Lou the okay to enter the shop. They followed the goon into a working garage with workers finishing for the day. The place was cluttered with a few old and new cars, a lift, a jack, jack stands, pole jacks, an engine hoist, and a few air compressors. Philly's Auto was the real deal.

Pike was working on a 1993 red Ford Mustang SVT Cobra R. The car's hood was up, and he was underneath it working on the engine. Pike was a grease monkey. He'd had a love for cars since he was 5 years old. Hunting Park and most of North Philly were his territories regarding drugs and vehicles.

"Yo, Pike," one of his men called out.

Pike removed himself from underneath the hood of the Mustang and stared at Nasir and Lou. He stood six feet one with a healthy build and was black like coffee with a bald head. He was clad in stained overalls and Timberland boots, and he held a socket wrench.

"Nasir, it's been a while," said Pike. "I heard you were locked up."

"Well, I'm home now," Nasir replied.

"And back in business, I see." Pike smiled.

Nasir looked at the Mustang, and Pike uttered, "This car always catches eyes, huh? That's a '93 Ford Mustang SVT Cobra R. It was the eleventh of just a hundred and seven units. It features a 5.0-liter V-8 engine paired with a five-speed manual transmission. One of the best Ford Mustangs of all time."

"Are we here to do business or talk about cars?" Lou interrupted.

He couldn't care less about a Ford Mustang. His purpose was quickly getting rid of ten kilograms without a fuss about it. Pike cut his eyes at Lou, smiled, and replied, "I see your friend is about his business. No love for cars, huh?"

"Pardon me for not being a gearhead," said Lou.

"Lou, chill out," Nasir uttered quickly. "He's my cousin," he added.

"Anyway, what do you have for me, Nasir? I was under the impression that you were down and out. So I'm a bit surprised you're back on your feet quickly, ready to move some keys," Pike proclaimed.

"I'm a natural-born hustler, Pike."

"Damn, ten keys to move. Maybe you need to write a book on hustling," Pike joked.

Lou handed Pike the small bag concealing the kilo. Pike looked inside, and it was a beautiful bird. He grinned. "How much?"

"For you, ten cents on the dollar," Nasir said.

"That's a very good price. But I'm curious, how are you able to sell it to me for so cheap?" asked Pike.

"We go back a few years, Pike. I respect you, and you were always fair, and I hear you're about to control North Philly. So consider this an appreciation for our longevity," said Nasir.

Pike nodded. "Ten cents on the dollar, huh?" Pike repeated.

"And not a penny less," Lou chimed.

"Okay. I'm good with that. When can I get the rest?" Pike asked them.

"We'll call you with a location to meet," said Nasir.

Nasir and Lou pivoted and left the premises. One of Pike's goons, Lamar, stared at them with suspicion, and when the two were gone, he said to Pike, "They think we're stupid."

"What you mean, Lamar?" Pike questioned.

"That's Zulu's shit. My people in Queens said two of his places got hit a week back. Muthafuckas took drugs and cash and killed several of his men in the process. Zulu's looking for these niggas, put a bounty on their heads," Lamar mentioned.

"How much?"

"From what I heard, fifty K, but it may be more," Lamar replied.

"Check it. We're still going through with the deal. So then contact your people in Queens and let them know what we know. Information is power and value. Plus, we earn some trust with Zulu with this. Give a gift, get a gift," Pike stated.

Lamar smiled. "I got you, and I'm on it."

Lamar walked away, and Pike was left behind feeling like a man who was killing two birds with one stone.

Chapter Thirty-three

Cook Gamble sat inside the interrogation room and stared into the mirror covering one wall. While he stared at the mirror, two agents stared back at him through the one-way glass. Cook sat silent, knowing what was coming next. He'd fucked up. This wasn't the local police. It was the DEA or FBI. They'd come at him hard and fast. He was nervous, but he refused to show it. Instead, he remained seated inside the bland room with a stoic gaze. This wasn't going to be pretty.

The room door opened, and two agents entered the room, Agent Monty followed by Agent Lee. Cook glared at them. Both agents took a seat at the table opposite Cook, where the fun began. Agent Monty spoke, "You know if you're sitting in here with us, you fucked up somewhere."

"He knows he fucked up," Agent Lee chimed.

Cook remained silent.

"The infamous Cook Gamble, a jack-of-all-trades and master of some," Agent Monty joked.

Agent Lee chuckled. "You've been a busy man, Cook," Lee uttered. "Right now, we have you dead to rights in possession of nearly twenty kilos of cocaine and heroin, a little over a million in cash, and two assault rifles."

"Damn. Pretty for us, but ugly for you right now," Agent Monty said.

"And that's just the tip of our big dicks beginning to push into the pussy. Once we're all the way inside at full thrust, I guarantee we'll make you holla," Agent Lee joked.

"And the Feds will always come to the party with a big dick," said Agent Monty. "So don't fuck with us. We already know everything about you."

"Amos and fucking Andy, the two of y'all," Cook retorted.

"He finally speaks," said Lee.

"Why am I here?" Cook asked gruffly.

Agent Lee and Monty shared a glance, then Lee uttered, "Because it's your turn, Cook. You want to play in the game, and we're the referees always ensuring our teams win."

"Look, we know you're working with Zulu, helping his organization to launder millions of drug money through various businesses and shell companies. You're a shrewd businessman. I'll give you that. But with the amount of shit we caught you with inside that stash house, I guarantee you'll be doing basic tax returns for federal correctional officers and inmates for the next thirty years," Agent Monty proclaimed.

"But it's not too late, Cook. A first felony offense, we can offer you a nice deal. You just got to be smart. So why don't you tell us about your friend Zulu," Agent Lee uttered.

Cook remained silent.

"You're supposed to be smart. So we did some digging into your life. You're an immigrant from Jamaica, came here with your grandmother when you were ten years old. You grew up poor in rough neighborhoods, but you were ambitious. Got yourself a scholarship to a fancy private school, huh? And then you received another scholarship to attend Pace University. Not bad for a kid from Kingston, Jamaica," Agent Lee proclaimed.

"And then you became stupid and greedy and got into business with the likes of Zulu, and then guess what, you decided to branch out on your own unbeknownst to Zulu. Your greed and ambition is your downfall. How do you think Zulu will feel with you going into business with two of our undercovers?" said Monty.

Cook frowned. Damn, his gut feeling was right. They were cops.

Agent Monty and Lee noticed his change of demeanor.

"You've been on our radar for months. You were a careful and meticulous individual, but eventually, you all will get sloppy down the road, and your partner, Winter, we arrested him in New Jersey a few hours ago, and guess what he had to say," Agent Lee proclaimed.

Cook knew he was fucked.

Agent Lee placed a manila folder in front of Cook. "Open it and see."

Cook opened the folder to reveal eight-by-ten glossy photos of him and his crimes. They were as clear as day and incriminating. There were pictures of him involved in several drug deals with Ricky and Tony. But the smoking gun was the kidnapped girl they found when they arrested Winter, and she had a lot to say, and they raided the motel in Far Rockaway. Smitty was singing like a canary, and Anna too. She was an underage whore connected to Cook.

Fuck me! was the only thing Cook could say to himself.

"There's enough here to get you a life sentence, Cook," Lee said. "As we said, you've been a busy boy on both ends of the spectrum. Now if you cooperate with us, then we can probably make some magic happen in your favor."

"Yeah, we can pull the big dick out of your ass a bit for you to breathe and give you some comfort," Monty joked.

"I want to speak to my lawyer," Cook uttered.

"Do you really want to do a life sentence for that asshole?" Monty asked. "Make it easy on yourself, Cook. Help us get Zulu."

"Because once we walk out of this room, there won't be any magic happening. You deal with us now, help us nail Zulu, and I promise you some leniency," said Lee.

"Besides, you know what they do to rapists of young girls in prison," Monty added.

"I'm no rapist!" Cook protested.

"You kidnapped, pimped, and trafficked young girls, Cook. Word gets out, and you're done. But you're the devil we're willing to work with."

The two agents were a dynamic duo when it came to interrogation. They could read their suspects, intimidate them, and finish each other's sentences. But unfortunately, Cook was another drop in the bucket regarding the criminals they interrogated and got to confess or cooperate.

Cook sighed heavily. He was in a position between a rock and a hard place. No matter how he looked at it, he was fucked. He didn't want to become a snitch, but he also didn't want to do thirty years to life in federal prison, and he didn't want to be labeled as a rapist.

"What's it going to be, Cook?" Lee asked.

Cook stared at both men. They had him by the balls and were squeezing, knowing he would pop soon.

"What is it that y'all need from me?" Cook relented.

Agents Lee and Monty smiled.

Bingo!

Chapter Thirty-four

The prison courtyard and exercise yard was surrounded by a fourteen-foot-high fence, a brooding, aged mass of concrete, beams, and mesh, topped by razor wire. There was no beauty in the design, only brutal efficiency. The only color in sight was on the warning signage. It was meant to keep inmates in. Where a piece of enclosed ground attached to the prison, prisoners could take in some fresh air, play basketball, or partake in the exercise area at certain times. Instead, the area was a breeding ground for spreading information and implementing destruction toward rivals.

Sincere was shirtless when he lay against the workout bench to bench-press nearly 200 pounds. He kept fit by lifting weights if he wasn't playing chess with Gent or reading. He had a lot of time on his hands.

"You got this," an inmate named Rock said.

Sincere gripped the long bar, pushed upward, and then brought the entire bulk of the weights against his chest and began doing reps of ten. He was strong and disciplined. Finally, he finished doing his set and arose. The workout bench was the only exercise equipment in the yard, thanks to the expense of equipment upkeep. However, inmates still found ways to stay in shape and build muscles. The prison yard was open for walking or running in place. Some prisoners did pushups on a chair or filled trash bags with water and used a broom to make a barbell.

Sincere sat upright and looked around at the activity happening in the yard.

"Let me get some," said Rock.

Sincere removed himself from the workout bench, and Rock took his place in bench-pressing. It was a breezy day, and everything was calm. The guards were doing their jobs, and specific routines were happening cleverly under the guards' watchful eyes. There was Teddy and his illegal gambling. Technically, prison gambling was banned. But given that it was unenforceable, most prisons looked the other way when inmates played cards for wagers, ran bookmaking operations, or wagered on prison happenings. Prisoners would wager commissary scrips, money they'd saved, cigarettes, or most likely food.

The blacks occupied one section of the yard, the Hispanics another, and the Aryan Brotherhood another. Everyone was one big happy family for now.

Rock finished his set and howled. Goons surrounded them, and while Sincere worked out among them, talk among them began about the robberies and murders in Queens. Whatever happened in the streets, it quickly made its way into the prisons. Once again, Sincere had this gut feeling that this was somehow connected to him.

"These muthafuckas got balls, I tell you that," said Rock.

"Niggas are stupid nowadays. Pussy got niggas slipping and tripping. Only a bitch can get that close to set some shit up," Kendrick chimed. He was doing a life sentence for murders and drug conspiracy.

"Word on the streets is the bitch used to be a stripper," said another prisoner.

Sincere listened to the gossip, but he kept his opinions to himself. With him becoming a shot caller, he established connections, power, and a conduit to information. People wanted to be in his good grace and favor, and many inmates owed him something, and all it took was a word to the right prisoner, a phone call to the outside, and Sincere was moving people around like they were pawns on a chessboard, and like one inmate said, the streets talk, and the truth and secrets traveled through the grapevine. Most of the time, shot callers and inmates knew more about what was happening in the hood than the detectives, neighbors, and the police.

While Sincere lingered in the workout area listening to his goons' gossip, Row entered the yard with some urgent news to share with him.

"What's happening, my nigga?" Row greeted him.

"C'mon, let's walk," Sincere said.

The two men trailed away from the group to talk privately. When they were away from the other inmates' hearing distance, Sincere asked him, "What did you find out?"

"I made some calls and had my peoples look into your sister," Row began.

Sincere was listening, knowing the news wasn't going to be good. "And?"

Row looked like he didn't want to share the bad news, but it wasn't his choice. "She's in deep. I mean, she's fuckin' around with your boy, Nasir. The word is that she stopped dancing at this club a few weeks ago, and my guess, she's doing licks with your boy Nasir and his cousin. They dropping bodies around the hood like raindrops," Row proclaimed.

Sincere became livid. "You sure it's her?" he questioned.

Row nodded. "My peoples are sure. She's a pretty girl, and you can't mistake her."

Sincere frowned at Row, but Row didn't mean any disrespect to him.

"The thing is, if I found out about her, it ain't gonna be too long until Zulu has this same information," said Row.

Sincere knew he was right.

"What you wanna do?" asked Row.

Sincere was processing everything. Hearing about his old partner in crime, his brother from another mother, hooking up with his younger sister and then involving her in murderous crimes was troublesome. Sincere wanted to decapitate Nasir and piss down his throat. He was hurt and felt betrayed. He believed Nasir took advantage of Denise, and he was dragging the only family he had left down the road to perdition.

"I got a number for you," Row said.

"For who?" he asked.

"Nasir."

Sincere nodded. He planned on making that phone call later from his jail cell from a burner phone.

When Nasir heard the news of Cook's immediate arrest, he felt slighted. The Feds got to him before he did, and it felt too late. Cook was out of his reach. Therefore, his revenge would have to wait.

Denise was nestled against Nasir in the back seat of the cab. They were on their way to the Marriott in Philly. The two decided to stay in Philadelphia for a while and spend quality time together outside New York City.

While they were cuddled together in the back seat eyeing the streets of Philly, Nasir's cell phone rang. He removed it from his hip and looked at the caller ID. It was an unfamiliar number, but he still answered the call.

"Yo, who this?" he answered.

"Nigga, you don't recognize my voice?" Sincere uttered coolly.

"Sincere?" he uttered in disbelief. Immediately, Nasir perked up and slightly removed himself from Denise's side. He was taken aback by the sudden phone call.

"Yeah, it's me."

"How did you get this number?" asked Nasir.

Hearing her brother's name come out of Nasir's mouth, Denise was shocked. Was it really him calling? Nasir looked at her and mouthed, "It's your brother."

What does he want? she thought.

"I trusted you, Nasir, and you do this to me, to my fuckin' family!" Sincere exclaimed. He wasn't going to sugarcoat the conversation.

"I don't know what you talking about, Sincere."

"Don't play stupid, muthafucka. You think I wouldn't find out about you and Denise. I may be locked down, but I got eyes and connections," Sincere hollered.

"Look, it ain't what you think," Nasir countered.

"So you're not fucking my little sister and don't have her committing crimes? You and your cousin pissed off some powerful people, and if I could connect the dots from inside here, how long do you think it will take them?" Sincere let him know.

Nasir was stuck on stupid for a moment. He didn't know how to respond. Sincere was his best friend, a brother to him, and the fact that he was angry with him was painful.

"I'm giving you the chance to walk away right now," Sincere said. "Leave my sister out of your shit. If you ever had love and respect for me, then do this."

Nasir was torn apart with guilt. But he was in love with Denise, and it was easier said than done. "I can't do that. I love her," he proclaimed.

"You what?" Sincere hollered.

"Let me talk to him," Denise chimed.

"Are you with her now?" Sincere asked.

"Yeah," Nasir replied.

"Nasir, she's all I have left in this world besides my children. I don't want to see anything happen to her," Sincere uttered.

"And I promise I won't allow anything to happen to her. She's family to me too, bro," Nasir countered wholeheartedly.

"You can't make that fuckin' promise to me when you're the one putting her in harm's way," Sincere argued.

The cab arrived at the Marriott on Market Street, a polished high-rise hotel less than a mile from the Liberty Bell and Independence Hall. Denise climbed out of the cab frustrated, while Nasir paid the cabbie. When Nasir finally climbed out of the cab behind Denise, he heard Sincere curse, "I thought you would always have my back, Nasir, but this is how you show your fuckin' loyalty to me?"

"I always had your back, Sincere, from day one. You're the one who got yourself locked up wanting to become Rambo in the hood and left Denise out here to fend for herself."

"They killed Marcus," Sincere protested.

"I understand, but you still had Denise in your life. What about her, huh? You ever thought about the consequences behind your action, nigga?" Nasir countered.

"So you're some kinda righteous muthafucka now?"

"Nah, I'm just someone who really cares about her," Nasir retorted.

The two men went back and forth, and the conversation became heated. Denise wanted to confront her brother, but Nasir wouldn't allow it. She'd been through enough, and their night was going good until the phone call from Sincere.

"I swear to God, Nasir, if anything happens to her, I'm gonna kill you myself, nigga!" Sincere heatedly threatened.

"You ain't gotta worry about that, nigga. She's in good hands right now," Nasir exclaimed.

"Put her on the phone and let me talk to her," Sincere said.

"Nah, I can't do that."

"Why not?"

"Because she doesn't want to talk to you," said Nasir.

"Fuck you, nigga!" Sincere shouted.

"So it's like that, nigga?" Nasir exclaimed.

"Yeah, it's like that!"

"Fuck you too, nigga. You're the one who fucked up. Don't worry about Denise. I got her back, muthafucka."

"Watch your back, Nasir," Sincere threatened.

Their phone call ended abruptly. Nasir sighed heavily. He was upset. He couldn't believe he had an argument with Sincere and threats were spewed. It was surreal. He wanted it to be a nightmare, but it wasn't.

"You okay?" Denise asked him. "What did he say?"

Nasir stood there quietly, refusing to answer her. His mind spun in so many different directions that he felt faint and dizzy. It wasn't supposed to be this way. Their friendship had gone down the drain that quickly. Denise was staring at him with worry.

"What did he say to you?" she reiterated.

"I need to go for a walk," Nasir told her.

She was baffled. *A fuckin' walk? Is he serious?* But he was, and he turned around and walked away from Denise.

"Nasir, are you fuckin' serious?" Denise cried out.

He continued to walk away from her. That argument with Sincere was painful, and it felt like a piece of him died tonight.

Chapter Thirty-five

Zulu grunted with his eyes closed as he pushed up into Tammy in a downward thrust. Her body was arched upward, and she opened her mouth in what looked like a moan of pleasure as Zulu shoved his black dick into her.

"Aaaah. Aaaah, fuck me," Tammy moaned.

She gripped the back of his head tightly and yanked Zulu closer to her skin. She tightened her grip behind his head and pulled him into a hard, lip-smashing kiss. Their mouths remained latched as she pressed her nude front to his. Her body molded to Zulu's, giving his flesh a strong sense of arousal. She was tight and wet, and it felt like every muscle was a machine.

"Oh, fuck!" he groaned, staying deep inside her.

Zulu rolled over on his back, pulling Tammy atop his dick. She was now riding him on the king-size bed, wrinkling and soiling the silk sheets. Her body was quite beautiful with curves, ass, and tits. Zulu thrust upward with his dick becoming harder inside of her. His hands grabbed her hips as he moved in and out of her. He closed his eyes, and a slight shiver raced up his spine, causing his body to shake slightly. Then Zulu opened his mouth and released a sensual moan. The pussy was so good his toes started to curl.

"Fuck me," Tammy cried out in excited lust. Tammy's hips swayed and gyrated with the guidance of Zulu's hands. It was a passionate moment inside Zulu's luxurious bedroom. The two were making up for missed years.

Zulu's bedroom was an oasis. There was a full-sized balcony overlooking Central Park. The large bedroom also boasted a king-size bed, feather pillows, a plasma TV, and a minibar stocked with snacks. The granite bathroom was complete with a deep soaker tub, brass accents, and a separate glass shower. It was the best that money could buy.

The two continued to fuck their brains out, and everything was going right until Zulu's cell phone rang.

"Don't answer it," Tammy uttered.

She was riding him forcefully, feeling herself about to come. His hands cupped her tits, and there was no going back. Zulu let his phone go to voicemail. But then it rang again.

"I need to take this," said Zulu while reaching for his cell phone nearby.

"Fuck!" Tammy cursed.

And just like that, their magical and brazen moment ended unexpectedly. She rolled off the dick onto her back while Zulu answered the call.

"This had better be fuckin' important," he shouted.

"The Feds are coming for you right now!" a cop named Beck shouted back.

"What?"

"I learned about it last minute. But they're coming to arrest you at this very moment!" Beck hollered urgently.

The news came out of nowhere, and Zulu was dumbfounded. Beck was a dirty cop he had in his pocket. He was one of several. Immediately, Zulu leaped from the bed and scrambled around the bedroom, looking for clothes. Tammy was taken aback by his sudden reaction.

"Zulu, what is going on?" she asked him.

"You need to hurry up and get dressed," he shouted.

"Why?"

"Bitch, do what the fuck I'm telling you and stop asking me questions!" he screamed.

Tammy was shocked and scared.

Zulu threw on some clothing and hurried to a vaulted safe in the bedroom. He opened it in a hurry and began removing essential documents from it. He had no idea how much time he had. But he needed to leave his place urgently. There was only time for him to take what was important and run. While he did that, he dialed Zodiac to let him know what was happening. When Zodiac answered, Zulu immediately shouted, "The Feds are coming for me."

"Now?"

"Contact my attorney right now," said Zulu.

"I'm on it."

The moment the call ended, there was a loud knock at the door followed by, "FBI! Open up!"

"Fuck me!" Zulu cursed.

He knew there was no escaping them, especially when they were raiding his penthouse. It was either leap from the twenty-first floor or face uncertainty. Of course, he chose the latter. His fate was sealed. The FBI was coming into his home by force or by him opening the door. Tammy was beside herself with worry and fear. This wasn't her world. She was an investment banker who wanted some dick from an old flame, and she scrambled to get decent before it was too late.

Zulu stormed into the main room as the Feds became impatient and broke the door. An army of heavily armed men wearing ballistic armor and carrying assault weapons with thirty-round magazines stormed into the penthouse. Zulu was a sitting duck in his own home.

"FBI. Marion Conner, aka Zulu," the agent exclaimed, "we have a warrant for your arrest."

"For what?" Zulu exclaimed.

They ignored him and started to read him his rights.

"Y'all couldn't wait another fuckin' minute for me to open my damn door? Y'all some ignorant muthafuckas! Who do you think I am, fuckin' Scarface?" Zulu cursed.

They arrested Zulu and wildly swarmed through the penthouse, leaving no stone unturned. They brought Tammy into the same room with Zulu, and he fumed.

"Be careful with her!" Zulu shouted. "She ain't got shit to do with this."

They handcuffed her and made her sit on the couch with Zulu. The look on her face was unpleasant. This wasn't happening.

"I'm sorry about this," Zulu said to her.

Tammy couldn't look at him. She was upset and scared. The only thing she wanted to do was disappear. It made Zulu furious. His romantic reunion with a beautiful woman had been completely ruined, and he'd be surprised if she ever spoke to him again.

Zulu was charged with multiple counts of drug racketeering, murder racketeering, narcotics trafficking, laundering drug proceeds, and extortion under the RICO Act. But what shocked him was when prosecutors hit him with an indictment for planning the murder of New York City detective Michael Acosta. Only three people knew about the murder plot of the detective, including Cook Gamble. Zulu knew Cook became a snitch.

"This muthafucka," he growled.

After processing in Metropolitan Correctional Center, New York—a twelve-story high-rise building located at 150 Park Row in the Civic Center neighborhood—Zulu knew it was urgent to meet with his lawyer, Richard Gillespie, and Zodiac. He was looking at life sentences for his crimes, and Gillespie was the best defense lawyer in the city. There was no way Zulu was doing a life sentence, and it was time for him to clean house. While incarcerated, he'd gotten word from the streets and Pike's crew about the trio's identities who robbed him and murdered his men, including Big Joe.

Zulu's arrest was a big deal, and it made headlines. He was housed in the 10-South wing. Inmates in the 10-South wing were locked inside single-man cells twenty-three hours a day and continuously monitored by CCTV cameras with lights on at all times. The prisoners were kept isolated. Their cells were equipped with showers, and the only time they were taken outside their cells was for exercise in an indoor cage.

It had been a long week, and Zulu was angry and frustrated. He was now a confined man who had been denied bail. The DA argued that he was a dangerous man on the streets of New York and a flight risk. He had the money, resources, and opportunity to intimidate witnesses and flee the country. Gillespie claimed his client was a law-abiding citizen and a businessman with too much to lose if he was remanded. But Zulu had priors and a record, so the judge sided with the DA. Zulu was a threat to let go, and now he was underneath the thumb of the law. The nail in the coffin was the intended hit on a police detective, and the DA had a State's witness willing to testify against Zulu in court.

Zulu walked into the isolated visiting room to meet with his lawyer, Gillespie, and Zodiac. He was clad in an orange jumpsuit and wearing bus shoes. The fashion, the jewelry, and the $600 shoes were all replaced with dismaying prison attire. He looked like a shell of himself. The moment Zulu entered the room with a guard escort, Gillespie and Zodiac stood up to greet him. Zulu scowled and sat opposite the two men when the guard left the room.

"I was able to convince them that Zodiac was one of my legal aids," said Gillespie.

"How you holding up?" Zodiac asked him.

"They got me in a fuckin' box nearly twenty-four hours a day until my trial," Zulu griped.

"My office is in the process of appealing the decision right now, Zulu," Gillespie stated.

"Fucking judge thinks he can keep me locked. I wanna snap his neck like a twig," Zulu exclaimed.

"Be mindful of where we are. We're working on getting you out of here. Just be patient with us," Gillespie replied.

"You want me to be patient while there's a fuckin' snitch out there ready to testify against me?" Zulu griped.

"The DA is keeping this individual a secret at the moment," Gillespie chimed.

Zulu stared at his right-hand man Zodiac and uttered, "He's no fuckin' secret from us. We know who he is. It's only a matter of finding him."

"He's a government witness, Zulu," said Gillespie.

Zulu and Zodiac looked at each other. There was a brotherly understanding between each other without saying too much. They needed him dead, but it couldn't be said in front of the lawyer. Even though there was the lawyer-client privilege, the less Gillespie knew, the better. He was highly aware of Zulu's involvement in the drug trade, but he was only there for legal support. The last thing he wanted to hear was a plot to murder a government witness.

"Zulu, keep a low profile. You don't need any more strikes against you. Early Monday morning, my office will file a motion to appeal for bail. I know this judge," Gillespie said.

"Just make it happen," Zulu said.

"We will. But I'll give you two a moment to talk. The less I hear, the better," said Gillespie.

He lifted himself from the table and knocked on the door, indicating to the guard that he was ready to exit. When Gillespie left, Zulu said to Zodiac, "You're my eyes and ears out there for the moment. Whatever is a threat to us needs to be taken care of. They're trying to bury me, Zodiac. No bail, a snitch, muthafuckas coming after my shit and still breathing. How does it make me look right now?"

Zodiac nodded. "I'll handle it."

"I want shit handled like yesterday, and you sure it's Nasir?"

Zodiac nodded. "He tried to sell ten kilos of our shit a few weeks back. Pike wants to make amends with us. He doesn't want any problems, wants to be in good favor with us."

"Of course, everyone does," Zulu replied. "But this cocksucker Nasir, I never did like that muthafucka. What is this, some kind of omen? First, Sincere comes after Mob Allah. Now this muthafucka wanna attack my shit. Make it happen to whoever was involved, and I want a message sent."

"I got you, and don't worry about Cook. We'll get to him."

Zulu nodded, believing his right-hand man would get the job done. Zodiac stood from the table, and the two men gave each other dap and a brotherly hug.

"One, my nigga," said Zodiac.

"One."

With that, Zodiac left the room with Zulu pondering his future.

Chapter Thirty-six

"Fuck her brother and fuck Zulu! I ain't scared of any one of those muthafuckas," Lou shouted. "And besides, they both locked up right now. What the fuck they gonna do?"

"You think because both men are locked up, they ain't dangerous?" Nasir exclaimed.

"And what the fuck do you think I am?" Lou retorted. "We out here gettin' this money, and there ain't no stopping it."

"Are you fuckin' crazy, Lou? There's a fuckin' price on our heads," Nasir shouted.

"They wanna hunt us? Then I'm gonna hunt them too. It's what we do and who the fuck we are!" Lou growled.

"And it's suicide!"

Lou grabbed a stack of cash, held it toward Nasir, and scolded, "Look at what we accomplished. This is what it's about: money, gettin' it by any means necessary. Like I said before, you and I deserve this life. We're putting that work in, and they gonna respect us, cuzzo. Fuck that, ain't no stopping us!"

Lou was insane.

"Ain't no stopping us, or there's no stopping you?" Nasir countered.

"What the fuck do you mean by that, cuzzo?"

"I'm just saying, you're not thinking rational right now. You're high off this shit. That's what you are. You're shooting dope without the needle in your arm. How long you think this will last, nigga?" Nasir exclaimed.

"And you're pussy whipped, nigga," Lou countered. "You let that bitch and her brother's treat get up in your head, got you faltering against family, against me, muthafucka! When you came home, I was there for you, and then you met that bitch, and you put that fuckin' bitch first before your own flesh and blood, your first cousin, nigga!"

"First off, watch your mouth, Lou."

"Or what, nigga? Huh? Look at you, ready to fight me over some fuckin' words over a ho!" Lou insulted her.

Nasir reacted without thinking. He threw a quick right and punched Lou in the jaw. The shock on Lou's face was fleeting, and he immediately countered with a sharp round punch to Nasir's chin. After that, the two men came to heated blows punching and tussling in the kitchen.

"Fuck you, nigga!" Lou screamed.

Nasir slammed Lou into the sink and began punching him repeatedly. Lou headbutted his cousin, then attacked his midsection, and Nasir flew backward. They continued to brawl and fell to the ground, arms and legs entangled, and Nasir's fist sank into his cousin's stomach. They were like two kindergarteners wrestling on the kitchen floor. Nasir tried to put Lou into a chokehold, but Lou was too strong.

"Get the fuck off me, cuzzo!" Lou shouted.

"Take it back!" Nasir exclaimed.

"Really, over some pussy?"

"I love her!" Nasir bellowed.

"Oh, my God, are y'all two serious?" Denise hollered when she entered the kitchen to see them fighting and tussling on the kitchen floor.

"He started it," Nasir uttered.

Denise huffed. She couldn't believe two grown men and first cousins were fighting like children. She glared at them. Nasir released his chokehold from Lou and exhaled.

"We got a contract on our heads, and y'all really fighting each other. This can't be happening," Denise exclaimed.

"Get off me," Lou muttered to his cousin.

Lou and Nasir stood up and coolly began collecting themselves.

"When you're done here, we need to talk," Denise said to Nasir.

"A'ight," Nasir replied.

Denise looked at Lou, and he told her, "I'm sorry."

"Whatever. Fuck you, Lou," she cursed, and then marched out of the kitchen.

"Look, she's right. We don't need to be fighting each other," Nasir uttered.

"I just want what's best for us. That's all I ever wanted. They shit on you, and you needed to let them know who the fuck you are. I love you, cuzzo, and I will always have your back, no matter what. We family, right?" Lou expressed wholeheartedly.

Nasir nodded. "Yeah, we're family. I love you too."

Lou smiled.

They hugged each other and made amends. Then Lou's cell phone rang. He glanced at the caller ID and said to Nasir, "I need to take this."

Nasir nodded.

"Yo, what's up?" Lou answered the call.

"Lou, it's Lexi. You remember that girl you was lookin' for, Iris? I know where she is."

"Oh, word, where are you right now?"

"I'm on Sutphin. She went into a hair salon," Lexi said.

"Watch her and stall her if you have to. I'm on my way there now," Lou replied.

He hurriedly ended the call and left the house, not even saying goodbye to Nasir.

***

Lou arrived on the corner of Sutphin Boulevard and South Road that night. He was familiar with the area and felt secure that his problem with Iris would end tonight. Lou couldn't afford to keep Iris alive with the heat they had on them. She'd become a liability, and the last thing they needed was the cops coming after them for homicide. Lou removed a Glock 17 from the glove compartment and checked the clip. He only needed one or two rounds to do the job. He placed the weapon on the seat next to him and watched the bodega on the corner. He didn't see Lexi or Iris. He removed his cell phone to call Lexi.

She answered, "Hey?"

"I'm here. Where are you?" he asked her.

"I'm coming out of the bodega now," Lexi replied.

Lexi exited the corner bodega, lighting a cigarette. She took a few pulls and saw Lou's Pathfinder idling across the intersection. She was dressed for the weather, wearing a short leather coat, winter boots, and a trendy top to entice her clientele. Lou noticed her and decided to drive closer to her. He stopped at the red light ahead with light cross traffic. While idling at the red light, he immediately noticed a pair of headlights following him. A black van pulled into the intersection to make a left, but it was too far into the intersection. Lou stared at the van, and he became wary. While Lou stared at the black van to his left, another black van came screeching to a stop at an angle behind his Pathfinder, blocking him. Suddenly, both vans' side doors slid open, and several assault rifles quickly protruded from both vehicles.

"Shit!" Lou shouted.

This is it. It is going down. They'd found him. Lou immediately reached for his Glock to react, but it was too late. Lou lifted his chin and braced himself for what was coming.

"Fuck y'all!" Lou screamed.

The assault rifles exploded.

Four men in each van opened fire with their heavy automatic weapons, AR-15s and HK-91s. Muzzled flashes strobed across their bandanna-covered faces and glaring eyes. A barrage of bullets punched through Lou and his Jeep, tearing through the vehicle, shattering glass, and demolishing Lou. The gunfire seemed to go on forever. It only ended after their weapons were emptied and gun smoke wafted through the intersection. Lou's Jeep became riddled with bullet holes. It had been shredded and looked like Swiss cheese, and in the driver's seat, Lou leaned forward against the steering wheel, his head against the horn. He took his last jagged breath and was dead.

The doors of the vans snapped shut, and the vans took off in different directions.

Chapter Thirty-seven

Detective Michael Acosta couldn't believe Zulu had put out a hit on his life. But it wasn't farfetched. Both men hated and despised each other, and although Acosta wasn't the one to bring him down, he was happy to hear that Zulu was finally imprisoned without bail. Fate had finally caught up to the drug kingpin, and he felt it was flattering that he'd become such a thorn in Zulu's side that the kingpin wanted to have him murdered. It meant he was doing his job efficiently and had gotten underneath the devil's skin.

Even though Zulu was incarcerated, the threat to Acosta's life was still active and viable. Cook's testimony was powerful. He gave them names, the Russians, the Shower Posses, including the supposed shooter, Dante, and how much Zulu was willing to pay to have an NYC detective killed: $50,000. The detective chuckled at the information and replied, "So my life is worth fifty grand." He had uttered it to his cohorts.

Detective Emmerson became upset with his partner because he believed Acosta wasn't taking the threat on his life seriously. The captain had placed two police officers outside of his home. They were adamant about protecting one of their own. It was happening whether Acosta was for it or not.

But the threat to Acosta's life was the least on his mind. He had other problems, meaning his mental health. Everything was taking a toll on him, from the job to his failed marriage and Cynthia's death. He felt alone. He was alone. There was so much on his mind and no escaping the pain. Once again, he was shirtless and stared long and hard at himself in the bathroom mirror. His police-issued Glock 19 was on the bathroom counter. He had seventeen years on the police force—that was seventeen years of seeing the worst humanity had to offer: murders, robberies, rapes, beatings, suicides, and pedophilia. Yet nothing shocked him anymore, not even the murder-for-hire on his life.

It was five years since his divorce, and he missed his wife and kids. His family was the only therapy and healing he had and needed after seeing the worst of society. Coming home to them was a blessing, but now, he came home to nothing but an empty house, and Acosta felt like an empty soul. Without his family to go home to and unwind with, without seeing his innocent and loving children, the world's darkness became consuming. He was a decorated detective with one of the highest clearances on the job. But there was no longer a balance in his life, something special to pull him away from the job. Acosta felt cursed. *What is left?* His wife had remarried, and he was a targeted man.

Acosta exhaled and continued to stare at his reflection in the bathroom mirror. The hurt, the pain, the ugly, and the loneliness all manifested inside him until the point of no return. It was simmering inside him, becoming a bottomless pit of discomfort and grief. Detective Acosta locked up some of the most dangerous people, yet he felt like a criminal. He failed his loved ones, and worse, it felt like he died himself, and any happiness became obsolete to him. There was the job, the badge, the streets, his credibility, and that was it.

Near his Glock was the pamphlet "Recognizing Symptoms of Trauma." Acosta felt there was no bouncing back this time, no rebounding from the trauma of his loss and the difficulties of the job. It felt like he could no longer build a healthy, intimate relationship outside of work. There was no leaving work and enjoying being with family, no separation. However, there was one absolute way Acosta knew how he could separate himself from everything.

Detective Acosta picked up his Glock 19 and remained focused on his reflection. He'd struggled for too long and could no longer keep it together. The department was adamant about protecting him from the threat to his life, but how would they protect Acosta from himself? He was emotionally exhausted and became a burned-out cop. Finally, he pressed the gun barrel to his temple, kept his eyes on his wounded image, exhaled, and then . . .

A gunshot echoed loudly through the bathroom.

Zodiac poured himself a drink, and then sat on the sofa and pondered his next move. It was a quiet evening, but he had a lot to think about. While Gillespie was trying to free Zulu from jail, he worked on keeping the organization together. With Zulu incarcerated, their drug organization was on the verge of collapsing. Still, Zodiac was determined to keep everything together by any means necessary.

First, Zulu raised the bounty on Nasir's and Denise's heads to $60,000. When he received news that Lou had been gunned down, it was only a drop in the bucket. He wanted them all dead. Second, he had to shut everything down. Nothing would move on the streets until he worked out the difficulties in their organization and eradicated any harm to their future. Their biggest problem was Cook. Trying to locate him was becoming difficult. He was a government witness, and Zodiac figured Cook would be in the witness protection program. His testimony to the grand jury and in court would damage the organization. Cook knew too much, and the snitch was willing to destroy everything they'd built to save his own ass, and if that happened, what would stop the Feds from coming for him too? But he wondered, *why didn't they come for me?*

Zodiac walked to the floor-to-ceiling windows and peered at the ocean from his waterfront co-op condo in Brooklyn. It was a beautiful view of the Atlantic Ocean on a cloudless night. Zodiac was a gangster but a man of substance and class. He was a discreet man but shrewd when it came to business and observant, and he enjoyed the finer things in life. His condo was an old-school, money-English stereotype, with an oversized leather Chesterfield couch and matching wing-back armchairs grouped around a handsome leather-inlaid mahogany table. A row of dark, polished bookcases lined the wall behind it, filled with thick, gilt-lettered leather volumes. It gave the impression of age and wisdom, like the quarters of an old barrister or a school headmaster.

"Damn," Zodiac muttered.

"What's wrong, baby?" Trina asked him.

Zodiac poured himself another glass of vodka and downed it like it was water. He huffed and became pensive. He had a lot on his plate. Then finally, Trina stood up from the sofa and walked toward him, clad in an elegant black lip-locked satin robe. She was a beautiful woman, but she was born a man. She was a trans woman, and it was hard to believe she was once a man. She started identifying as a woman when she was 6 years old. Trina was tall and curvy with long, opulent black hair, and she had tits that could rival Dolly Parton's.

"I asked you what's wrong, and you're going to ignore me, Zodiac?" Trina barked.

"You know what's wrong, Trina. Don't come at me with thoughtless questions," Zodiac griped. "I got people looking all over this city for Cook, but he's protected right now. So how should I deal with this problem if I can't find him?"

"Maybe you don't," said Trina. "Perhaps you let everything play out."

Zodiac looked at her as if she were crazy. "Are you high or something?" he replied.

He poured himself another glass of vodka and sat in his high-back leather chair behind his mahogany desk. Trina approached him, took a seat on his lap, and then wrapped her arms around him to show intimacy with her boo.

"Listen to me, baby," she began. "Possibly, this is a sign telling you that it is your time to shine. You're respected, smart, and feared, like Zulu. In fact, all these years, you were the brains behind everything. It wasn't Zodiac or Mob Allah, but you. You have a mind for business, and you know these streets better than anyone. Aren't you tired of playing second fiddle?"

"Are you trying to create a civil war between Zulu and me? Because that is what's going to happen," said Zodiac.

"He's locked up right now, and from my understanding, the cards are stacked against him. So when Cook Gamble testifies against him, Zulu is done, and for those who don't wanna play ball with you and are loyal to Zulu, then you know what needs to be done. A message needs to be sent for anyone to take you seriously," said Trina. "Think about it."

Zodiac sighed. Trina had planted the seed into his head, which wasn't a bad plan. He threw back the vodka and began thinking.

"I'm here, baby, and together we can do this," Trina added. "We can own this fucking city. So let him fuckin' rot."

Chapter Thirty-eight

A deep gloom overcame Nasir when he heard about Lou. He couldn't believe it. His cousin was gone, gunned down in the street. Nasir knew Lou was set up. He thought about his cousin's phone call right before he was killed. He had no idea who had called him, but he wanted to find out. Nasir's heart was flooded with sadness, and his eyes were dull with grief. Next to him on the bed was a 9 mm Beretta and a .45. He and Denise were staying at a cheap Brooklyn motel in Flatbush. They couldn't stay in Queens anymore. It had become too hot.

Nasir took a swig of Bacardi straight from the bottle while he sat at the foot of the bed. Denise was taking a shower in the bathroom, leaving him alone with his disturbing thoughts. The anger and regret started to swell inside him. He wished he had been there with Lou to have his cousin's back. Maybe the outcome would have been different. But Denise assured him that if he'd gone with his cousin that night, he would be dead too. Lou knew the risks. They all did. Still, Nasir felt guilty.

He heard the shower stop, meaning Denise was finally done showering. Nasir took another swig of Bacardi. First, he had a falling out with Sincere. Now he'd lost his cousin. When Nasir looked at himself in the mirror, his eyes had a haunted look. His grief continued to come in waves trying to sweep him away.

"Baby, are you okay?" Denise asked him.

She came out of the bathroom wrapped in a white towel. Her body was still glistening from her shower. She was beautiful, there was no denying that, and Nasir knew he couldn't lose her too. The couple planned on leaving New York. They had the money to do so. In a small black duffle bag in the corner was $140,000. It was blood money, but it was the kind of cash that would allow them to start over somewhere different and far away from Queens, New York.

Nasir took another swig of alcohol while Denise approached him. She removed the bottle from his hand, placed it on the floor, and then straddled him at the foot of the bed.

"You need to remain sharp and focused," she told him.

Nasir stared at her with passion and affection but also with regret. Then he uttered, "I'm sorry, baby."

"About what?"

"I got you mixed up in this life, and now your brother is upset with me, and we have a contract on our heads. You didn't deserve this life. You deserve better. You should have been with a man who could give you the life you need without the risk. You're a beautiful woman, baby, and I love you so much, and I don't want to see anything happen to you," Nasir proclaimed emotionally.

"Nothing is going to happen to me or us. We're leaving this place, baby, and we're not looking back, and the only man I deserve and love is you," Denise replied unequivocally. "We protect each other until the end."

Nasir sighed heavily. Then he proclaimed to her, "I love you so much."

"I love you too, baby. More than anything. More than life itself," Denise replied clearly.

She leaned closer to Nasir and placed her mouth on his. Their lips gently parted, and their tongues found each other. Electricity shot through Denise's body, and immediately her pussy began to throb and pulse. Nasir's hand began to roam, and they gently caressed her curves while their kissing became more passionate and extraordinarily sensual. Finally, Nasir unknotted the towel and allowed it to fall from her body onto the floor to reveal her heavenly grace. Now she was naked and craving him.

"Make love to me, baby," Denise whispered to him.

Nasir cupped her breasts, toyed with her body, and then lowered his mouth to her hardened nipples. Softly, he sucked on them with his mouth filled with her sweetness. A pleasurable and aroused moan escaped from Denise's mouth. It was about their intimacy, connection, and passion. Denise's pussy flowed freely as Nasir humped his thigh against her mound.

"I want you inside of me," she said.

She undid his jeans and tossed them to the floor. Nasir was so hard it looked like a steel pipe. Denise straddled him again. This time, she gripped his hard dick and guided it inside her. She pushed the head in inch by inch, continuing their passionate connection, intimacy, and truth. Nasir licked, kissed, and softly sucked her nipples like she wanted them to be sucked while Denise was wet beyond her wildest dreams. He pressed his body to hers with Denise's legs wrapped around him, pulling him closer, tightly. He let her control the action. Denise felt like Nasir was her breath, that he was her life force.

"Fuck me," she cried out.

He went deeper into her until Denise felt she couldn't breathe anymore. She released a guttural moan while experiencing a mind-blowing, heart-stopping sensation with someone she loved very deeply, and the pleasure was indescribable. For a moment, the two connected with their eyes.

"Mmm, that feels so nice. Don't stop. Oh, yeah, fuck me," Denise cried out.

It was the distraction they both needed. Nasir's big dick continued to thrust between the folds of her beautiful, engorged, slippery lips, intending to give her an earth-shattering orgasm. He was entirely inside her and rhythmic and graceful. In and out, in and out, in and out. *Fuck!* The passion consumed them. They met each other's bodies, connected, and joined.

"Ooooh, God," Denise hollered.

She was about to come. Finally, it was time, and Nasir thrust into her like a rocket. The intensity of the dick made Denise bite into his flesh and claw his back like some animal unable to control herself and her arousal. There was groaning, chanting, and cursing. The weight, the fullness, the feeling of Nasir's erection deep inside her—she was fighting a losing battle of pure sensory overload. Pleasure consumed her entirely, and her legs shook and trembled. She held on to Nasir for dear life, demanding that he not move, not stop, as he was lovingly coaxing her orgasm out with his hard dick, and soon, Denise released her passion. Waves of impending pleasure overtook her, her body exploding with an intense orgasm that made her body light up like fireworks going off on the Fourth of July.

Denise froze momentarily against Nasir and took a deep breath. He'd scratched that itch. Together, they collapsed onto the bed on their sides and stared at each other. Once again, Denise proclaimed, "I love you, Nasir."

"I love you too," he replied.

Half an hour before midnight, the couple decided to check out of the motel and leave the city. The plan was to head west, maybe settle in Arizona or Nevada. The desert seemed like the perfect place for a new start. It was far from the big eastern cities, and Nasir and Denise believed Zulu or Zodiac's influence wouldn't reach that far. Their bags were packed, the gray Honda Accord was filled with gas, and they had a duffle bag of cash. Nasir stuffed the 9 mm into his waistband and handed Denise the .45. They looked at each other, and there was hope, love, and faith.

"We got this," Nasir said.

Denise smiled. "I know."

"Once we're gone, we can never come back here, Denise. We can't look back. Our lives are no longer here," Nasir added.

Denise nodded. "Why would I want to look back? This place took everything from me. Let's just go."

Nasir picked up the duffle bag with cash, and Denise grabbed their other belongings. As they headed out the motel door, the motel phone rang. It startled them. There was no reason for that phone to ring. They both stared at the ringing phone like it was some kind of omen.

"Don't answer it," said Denise.

"I'm not. Let's get the fuck outta here," Nasir uttered.

They hurried out of the motel room and walked toward the Honda parked in the parking lot. It was a cold night and quiet. Everything seemed okay. Nasir tossed the bags into the car's trunk and got behind the wheel with Denise by his side. He started the ignition and drove off without a second thought. For days they'd kept a low profile at the motel and mainly ordered in. Nasir was upset that he couldn't bury Lou properly. It was too risky. So instead, his cousin's body would be cremated by the State.

Nasir headed toward the Belt Parkway. The roads were sparse and quiet on the chilly autumn night, and they traveled down Flatbush Avenue and stopped at a red light. Unbeknownst to them, they were being followed. Before the light changed, a dark-colored SUV with tinted windows pulled up parallel to the passenger's side. Denise glanced at the vehicle but didn't sense any danger. However, the rear and driver's side windows rolled down when she removed her glance from the SUV. Immediately, semiautomatic pistols protruded from the SUV and opened fire on the Honda.

A barrage of bullets tore into the Honda. Under attack, Nasir pressed against the accelerator and floored it through the red light. Gunfire continued behind them, and Nasir panicked. He lost control of the car and slammed into another parked car at full speed. The SUV sped away in the opposite direction. At the same time, twisted metal, mangled bodies, and smoke came from the Honda Accord.

Chapter Thirty-nine

The news hit Sincere like a ton of bricks, but he kept a stoic look about him. His sister was dead. That afternoon, he'd been called into the chaplain's office to receive the news.

"I'm sorry to be the one to inform you," said the prison chaplain. "If there's anything I can do within my power, let me know."

"I wanna see her body," said Sincere. "She was the only thing I had left in this world."

The chaplain sighed. "We'll see what we can do for you," the chaplain replied.

"Please do."

It was challenging, but he was a man of God and faith.

"Did she die alone?" Sincere asked him.

"Unfortunately, she was found alone," the chaplain replied.

Sincere didn't want to hear any more. He stood up from the pew, uttered, "Thank you, Chaplain," and then removed himself from the room.

He frowned when he was alone, but that frown quickly turned into deep sadness and hurt. What he'd predicted had come true. Her lifestyle with Nasir caught up to her. Now she was dead, and Nasir was believed to be still alive. Sincere collected himself and marched away. When Sincere entered the dayroom, he didn't care about chess or anything. What he wanted was revenge. He wanted Nasir dead.

Row approached Sincere with his deepest sympathy and said to him, "We'll find that nigga, Sincere. Best believe that. I'ma put the word out everywhere. If he's locked up, we'll know. If he does any business on the streets, we'll fuckin' know."

"I don't give a fuck what it takes. I want him dead, Row. I know he's out there, still breathing while my sister's body lies in a fuckin' morgue unclaimed," Sincere griped.

"We gonna find that muthafucka," Row repeated.

A deep sadness came over Sincere. He walked away, wanting to be alone. But there was no one left in his life.

Zodiac sat in the back of the courtroom to witness Zulu's sentencing: life imprisonment. It was utterly shocking and a blow. Zulu was furious. Cook Gamble had been successful in testifying against Zulu in the courtroom, and what Cook had to say about Zulu and his drug empire was crippling to his defense. Cook was a waterfall with information, giving the DA everything they needed, from money laundering, shell companies, murders, to racketeering, and Zodiac sat quietly in the back, watching it all unfold.

Before the marshals could escort Zulu out of the courtroom shackled, Zulu looked back at Zodiac sitting comfortably in his position. Both men locked eyes, and there was this broken brotherhood between them. Zulu wasn't a fool. He knew what had transpired. Cook should have been a dead man, but Zodiac allowed him to live to become the final nail in Zulu's coffin. Cook was a monster. His transgressions were so great that it was unbelievable the DA would make a plea deal with him. He'd kidnapped and raped young girls and forced them into sex trafficking, along with selling drugs. But Zulu was the king on the chessboard law enforcement wanted to topple.

"I guess it's your turn to wear the crown, nigga," Zulu exclaimed to Zodiac.

Zodiac was a bit disheartened by everything, but Trina was right. Now it was his time to shine.

To be continued in *King of Kings*.